Please feel free to send n
publisher filters these em

B. D. Fresquez - bd_fresquez@awesomeauthors.org

Sign up for my blog for updates and freebies!
bd-fresquez.awesomeauthors.org

Copyright © 2017 by B. D. Fresquez

All Rights reserved under International and Pan-American Copyright Conventions. By payment of required fees you have been granted the non-exclusive, non-transferable right to access and read the text of this book. No part of this text may be reproduced, transmitted, downloaded, decompiled, reverse-engineered or stored in or introduced into any information storage and retrieval system, in any form or by any means, whether electronic or mechanical, now known, hereinafter invented, without express written permission of BLVNP Inc. For more information contact BLVNP Inc. The publisher does not have any control over and does not assume any responsibility for author or third-party websites or their content. This book is a work of fiction. The characters, incidents and dialogue are drawn from the author's imagination and are not to be construed as real. While reference might be made to actual historical events or existing locations, the names, characters, places and incidents are either products of the author's imagination or are used fictitiously, and any resemblance to actual persons living or dead, business establishments, events or locales is entirely coincidental.

About the Publisher

BLVNP Incorporated, A Nevada Corporation, 340 S. Lemon #6200, Walnut CA 91789, info@blvnp.com / legal@blvnp.com

DISCLAIMER

This book is a work of FICTION. It is fiction and not to be confused with reality. Neither the author nor the publisher or its associates assume any responsibility for any loss, injury, death or legal consequences resulting from acting on the contents in this book. The author's opinions are not to be construed as the opinions of the publisher. The material in this book is for entertainment purposes ONLY. Enjoy.

Praise for Outcasts

This book is so amazing It definitely deserved to be
published! I recommend it to everyone!
—Jasmine, Goodreads

This book is awesome. I will keep reading it without getting
bored.
—Vaishnovi, Goodreads

I love this book so much, and I'm so happy it's getting
published.
—Sidra, Goodreads

Oh my God, best book ever. I read it 2 times; it was that
good.
—Aria Sultani, Goodreads

Outcasts

By: B. D. Fresquez

BLVNP

ISBN: 978-1-68030-899-0

©B. D. Fresquez 2017

Table of Contents

For my Aunt Ruby, who I know is watching over me and celebrating this achievement with me. You inspired me every day with your strength. I love you, Auntie.

FREE DOWNLOAD

Get these freebies and MORE when you sign up for the author's mailing list!

bd-fresquez.awesomeauthors.org

Chapter 1

There's something oddly satisfying about sitting at my desk and seeing the same pencil-written letter K that's scrawled in the upper right corner. There's always a nice feeling of familiarity to it. When I sit at my desk again today, it's not there. The desk seems to be wiped clean; the pencil marks and eraser shavings are nowhere in sight. This bothers me. I like familiarity, and now this desk doesn't even seem like it's mine anymore. Even though I didn't write the K in the first place, I became accustomed to seeing it.

Familiarity always seems to get me through the long school days. It might bother other people to see the same thing and the same people over and over again, but it soothes me. Change is something I don't like.

It's like walking down the hallways of Fairfield High and seeing the same groups of people standing in the middle of the hallway like they don't have a class to get to in the next three minutes. This is the familiarity of high school. Every day, I hear people talking about last weekend's party, the homework they had to cram on Sunday night, and who's hooking up with whom. I push past these people to make it to class on time. Grades are all that matters to me right now. I don't play any sports, so I can't depend on my athletic ability to get me into a decent college. I want to get the hell out of this town, and I have to work hard to do it.

Jesus, I *am* a nerd.

I waltz into my last class of the day, and I pray time will go by quickly. Exhaustion has taken over my body, and I just want to go home and lay on my bed. Thankfully, class goes by swiftly, and I'm soon gathering my things. My teacher, Mrs. Clarke, stops me on my way out and hands me a book she thinks I'll like. I thank her and walk home. I've never bothered my mom for a car. My house is within walking distance from the school, and I never go anywhere outside of school, so what's the point?

As I round a corner, I open the book Mrs. Clarke has given me. I start to read the first chapter. When I hear footsteps behind me, I don't think anything of it. But the footsteps increase in speed and sound like they're getting closer. Before I can turn around to investigate, I'm knocked to the ground, and my book falls out of my hands onto the side of the road.

"What the hell?" I say as I frantically stand up to dust myself off. My only injury is the scratch on my forearm. No blood seems to be gushing anywhere, so I whirl around to face the person who knocked me down.

Aiden Callaway, Fairfield High's known troublemaker, is standing in front of me and looking around wildly. His eyes travel to the ground where my book is still laying. He hastily picks it up and shoves it in my chest. "Here," he grumbles.

He runs into me and has the nerve to snap at me? I feel like giving him a piece of my mind, but I decide against the idea. He isn't someone I want to be acquainted with in any shape or form. His whole demeanor screams *trouble*. Instead of yelling at him, I simply walk away without saying a word.

"What? No 'thank you?'" I hear him ask me.

"Thank you," I say without turning around. This ends up being a big mistake. I know when to pick my battles, but he clearly doesn't.

My shoulder is yanked back, and I'm facing Aiden yet again. The irritation on his face is evident as he says, "You don't have to be bitchy about it." He glances around suspiciously before looking at me again.

I scoff. "I think I can. You're the one who ran into me and never bothered to apologize or ask if I was okay." *The nerve of this guy!*

"Stay out of my way next time."

"Or next time you can run *around* me like a normal person would."

"Like you would know anything about being normal."

"Excuse you?" I say loudly. "You're being rude, and just for that, you're not a normal person either!"

He stares at me, and I'm immediately embarrassed by my lame comeback. He bursts into laughter, and I feel my cheeks heat up even more. "Wow," he chuckles. "You really aren't normal."

"There he is!" someone yells in the distance. I glance behind Aiden's tall figure and see two guys running in our direction.

"Shit," Aiden mutters when he sees them. He grabs my arm and starts to run, bringing me along with him.

I run with him until I realize what a stupid idea it is. I try to pull my arm away, but his grip tightens. "Let go!" I yell at him.

"Stop struggling and run!"

A car halts and the passenger side window rolls down, revealing a driver with sunglasses and a baseball cap. "C'mon, Aiden!"

Aiden jerks the door open to the backseat of the car and the panic rises in me. I try once again to tug my arm away from Aiden's grip, but I can't match his strength. He pushes me into the backseat and flings himself in next to me. The car takes off, and Aiden quickly shuts the door.

I sit up in the seat and start to breathe heavily. I glance around, thinking of ways I can escape. There is no way in hell I'm getting kidnapped today.

"Jesus, calm down," Aiden says to me. He leans back in his seat, seemingly unbothered that he was just chased down by two crazy people.

The anger wells up inside me, and my fists connect with his arm repeatedly. "Do not tell me to calm down. I just met you, and you pulled me into a speeding car while being chased by two maniacs! This is practically kidnapping!"

My small hands do little to no damage; he doesn't even flinch. He laughs instead then says, "Relax. Those guys are gone."

"Why were they chasing you in the first place? Who were they?"

"Just some guys I owe money to." He casually shrugs.

I look out the window and see that we're going in the opposite direction of my house. I groan and slump into the seat.

Chapter 2

"I heard the weather is supposed to be weird for the next couple of days. It might rain one day and the next it might get up to eighty degrees."

"Can we talk about something else, perhaps?" The guy driving groans. His sunglasses were off, giving me a better look at him. He drove as if Aiden and I weren't just chased by two psychos. Well, chasing *Aiden*.

I cross my arms defensively before letting out a long sigh. It's not my fault I tend to talk a lot when I'm bored. At first, it was strange being in here, but now it's just boring. We've been driving around aimlessly, and it's getting late.

"Just shut up and drive, Alex," Aiden tells him. He then looks at me. "Seriously, why are you talking so much?"

"I talk a lot when I'm bored." If I ever do get kidnapped, hopefully, I'll talk their ear off to the point where they'll get annoyed with me and they take me back home. "Besides, what else am I supposed to do? And where are we going anyway? I need to get home and feed my dog."

"We aren't going anywhere specific," Aiden says as he looks out the window.

"I still don't understand why you had to drag me along with you. That was your problem, not mine," I say to him. "I'd like to go home now if you don't mind." I don't say this out loud, but I have too much homework and I can't waste time doing absolutely nothing.

Aiden leans forward in his seat. "Drive to your house. I'll take her home after we drop you off."

Not going to argue with that. I lean back in my seat and relax a little.

About ten minutes later, Aiden is in the driver's seat and I'm sitting in the passenger's. He asks for my address and I reluctantly tell him. He glances at me and smirks. "I live on the same street."

I cross my arms. "Good for you. It's a decent neighborhood."

"Are you always like this, or did I catch you on a bad day?"

"I'm not always like this. When you're dragged along with someone you just met while there are two guys chasing after you, wouldn't your mood turn sour also?"

His gaze lowers to my chest, and I almost call him out until he turns his eyes back to the road and says, "Nice shirt, by the way."

My Led Zeppelin t-shirt has proven to be very comfortable in this dire situation. "Thank you," I tell him. "And my house is the second one, right there."

He parks along the sidewalk and I quickly unbuckle my seat belt. "Well, it was just lovely meeting you, Aiden. I doubt we'll ever talk again, so have a nice life." I smile and nod at him before hustling out of the car. I rush into my house and I lock the door behind me.

Sassy, my Pomeranian, runs up to me and I pick her up immediately. "Let's get you some food!" I say in an embarrassingly high-pitched voice.

After Sassy is fed, I run upstairs to my room to start on my homework. My mom is still at work and won't get home until later, so I still have a couple of hours to myself. My dad left us when I was about three years old, so I don't remember him too much. Mom never talks about him and I never bug her about it. We've done pretty well without him, so it doesn't bother me too much.

The walls of my room are covered in band posters, abstract paintings, and some sketch drawings that were supposedly drawn by my great, great grandma. My favorite posters display bands such as Led Zeppelin, The Eagles, Fleetwood Mac, and Nirvana. I plug my iPod into the dock on my nightstand, and my music softly plays throughout my room. A little background music usually helps me focus.

Today is different, though. My mind is still racing with flashbacks of what happened earlier with Aiden. I'm still not sure what possessed him to drag me along with him, but I'm so sure Aiden isn't a person I want to encounter again.

***

When I wake up the next morning, I feel physically and mentally exhausted. My body is running on about four hours of sleep, so my morning starts off slower than usual.

Once I'm ready to leave, I make sure I have everything I need for the day. I drag myself outside the front door, locking it behind me. The air is cool, but it feels good against my tired skin. It's like a natural wake-up call. I make my way down the driveway to the sidewalk where I head to my next destination: hell. Or in other words, school.

I enter the main building and I prepare myself for the day. As I weave my way between everyone, I realize Fairfield isn't really the stereotypical high school you see in movies. Our football players aren't cocky and arrogant, and our cheerleaders aren't snobby. Our soccer players and our volleyball players are actually a bit more intimidating, but I can't complain.

I guess we sort of have the typical "it girl." Her name is Nicole Sanders. She's not the cheer or dance captain, but she is Fairfield's own student body president. I hear she can be a really sweet person, but get on her bad side and she can turn into a major bitch. Obviously, she has a boyfriend. First-string running back on the football team and overall nice guy, I guess: Ryan Dixon. It's obvious why those two wound up together. Both of them are popular, attractive, and are seemingly Ivy League-bound. Every girl in school drools over Ryan and his bright smile and blue eyes. Every guy wishes Nicole would give them the time of day.

When lunch finally rolls around, I figure a stop at my locker is much needed to switch my textbooks. Once they're nicely shoved into my locker, I shut it and start to walk in the direction of the library. I hear a crashing noise that makes me jump in surprise. I glance around to see where the noise came from, but everything seems intact. I continue to walk down the hall, but it's not long before I hear the noise again.

This time I round a corner to the next hallway, but I stop dead in my tracks when I see Aiden and another guy, who is currently on the floor in front of Aiden. The guy on the floor has a bloody nose. He stands up swiftly and leans against the lockers next to him. A black eye is forming on his face already along with a busted lip. My gaze shifts to Aiden and notice that his clothes are disheveled and he has a busted lip also. He doesn't look as bad as the other guy though.

Aiden delivers a deadly glare to the guy until he finally speaks, "Get the hell outta here."

The guy pushes himself off the locker and heads in my direction. I hide behind the corner as Aiden's human punching bag disappears down another hallway. I lean against the wall and release a breath I'd been holding.

"How much did you see?"

I jump when I hear Aiden's voice. I look to my left where he's now standing. I'm at a loss for words. Nothing comes to mind as my excuses get jumbled. I didn't even hear him walk over here.

I blink and clear my throat. "I didn't—I mean, I just got here," I stammer. I want to kick myself for coming up with such a lame excuse.

"You aren't going to tell on me, are you?" He steps closer to me. His tone is challenging yet mocking.

I shake my head, not trusting my voice.

He walks around me without a word and I sigh in relief. He's now starting to live up to the reputation everyone else has placed on him. I don't think I want to know what he does in his spare time to keep that rep up. Once my body recovers from the shock, I quickly walk towards my sanctuary: the library.

Chapter 3

Seeing my mom's car in the driveway surprises me as I approach my house. When I walk into the house, I hear noise coming from the kitchen. My mom is snacking on some crackers when I peek into the kitchen. She shoots me a smile.

"Hey, sweetie. How was school?" She holds the box of crackers out to me.

I shake my head, denying the crackers. "School was school." I shrug. "What are you doing home early?" Being a nurse, my mom always works weird hours. I wasn't expecting to see her until tomorrow morning.

"I decided to take the rest of today and tomorrow off from work. Exhaustion has taken over and I felt like a mini vacation was in store." She smiles. "Plus, we haven't had any mother-daughter time in a while."

I nod, understanding. I take this opportunity to really look at my mom. It seems as if age has no effect on her. Her dark brown hair hangs loosely around her shoulders as it frames her face, which has little to no lines. Her brown eyes don't look as lively as usual, but that's probably because she's tired.

"Is there anything exciting going on at school?" she probes. She asks this question all the time and my answer is always the same.

"I wouldn't know. I'm not exactly *involved*." I mean, I do know that the big homecoming game and homecoming dance is coming up, but that's all I know.

"It's your last year of high school, Riley. You should make this year an unforgettable one."

"I'll try, I guess."

Her lips form a tight line, seeing how the subject isn't going any further. Then her eyes brighten. "Oh! I almost forgot to tell you. We've been invited to a wedding."

I raise an eyebrow. "Who's getting married?"

"My friend Anna at work."

Dressing up and attending special occasions aren't exactly my favorite past times. "Oh. That's cool," I say, not knowing how else to react. "I have to go finish some homework."

"Okay." She stands up and makes her way to the cabinet to put the crackers away.

Before I climb the stairs, I pick Sassy up, and I don't let her down until I walk into my room. I throw my backpack on the bed and I start on my homework.

Around five o'clock, I decide to take Sassy for a walk. I hook the leash onto her collar and we run down the stairs together. "Mom, I'm taking Sassy out for a walk," I call out as I open the front door.

"Okay, be careful!" she yells back.

I take a deep breath of fresh air as we walk outside. As much as I love to stay in and read, I still need my dose of fresh air, and walking Sassy is always the perfect opportunity.

The houses around me are familiar but the people inside aren't. I only know a couple of neighbors, and even they aren't around much. It's always too quiet.

We get to the park that's located in the middle of the whole neighborhood. It's nothing too extravagant, just a small play structure surrounded by a modest area of grass. There are also a couple of benches near some trees. Sassy and I circle the play structure a couple of times before I sit on one of the benches.

I let Sassy loose from her leash before I look at my phone to check the time. When I put my phone back in my pocket, I notice Sassy isn't around me.

"Sassy?" I call out nervously. "Sassy, come here, girl!"

I stand up and walk toward the play structure. Before I get too worried, I take a deep breath and I tell myself to calm down. But where could she have gone?

"Hey, is this your dog?"

I whirl around and meet a pair of blue eyes towering over me. Standing in front of me is Ryan Dixon with Sassy in his arms. I sigh in relief. "Yeah."

He hands her to me and I quickly clip her leash back onto her collar. I set her down before looking at Ryan again. "Thanks," I say awkwardly. I'm not one to drool over hot guys, but Ryan is definitely easy on the eyes.

He flashes a smile at me. "No problem."

Before I can even think of my next sentence, a voice yells out, "Dixon! Where the hell did you go?"

Lo and behold, none other than Aiden Callaway himself approaches us with confidence in his stride. What are these two doing here together? It's an unusual pairing. I catch Aiden's eye and a flash of recognition crosses his face. "Led Zeppelin girl," he instantly says to me.

Right, I never told him my name. "Hi." I wave to him, not knowing what else to do. I'm awkward once again. After seeing what he did earlier today, I can't help but feel wary.

"You know each other?" Ryan looks at Aiden and me. He looks as confused as I feel right now.

Aiden gets a mischievous smile on his face. "We've run into each other before," he says to Ryan but doesn't tear his eyes away from me. His tone is mocking once again, just like earlier. It's like every instance in his life is a game to be played.

Instead of disputing his version of the story, I decide that this is all too weird for me. "Well, this has been interesting. I should probably head home now." As I say this, Sassy walks up to Ryan and paws at his shoelaces.

He bends down to pet her. "What's her name?" he asks as he scratches her behind the ears. She practically melts into his hands.

"Sassy."

He continues to pet her as Aiden and I watch him. I steal a quick glance at Aiden, who is frowning slightly at Ryan.

Ryan stands up again and looks at me, completely ignoring Aiden's stare. "I don't think I caught your name."

That's because I didn't tell you. "It's Riley."

He grins. "I'm Ryan."

"And I'm Aiden." Aiden visibly rolls his eyes. "Now that we've settled the obvious, we need to go," he tells Ryan.

Before I can make a fool of myself, I start to walk backwards. "I have to go too."

"I'll see you around, *Riley.*" Aiden sends me a strange smile like we have some inside joke between us.

"Bye, Riley." Ryan waves.

I wave before quickly turning around to walk down the sidewalk to my house. A million questions are raised in my mind. Why were Aiden and Ryan hanging out together? I never see them hang out at school. Hell, they don't even look in each other's direction at school. Everything seems out of the ordinary, and I can't decide whether or not it settles right within me.

***

The light breeze sends chills throughout my body as I walk out the front door. Mid-September mornings are probably the best thing in this town. Fall is just around the corner and I can't wait for it. Things seem livelier in the fall.

I listen to my iPod as I make my way down the sidewalk. Today's song of the morning is New Slang by The Shins. I hear something that isn't part of the song, prompting me to take out one earphone. That's when I hear shouting from one of the houses. I look to my left, and the front door to someone's house opens furiously, and someone stumbles out. That someone is Aiden Callaway.

He's a wreck. His clothes are lopsided and his hair is sticking up in several directions—and not in a good way. His back is to me as he looks into the house.

"Why don't you just piss off already," he yells, I'm assuming, at someone in the house. The front door is slammed from the inside as Aiden walks heatedly down his driveway.

His gaze meets mine and I panic. I ignore what I had just seen and I make my way down the sidewalk, just a bit quicker this time.

"Hey!" I hear Aiden's voice call out to me. His footsteps get louder with each passing second.

I turn the volume up on my iPod, ignoring him as I try to walk faster. A hand grabs my shoulder and forcibly turns me around. My mind is spinning and before I can even think I blurt out, "I didn't see or hear anything! I was just passing by! Please don't hurt me!"

Aiden frowns and reaches out, pulling an ear bud from my ear. "I'm not going to hurt you, weirdo."

A sigh escapes my lips. "Oh, okay." I start walking again and he falls into step with me.

"Have you always lived on this street?" he asks me as he adjusts the strap of his backpack.

As strange as it is for Aiden to be walking with me and making conversation, I nod. "My mom and I moved into this neighborhood when I was in the first grade." How did I not know that Aiden Callaway lived on the same street as me?

"Do you always walk to school?"

Once again, I nod. "My mom tells me I should take the bus, but I like walking better. What's the point in taking the bus anyway? We only live a couple of minutes down the road, you know?"

"Right," he drawls out.

The school comes into view and I look at the time on my phone to make sure I won't be late. I realize the awkward silence that has fallen upon us and I clear my throat uncomfortably. "Why were you yelling when you came out of your house?" Oh God, why did I even ask that? "I'm sorry. You don't have to answer."

Aiden shrugs and doesn't meet my eyes. "There's just a lot of shit going on right now."

"Oh." I don't know what else to say.

He looks at me with a strange expression, but it quickly fades away. "It's whatever," he says before glancing around. "Listen, I'm gonna split here. I don't feel like going to first period today."

I figure there's no point in trying to convince him not to skip class, so I simply nod.

Aiden takes off in another direction before we walk onto campus. The curiosity still burns in my mind about earlier, but it isn't my business, so I'll have to stay curious.

At the beginning of lunch, I see Aiden saunter down the hallway with his head held high. Confidence radiates off him, earning the stares of a few girls. Sometimes I wish I can hold my head high like that. Others look at him as he passes by. Some look with envy, some with hatred, and some look away with fear in their eyes.

If I can go unnoticed by the student body until graduation, I'll rejoice. I don't need any attention drawn to me. My mantra for the past three and a half years has been to stay unexciting and don't get noticed. It's worked so far.

Aiden makes a beeline in the hallway, clearly on a mission. He stops in front of Ryan and the two share some words. Ryan looks annoyed but amused at the same time. Aiden is totally serious and has the final word before stalking off. Ryan's eyes meet mine and my cheeks burn out of embarrassment from being caught watching them. He offers me a smile and I quickly turn away.

I continue down the hall until I make a right down the next hallway. Aiden is walking in my direction. I steal a glance at him and he gives me a nod of acknowledgement.

Things are getting stranger by the second, leaving me to wonder where all of this will end up.

Chapter 4

The fiction section in the school library holds a special place in my heart. A well-written, inspiring novel can always be found on these shelves, and I desperately need a good read at the moment. I finished my lunch quickly just so I can scan the shelves in depth.

My fingers run across the spines of the books as I examine the titles. Nothing is really catching my eye. I've seen these all before.

As I go around the bookshelf, I bump into someone. I keep my head down and mumble a quick "Sorry." I continue to look at the books on the next shelf as I curse at myself for not paying attention.

"Hey, it's Riley, right?" a voice asks.

Recognizing the voice, I turn around, and lo and behold, Ryan Dixon is standing next to me. He smiles when my eyes reach his.

"Right," I say slowly. I avert my eyes and fix my gaze on the books in front of me. What is he doing here?

"So," he starts, "looking for a specific book?"

It puzzles me why Ryan is even talking to me in the first place. Might as well get my thoughts out in the open so I can figure out his angle. "Listen"—I look at him seriously— "just because we had a short conversation in the park doesn't mean we're all buddy-buddy now. We never acknowledged each other before, so why start now?"

He stares at me before clearing his throat. He looks genuinely surprised. "Wow. I'm going to pretend you didn't just hurt my feelings."

"Oh please, like *I* could hurt *your* feelings." I go back to looking at the books, but my brain is muddled and I can't focus on the titles. Damn you, Ryan.

Ryan takes a step closer to me, getting a little too close for my liking. "Is this your thing? Pushing people away? Because if so, it's a little cliché."

"*Cliché?*" I can practically feel my eyes popping out of my head. "What's cliché is the popular guy following the quiet girl in the library so he can get her to do his homework or something."

"I'm not following you, first of all. And I don't want you to do my homework for me. I don't know what your grades look like, but I have straight As." He chuckles. "I just want to be your friend."

"My *friend?*"

"Yeah, you don't seem like you have a lot of those…"

I turn around and walk away from him. I don't need his charity. It's never bothered me that I don't have any close friends. Sure, I talk to people in some of my classes, but I'm doing fine without any best friends. I'm definitely not going to take up Ryan's offer. How would his friendship benefit me anyway?

"Riley, I was kidding." He catches up to me. The amusement is evident on his face.

I feel myself scowling at him. "It's not funny."

"So, how do you know Callaway?" he asks, noticeably switching the topic of conversation.

This must be what he *really* wants to talk about. "I don't *know* him. We just kind of...ran into each other." It isn't a lie. There's no use in explaining the extent of our acquaintanceship, if it's even that.

"I see." He looks confused as he says this.

I want to ask him why he was with Aiden at the park, but he suddenly reaches into his front pocket and pulls out his phone. He sighs when he looks at the screen. "Hey," he answers. He looks a bit annoyed with the person he's talking to.

I take this chance to walk around the different shelves until I land in the biography section. I watch Ryan as he walks out of the library. I can't understand Ryan's personality, so it's frustrating trying to figure out his motive. Why is he so concerned about Aiden? Are they friends? Or more? I let out a deep breath as the bell rings overhead, signaling the end of lunch.

So much for finding a good read.

***

My mom is sitting on the couch and talking on the phone when I walk in that afternoon. I throw my backpack down next to the front door before I walk into the kitchen.

Sassy doesn't have any food in her bowl. My mom never feeds her. Sassy is practically my child because I'm the only one who takes care of her.

I grab the bowl from the ground and I pull the bag of dog food from the pantry. As I'm doing this, I hear my mom saying goodbye to whoever she's on the phone with.

"How was school?" she asks as I scoop some food into the bowl.

"It was the same as yesterday, and the day before that." Nothing too exciting happened. It was out of the ordinary since Aiden walked with me to school and Ryan talked to me in the library, but I'm not about to tell her that.

She gives me a strange look before speaking again. "I have something to tell you, Riley."

Oh great. The last time she spoke like this was when she "accidentally" threw my Harry Potter poster away. "What?" I ask slowly. I hope it isn't anything ridiculous.

"Remember that wedding I told you about?"

"The wedding we got invited to, right?" The bag of dog food doesn't fit back into the pantry and it's starting to frustrate me.

"Right." She nods. "Well, Anna, my friend who is getting married, lost a bridesmaid. She asked me if I would be in the wedding, but I told her I'd look ridiculous in the bridesmaid dress she picked out. So I volunteered you for the job."

My jaw drops just as the bag falls over and spills dog food around me. "What?" She cannot be serious. There's no way. "Why would you volunteer me without even talking to me about it first?"

"I just figured it would give you something to do. You never go out, and when you do, it's to take Sassy for a walk, or you end up at the library. I want you to be involved, Riley. I don't want you spending the rest of your teen years reading in your room. I appreciate you staying out of trouble, but I want you to try something different. Besides, the wedding is soon anyway, so it'll be over and done with before you know it." She lets out a breath as she finishes her rant.

It doesn't surprise me that she would pull something like this. I knew she would try to take control of my life somehow. And this is her doing exactly that. "I don't know..." Being in a wedding requires talking to people and being in front of people—two things I don't especially like doing.

"If you don't do it, then she'll be left with no fifth bridesmaid. She needs someone, Riley."

Now she's trying to give me the guilt trip.

I can't believe I'm even considering this. "Fine. I'll do it."

She claps her hands. "Thank you, Riley! I'll call Anna back and tell her you're filled in." She runs back into the living room. I swear, *she* acts like the teenager in this house sometimes.

What do bridesmaids even do? How do they function? My head begins to hurt and I automatically blame it on my mom. I'm about to run up to my room when I hear something crunch beneath my feet. I remember the spilled dog food, let out a long sigh, and start to clean the mess I made.

***

"Riley, wake up! Riley!" Someone is shaking my shoulders.

"Leave me alone," I grumble. It's Saturday. The day I get to sleep in as late as I want to. I don't know why my mom is trying to wake me up earlier than I have to.

"Get up, Riley! You need to get fitted for your bridesmaid dress today," she says.

Oh, right. The wedding. The wedding that I'm now regretting being a part of.

"Riley Summers, if you're not up and out of your bed in the next thirty seconds, I am taking all of your t-shirts out of your closet and burning them. I won't hesitate to buy new, *girly* clothes for you."

I instantly jump out of bed. My head spins from the sudden movement, so I lean against the wall. "I'm up." I rub my eyes clear of the sleepiness. My clock on the wall reads seven thirty. It's way too early to be out of bed. What an unholy hour.

Mom smiles at me. "Good. Now get dressed. I'm taking you to Anna's house in about fifteen minutes, and from there, you'll go get fitted for the dress." She walks out of my room and shuts my door behind her.

Sassy jumps onto my bed and stares at me. I sit down next to her and sigh. "I wish I were like you, Sassy. I wish I could just lounge around the house without a care in the world."

"Stop talking to the dog and get ready, Riley!" Mom yells at me from behind the door.

I let out a dramatic sigh and make my way to my closet where I pull out a pair of light wash jeans and my Guns N' Roses t-shirt.

I throw on the clothes and my pair of old Converse, then I run a brush through my long hair. I quickly brush my teeth and head downstairs.

Mom is standing in the kitchen, eating a bowl of cereal as she reads the newspaper. She looks at me and scans my clothes. "Someday, I *will* get a hold of your clothes."

"I'll be out of the house before you can even act upon your evil doing," I tell her, crossing my arms.

"Are you ready?" she asks, and I nod. She puts her bowl into the sink. "Let's go. Anna's house is a bit further out of town."

"I don't get to eat breakfast?"

"If you'd gotten up earlier, you would've had time."

I run to the pantry and grab a granola bar. For good measure, I snag an apple from the fridge.

We're out the front door and in my mom's car in a flash. I stare out the window as we head to Anna's house. I plug my earphones into my iPod, and before I know it, I'm drifting off to Led Zeppelin's Stairway to Heaven.

Chapter 5

"Riley, wake up. We're here."

I groan and curl myself into a ball. "Five more minutes," I mumble.

"Riley, c'mon. They're leaving in a few minutes and you still have to meet everyone."

I groan louder at the mention of meeting people. I open my eyes and reluctantly unbuckle my seatbelt. "Fine. Let's get this over with."

My mom gives me a bright smile before exiting the car. When I'm out of the car, I stretch my limbs and instantly feel tired again. My shoulders slump as I walk around the car.

"You really need to work on your posture, Riley. You look like an old man when you walk like that."

Mom always wanted a girly, outgoing daughter. Instead, she got me.

Ignoring her comment, I whistle when I see the house. This place is huge. Our house isn't small, but it certainly isn't as big as Anna's.

We walk up the concrete steps and approach the front door, which has an oval-shaped piece of glass in the middle with delicate gold designs. I take a deep breath as Mom rings the doorbell.

"Don't be afraid to make new friends and have fun. You need some girl time instead of being locked up in your room," she says to me.

Before I can respond, the door opens and I instantly hear girls laughing from inside the house. Please shoot me now.

"Carol!" the woman who opened the front door exclaims. She hugs Mom before they look at me.

"Anna, this is my daughter, Riley. Riley, this is Anna," she introduces us.

I hold out my hand. "It's nice to meet you," I say as politely as I can.

Anna gently shakes my hand. "Pretty and polite." She beams. She looks at Mom. "We shouldn't be out too long, but who knows with them." She gestures behind her. "I can ask one of the boys to take her home after we're done."

"Sounds good to me." Mom grins at Anna before looking at me. "I'll see you later, Riley. Have fun." She winks.

I'm pulled inside by Anna and the smell of sweet candles and perfume hits me like a truck. I want to plug my nose, but that would probably be rude.

Anna looks at me excitedly. "I really appreciate you doing this, Riley. I don't know what I would've done without a fifth bridesmaid." She chuckles.

I take in her appearance as she speaks. Her blonde hair is swept up into a ponytail and her blue eyes match the light blue blouse she currently has on. She looks fairly young. I can't guess how old she is.

"It's no problem," I tell her.

"Alright, I'll introduce you to the girls," she says. "And don't feel nervous, hun. I promise we're not a bad crowd."

We walk into what I assume is the living room. Then I see them. Blondes. All the girls in the room are blonde. Which means I'm going to be the only bridesmaid who is a brunette. I'll stand out. Great.

"Our new bridesmaid has arrived! Everyone say hello to Riley," Anna announces.

One girl walks up to me. She looks younger than the others. "Hi, Riley." She grins and sticks out her hand. "I'm Kelly."

I shake her hand. "Nice to meet you."

She stands by my side and points to another girl who looks a bit older than me. "That's my older sister, Jenna," she says before gesturing to the other two girls. "The girl with the blue tips in her hair is our cousin Halle. Next to her is her twin sister, Holly."

"Jenna and Kelly are mine," Anna pipes in. "The twins are my nieces, who are both twenty. Jenna is twenty-one and Kelly is sixteen."

"How old are you?" Kelly asks me.

"Eighteen."

She smiles. "Finally, someone a little closer to me in age."

"Well, I need to call Robert and tell him we're ready to leave," Anna says then excuses herself.

Kelly drags me to the couch and we both sit down. "So, Riley, what school do you go to?" she asks.

"Fairfield High," I tell her. Now that I think about it, I don't think I've ever seen her around Fairfield.

"My brother goes to Fairfield. Maybe you know him." Before I can ask who her brother is, she speaks up again. "I go to Maxwell Academy."

"That's the all-girls private school, right?" Mom considered putting me in Maxwell until she saw how much it would cost her.

Kelly nods. "Right. I thought it would totally suck, but it's actually not that bad."

I feel the couch dip to my left. I look over and see Jenna sitting next to me. "You haven't scared Riley off, have you, Kelly?" she asks with amusement in her eyes. She looks familiar somehow. She looks an awful lot like Anna. Kelly too. They all have the same blue eyes.

Kelly crosses her arms. "No."

Jenna glances at me. "I'm glad you're not another blondie." She chuckles. "That's basically our whole family."

"Except Ryan and Dad," Kelly says. Something in her tone changes. For a split second, Ryan Dixon enters my mind, but I push the thought back.

I feel a presence behind me, so I look back. A tall figure creeps up behind Kelly and begins to mess with her hair, tangling it from the looks of it.

"Aiden, stop!" Kelly shrieks.

I do a double-take at the figure, and lo and behold, it is, in fact, Aiden Callaway. My eyes widen at the sight of him.

He laughs at Kelly's despair before he meets my gaze. His eyebrows rise in surprise.

"What are you doing here?" we ask at the same time.

"I asked first," I say before silently judging myself for sounding so childish.

He smirks. "Well, this is my soon-to-be stepmom's house. What are *you* doing here?"

"She's the new bridesmaid," Kelly says as she tries to smooth her hair out.

Wait. Anna is going to be Aiden's step-mom?

"Really?" Aiden looks at me.

"You two know each other?" Jenna asks us both.

"Not really," I say at the same time Aiden says no.

He goes back to tangling Kelly's hair, making it look like a mess from the '80s. She finally shoves him away and glares at him. "Aiden, you jerk."

"Aiden, stop harassing my sister."

I turn around and see Ryan walking into the room. What the hell is *he* doing here? What is even going on right now?

"Having two brothers will be so much fun," Jenna says sarcastically.

Ryan's eyes meet mine and he smiles. "Hey, Riley. What are you doing here?"

"Riley is Mom's new bridesmaid." Jenna fills him in. The word *bridesmaid* is beginning to make my head spin.

Wait, wait. So, Ryan is Jenna and Kelly's brother. Aiden is going to be their step-brother. Which means that Aiden's dad or mom—who knows—is marrying Anna.

"Oh, cool," Ryan says distractedly. Something is definitely on his mind.

"Okay, kids. Let's get this show on the road." Anna claps her hands together as she enters the room again. "Oh, good, Ryan and Aiden are here. Robert said he'll pick you two up at the bridal shop." She looks at Ryan. "Do you mind driving three people over there with you? I'll take Kelly and the twins."

"I want to go with Ryan," Kelly whines.

"I'll go with Mom," Jenna says to Kelly, rolling her eyes.

"Let's get going," Anna says. We stand up and follow her out of the house. She practically shoves us out the door. I wring my hands together nervously.

Kelly walks next to me as we make our way to Ryan's black BMW. "I can't wait to try on the bridesmaid dress. Don't you love dresses, Riley?"

I nod slowly. I hate dresses with a passion.

***

On the way to the bridal shop, Kelly talks my ear off. She decided to sit in the back with me, while Aiden sat in front with Ryan. Kelly is nice and all, but she sure knows how to talk. I don't have the heart to tell her to slow down a bit. Thankfully, Aiden does this for me.

"Jesus, Kelly, can you shut up for one second?" he asks her without turning around in his seat. I've caught his eye a couple of times in the rearview mirror. Maybe he senses my silent plea for help. Or maybe he is annoyed too. Probably the latter.

She huffs. "Can you be any more rude? I'm talking to Riley."

"I'm sure Riley doesn't like having her ear talked off," Aiden says. I get a weird feeling when he says my name. It sounds strange rolling off his tongue.

"Both of you shut up. I'm pretty sure Riley doesn't like hearing you two arguing." Ryan snaps.

Since when is this all about me?

"Sorry about my soon-to-be step-siblings." Aiden shifts in his seat so he's looking at me. "Maybe I should've sat next to you." He gives me a weird smile.

I return the smile, against my better judgment.

"And we're here," Ryan announces as he drives into the parking lot of the bridal shop. "Robert is already here," he says as he parks the car.

Aiden frowns as Ryan says, "Fantastic." The sarcasm is dripping from his tone.

Kelly and I get out of the car, and I glance at the shop in front of us. There's a huge window in front, showcasing a long, flowing wedding dress. Behind that are two bridesmaid dresses in teal but in different styles.

"I'm so excited!" Kelly exclaims.

I feel someone's arm brush against mine as they stand next to me. Aiden looks at the shop also and smirks. "Are you excited, too?" He mocks Kelly.

"Not really," I whisper to him.

He chuckles.

"Ryan! Aiden!" someone yells in the distance. Aiden and I both turn and I see a tall man with dark brown hair standing next to a navy blue truck. I assume this is Aiden's dad, as he looks exactly like him.

Aiden sighs. "Here we go." He walks off in the direction of the truck.

Kelly grabs my arm and pulls me toward the shop. "I've only seen the dress in the magazine, but it looks amazing!"

"That's good." I nod, not knowing how else to respond.

"I can't wait to see it in person. It's probably beautiful."

***

Beautiful? Yeah, sure. Extremely feminine and something I would never wear? Definitely!

I look at myself in the full-length mirror in the dressing room and I scrunch my nose. The dress is strapless, with what I think is a sweetheart neckline. In the middle of the bust is a giant flower. Beneath that, ruffles cascade down the length of the dress. It's a short dress, only going up to the top of my knees. The whole dress is a dark peach color. Definitely not something I would pick out, but then again it's not my wedding.

Is it too late to back out of this thing?

"We're waiting on you, Riley!" I hear Kelly yell from the other side of the door.

I unlatch the door and I brace myself.

When I see what the others look like in their dresses, I instantly feel insecure. These girls have the perfect tan, the pretty blonde hair, the shapely body, and they all look beautiful in the dress.

And here I am: a bit too skinny, with little shape to my body, and with lifeless brown hair that currently feels like a mess. I'm usually not one to feel insecure, but I really feel it at the moment. All I can think about is how I'll stand out compared to them, and not in a good way.

"Riley! You look absolutely amazing!" Kelly exclaims, snapping me out of my thoughts.

She brings everyone's attention to me when she says this. I hate being the center of attention. Everyone's gaze is on me, and I cross my arms.

"Wow, Riley." Jenna smiles brightly. "You look gorgeous."

The twin with the blue tips—I think her name is Halle if I remember correctly—sighs dramatically. "I wish I was eighteen again."

Holly rolls her eyes. "Shut up. That was only two years ago."

"College fucked me up. I'm not skinny anymore." Halle pouts.

Anna gives her a stern look, probably for her language. She then looks at me and grins. "I knew it. All of you look fabulous in the dress. Peach is definitely the right color for all of you." She reaches out and grabs a section of my hair. "Especially for you, Riley. Your hair color is beautiful with this shade."

"Thank you," I mumble shyly.

She walks over to Jenna, and I steal another glance at myself in the mirror behind me. I move and the dress sways with me. I feel like a different person with this dress on. The dress is pretty and all, but I need to get back into my jeans and t-shirt.

***

We walk out of the shop and Anna gathers us around her. "Don't forget, girls, the day before the wedding you all need to come back and pick up your dresses."

We all nod.

The navy-blue truck pulls up next to us, and Ryan and Aiden jump out. Aiden snaps at someone in the truck before slamming the truck door.

"Here we go again," Jenna says quietly behind me.

Ryan comes up to us and looks at Kelly and me. "Ready to go?"

"You can take Riley home, right, Ryan?" Anna asks him.

He nods. "Yeah, sure."

Anna, Jenna, and the twins all hug me before they leave. It's odd that they have accepted me so quickly. I guess Anna is right. I don't need to be nervous around them.

Kelly and I walk with Ryan and Aiden back to the car. Aiden is deadly silent. There's a permanent frown on his face, so I'm assuming things didn't go well today.

"Take me home first," Aiden tells Ryan when we're all buckled in the car. "Riley's house is on the same street anyway."

Ryan just nods.

Relief washes over me as Ryan turns onto my street a few minutes later. He parks in front of Aiden's house first, just as he was asked.

Aiden is about to get out of the car when Ryan grabs his arm. Aiden glares at Ryan's hand on him, and Ryan quickly lets go. "Just chill out, dude. Don't freak out over everything."

Aiden's jaw ticks. "Leave me alone," he says slowly before getting out and slamming the door, just as he did with the truck. He walks straight to his backyard.

Some metaphysical force is pulling me toward Aiden, and I know this is going to be a bad idea. Once again, against my better judgment, I open my mouth. "Um, I'll just get out here. My house is just down the road."

"Are you sure?" Ryan twists in his seat so he's looking at me.

I nod and open the door.

Kelly waves at me. "See you soon, Riley."

"Okay." I give her a quick smile before shutting the door.

I walk along the sidewalk until I know Ryan and Kelly are out of sight. I turn around and make my way back to the Callaway residence. I walk hesitantly to the backyard, nervously wringing my hands together. I take a deep breath.

What am I doing?

Before I can escape, I see Aiden leaning against the side of the house with a small bottle of what looks like some type of alcohol in his hand. He brings it to his lips and takes a long sip.

"Drinking at a young age can kill brain cells, you know." I let it slip between my teeth before I can stop myself.

Aiden's eyes drift toward me. "What are you doing here?"

I'm asking myself the same thing. "You looked pretty angry a while ago. Just wanted to see if you were okay, I guess." I shrug like it's no big deal.

He smirks as he puts the cap on the bottle. "I'm fine."

"Clearly." I gesture to the bottle.

He walks up to me and I feel intimidated by his height. "Why do you care? None of this is your business anyway."

I knew this was a bad idea. "Whatever." I roll my eyes. "I'll go now." I duck my head and I move quickly away from his house. I shouldn't have followed him in the first place. Why would I even try to talk to Aiden Callaway in the first place? Such a stupid mistake.

I hear footsteps behind me and I feel his now familiar presence next to me. He doesn't say anything as we walk, but he doesn't need to. The silence between us is comfortable and I'm okay with it.

Chapter 6

It's Monday afternoon, so I don't expect anyone to be in my house. When I walk in, however, I hear two voices. My mom's and another familiar high-pitched voice.

In the living room, Kelly is seated on our couch, playing with Sassy as she talks to my mom. Kelly sees me first as I walk in.

"Riley!" Her eyes brighten and she stands up. She's soon barreling toward me, and her arms are around me in an instant.

My insides are being crushed!

I widen my eyes and mouth 'help' to my mom, who just laughs. Thanks, Mom.

Kelly lets go of me and grins.

"What are you doing here?" I ask, trying not to sound rude.

She clasps her hands together. "I thought we could hang out. You know, get to know each other a little better."

"Oh" is my response. I think of using homework as an excuse not to hang out with her, but Mom gives me a stern look, and I mentally sigh. "Okay. What do you want to do?" I ask awkwardly. I've never hung out with someone so spontaneously.

She shrugs. "I don't care."

Well, she is certainly no help. "How about we take a walk to the park?" I suggest. "I need to take Sassy for a walk anyway."

"Okay." She's still smiling.

I excuse myself before running up to my room. I throw my things onto my bed and I quickly grab Sassy's leash. When I walk back downstairs, Kelly already has Sassy in her arms. I clip the leash on her collar before I open the front door.

"We'll be back in a bit, Mom," I call out. We walk out of my house and start walking in the direction of the park.

Kelly puts Sassy on the ground and holds the leash in her hands. "So, Riley, tell me about yourself."

"Um…" What do people usually say in situations like this? "I like to read and listen to music."

"What kind of books do you read?"

"I like reading romance and mystery novels." I'm a sucker for the mysteries and the romances. I don't seem like the type who would melt over a romance novel, but I definitely am.

"How about music? What do you listen to?" she asks.

I shrug. "A little bit of everything, I guess. Mostly classic rock and alternative." I don't think I'm giving interesting answers, so I switch the attention to her. "What about you? What do you like to do?"

Her eyes shine. "I love to dance. I've been in ballet since I was three. I was into cheerleading until I came to Maxwell. I would read more, but I can't seem to find the right books to read. My favorite TV shows are *Pretty Little Liars*, *The Vampire Diaries*, and *Gossip Girl*. My favorite movie ever is *LOL*, and someday I want to go skydiving."

Wow. She is the complete opposite of me. I hate all the shows she named; I have never even seen *LOL*; dancing has never crossed my mind, and I would never go skydiving, not even for a million dollars.

"And you also have a mom who is getting married soon," I say, switching the topic to something we can relate to.

She nods. "Right."

"Are your parents..." I don't know if I should ask this question.

"Divorced?" She finishes for me. "Yeah, they are."

Curiosity gets the best of me. "Do you see your dad a lot?"

She shakes her head. "Jenna and Ryan visit him sometimes, but I don't feel like I need to see him. He left us, so why should I bother making the effort to see him and his Barbie wife?" she says bitterly.

Ah, something else we have in common. "My dad left us too. He left when I was three years old."

"Do you remember him?"

"Nope, not at all. I've only seen pictures of him." Mom has a box of old things from her first apartment with my dad. I've gone through it once, just to satisfy my curiosity about him.

"Seems like both our dads ran out on us." She looks at the ground. "I guess it's okay now. Robert is pretty cool with us."

Robert? "Aiden's dad?"

She nods. "Mom's happy with him, so I'm happy for her."

Mom has never even mentioned another man in her life. I think she's still hurt about my dad leaving us. She talked to him on the phone last year for some reason. I don't know what they talked about, but she looked as if she were crying after she hung up.

"That's good," I say as I glance at the houses we pass by. I notice we're getting closer to Aiden's house. "How long has your mom been with Aiden's dad?"

She hesitates. "About five or six years." Her eyes flicker to the houses. "Let's stop by Robert's house, yeah? I don't think you've officially met him, have you?"

I shake my head.

She grasps my arm and tugs me toward the Callaway residence. There's a 'for sale' sign in the yard that wasn't there a couple of days ago. The navy-blue truck from the other day is in the driveway also.

We approach the front door, and Kelly rings the doorbell. A few seconds later the door opens, revealing the same man I'd seen at the bridal shop.

He smiles at Kelly. "Kelly." He sounds surprised. His eyes flicker to me. "And Kelly's friend."

"This is my friend Riley. She's mom's new bridesmaid," Kelly explains.

I smile and give him a small wave. "Hi."

"It's nice to meet you, Riley." Now I know where Aiden gets his looks from. Aiden looks just like his dad, except for the few gray hairs. There are some slight wrinkles by his eyes that are noticeable when he smiles. "Come on in," he tells us as he opens the door wider for us.

I pick Sassy up from the ground and I take the leash from Kelly.

We walk in and I examine our surroundings. There's a staircase to our left, a long hallway to the right, and a hall in front of us. Similar to my house, just switched around a bit. Kelly seems to know her way around, as she walks straight. I follow closely behind her.

"I see you've still got a lot of packing to do." Kelly observes. That's when I notice the few boxes that are stacked in a corner in the kitchen.

Robert chuckles. "Well, it's pretty much just been me packing things up. Aiden is still, uh, adjusting."

"Yeah, he's made that very clear." She sighs.

And speaking of the devil, Aiden appears from the long hallway and scans the room. His gaze stops on Kelly and me. "What are you guys doing here?"

Robert clears his throat. "I'll be upstairs if you all need anything." He looks at Aiden expectantly, but Aiden doesn't turn in his direction.

"It's good to see you too, bro," Kelly says sarcastically.

Aiden gives her the middle finger then looks at me. "Aren't you tired of her yet?"

She shoves his shoulder. "Ha-ha. You're absolutely hilarious."

"But really, what are you guys doing here?" Aiden's eyes flash to Sassy, who is squirming in my arms.

"We were in the neighborhood and decided to drop in real quick." Kelly shrugs.

He crosses his arms. "Riley lives in the neighborhood. Did you ambush her to get her to hang out with you?"

Yes.

"I did not ambush her. Anyway, we were walking the dog when I thought we should stop by to say hello. We're heading to the park after this."

Aiden's attention is on Sassy. He reaches out and starts to pet her. "What kind of dog is this?" He looks genuinely confused.

"She's a Pomeranian," I tell him.

Kelly then grabs Sassy from my arms. "She's a pretty dog. Yes, she is," she talks to Sassy like the dog is a baby.

Aiden rolls his eyes. "God, Kelly, can you get any girlier?"

Tell me about it.

"Shut up, Aiden." She snaps at him. "Let's go, Riley."

"Actually, I need to head that way too," he says, reaching into his pockets and fishing out his phone.

"Really?" Kelly groans.

"Yes, really," he says, pushing past us.

***

Kelly and Aiden bicker over who should hold the leash as we walk to the park. Even though Sassy is my dog, I continue to listen to their argument. Kelly thinks that Aiden should walk Sassy since he's a guy and it would be the gentleman thing to do, but Aiden argues that walking a dog like Sassy will damage his reputation. He says she's too *fluffy*.

I silently take the leash from Kelly as they argue. They don't even notice that I have the leash now. "Or I can walk her. She's my dog after all," I pipe into the conversation.

Aiden smirks at Kelly, and she sticks her tongue out at him. "So, Riley," she says, turning her attention to me. "Tell me about Fairfield."

"It sucks ass," Aiden says as he kicks a rock on the sidewalk.

"I didn't ask you." She snaps at him before looking at me again. "Are there a lot of cute guys there?" She winks at me.

"Um, I don't really pay attention," I tell her honestly. It's not that I'm *not* interested in boys. The boys that go to Fairfield High aren't the sharpest tools in the shed.

Aiden looks amused. "You see, Kelly? Riley here actually focuses on school and not the douche bag population that attends Fairfield."

"C'mon, Riley." She ignores him. "There has to be at least one guy you think is cute."

"She likes me." Aiden flexes his arms.

I frown. "No, I don't." Aiden Callaway is the last person I could ever see myself dating. Sure, he's obviously gorgeous, but his attitude takes away from that.

Kelly cracks up laughing and Aiden huffs. "Did I just witness someone rejecting Aiden Callaway?" She continues to laugh.

"Whatever." He's completely serious. "There are plenty of girls who like me."

Soon enough, we reach the park and Aiden leaves with a guy who's already waiting here. I wonder what kind of lifestyle Aiden has when he's not around his family, or step-family. What could Aiden Callaway possibly do for fun?

Kelly and I hang out at the park for a while after Aiden departs. Kelly plays with Sassy and confesses that she's tempted to dognap Sassy. I quickly protest and I make sure Sassy is in my line of sight at all times.

Once it gets dark, Kelly calls Jenna to pick us up. I convince her that I'm fine walking home by myself.

"Sassy doesn't seem much like a guard dog, though." Kelly laughs.

Jenna soon shows up and takes Kelly home. It's now eight o'clock and I'm walking Sassy along the sidewalk. The cool air feels good against my skin as I walk. I close my eyes and breathe in the fresh air. Nights like this make me feel serene and calm. It's peaceful.

That peacefulness is shattered when I hear angry shouts behind me. My eyes pop open and I steal a glance behind me only to find that there's no one in sight. I continue walking, but the shouting again pierces the air. That's when I learn that the shouting is coming from inside of one of the houses.

Specifically Aiden's house.

I tell myself it's none of my business, but a door opens and the shouting grows louder.

"Get back in this house now, Aiden!" I go ahead and assume Robert is yelling from inside the house.

"I'm fucking done talking to you!" Aiden yells back from the doorway. He slams the door behind him and he starts walking down the driveway. He then turns and walks in the opposite direction I'm walking. If he saw me, he isn't making it obvious.

Part of me wants to follow him and make sure he doesn't get into trouble. The other part of me knows he wants to be alone, so I continue to walk to my house.

Chapter 7

I leave the library before lunch is over so I can stop by my locker to switch out a few books. While at my locker, I notice Ryan walking by with Nicole Sanders hanging on his arm. They stop by the girls' restroom and Nicole goes in, leaving Ryan to wait in the hall.

I'm shutting my locker when I see him approaching me.

"Hey, Riley," he says casually.

The fact that Ryan Dixon addresses me so nonchalantly now is still a strange concept to grasp. "Hi," I say as I slowly face him. I immediately see that something is off about his demeanor.

He rubs the back of his neck. "Have you heard from Aiden at all?"

Why would I know anything about Aiden's whereabouts? "No. Why?" I ask curiously.

"Kelly hasn't told you?" he asks instead of answering me. "Aiden got into another argument with Robert, and he ran off somewhere. He hasn't been home."

The feeling of guilt instantly settles within me. I should have talked to Aiden when I saw him run out of his house. "What were they fighting about?"

Ryan rolls his eyes. "Aiden doesn't exactly like the fact that Robert is marrying my mom. He's constantly fighting with Aiden about the whole thing."

"He got angry and just took off?"

He nods. "I'm pretty sure Robert is close to dumping him from the wedding completely. My mom wants him to be a part of everything, but Aiden obviously doesn't want any part of it."

I wonder what Aiden's problem is with Anna. She doesn't seem like a horrible person.

I'm about to respond to him when I see Nicole walk out of the restroom. She sees Ryan talking to me and I can tell by her gaze that she's sizing me up. Her expression is unreadable. She puts a hand on his shoulder and tears her eyes away from mine.

"Ready to go?" she asks him.

"Yeah," he says. "I'll see you later, Riley."

I give a small wave to him before I continue in the opposite direction in the hall. My mind is swirling with the thought of me going up to Aiden when he ran out of his house. Maybe I could've stopped him, convinced him not to run off somewhere. Would he have listened to me?

***

When I get home, I'm once again greeted by Kelly. After a quick chat with my mom, we head upstairs to my bedroom.

"Your room is so hipster." She stares at my walls in awe. "I love it."

"Thanks," I say as I throw my backpack on the floor.

We sit on my bed as Kelly sighs dramatically and throws herself back. "I get that boys aren't any of your concern right now, but I need to vent about one."

"Go ahead."

She continues to tell me about some guy who reached out to her on social media and goes to a different school in our city. She says he's frustrating but cute at the same time and she doesn't know what to do about it.

She's telling the wrong person about this, obviously.

She sits up suddenly and pulls her phone out of her pocket. She sighs when she looks at the screen. "Hold on," she tells me. "Hello? Aiden?"

Aiden might not like that his dad is marrying Anna, but I'm certain he has a soft spot for Kelly.

"Where the hell are you, dude?" she asks him. "Aiden, everyone is worried sick about you. Just come home, okay?" The frown on her face deepens. She then holds the phone out to me. "Here. You try to knock some sense into him."

I slowly grab the phone from her, and I put it against my ear. "Aiden?" I ask awkwardly. I don't really do well on the phone. I actually can't stand phone conversations. Or conversations in general, but what can you do?

"Put Kelly back on," he demands.

"Aiden, maybe you should—"

"Listen, you tell Kelly that I'm done with this wedding shit and that I'm done dealing with everyone. I'm fine on my own," he says angrily.

I sigh. "Aiden, you know the whole world isn't against you, right?"

"None of this even concerns you. Just stay out of my business. We're not friends and we never will be. Now, let me talk to Kelly again."

I hand the phone to Kelly, and she talks to him for a good five seconds before she looks at the screen and puts her phone down.

"He hung up on me." She presses her lips together. "I was sure he'd listen to you."

"Aiden and I aren't friends or anything. He'll never listen to me." I look down. It doesn't hurt my feelings. I don't need a friend like Aiden Callaway anyway.

Kelly invites me to a party. I try to refuse, but it's kind of hard with her. She has already brought clothes for me and a huge briefcase that is filled with who knows what. My mom had told me that she would be working late.

Apparently, Kelly had told my mom that I would be spending the night with her at her house, so I would have to go to the party.

Sneaky that girl, let me tell you.

I also refuse to wear a dress. I don't like dresses and dresses don't like me. So I reluctantly decide on black jeggings, a denim cut-off shirt, and some light-colored ballet flats. Kelly slips on a short blue sparkly dress with one sleeve. She puts loose curls in her blonde hair while my brown hair is given what Kelly calls beach waves. I complain to her how I don't want to go to the beach, and she rolls her eyes.

A friend of hers meets us at my house and we all make our way to the party. My hands are sweaty in my lap as we drive there. I am extremely nervous, not only because this is my first party, but because I have a bad feeling about tonight.

The music playing at the party location can be heard down the street it is on. I don't know how they can even have this party without neighbors complaining. They must be used to it or something.

Kelly squeals once the house comes into view. "I'm so excited!"

I'm not.

At least I don't have to wear a dress. But these jeggings are skin-tight on me and this shirt is exposing my shoulders, which isn't really me. I don't feel like myself right now.

We pull into a space between two cars about two houses away and get out. Kelly grabs my arm and smiles. "You'll have fun, Riley. I promise."

"Have you ever been to a party before?" I ask her.

She smirked. "Once or twice. But don't tell Ryan or Jenna. They'd kill me if they found out I was here."

Kelly is only sixteen, two years younger than me, and she's already been to her first party.

We walk up to the house and enter without even knocking on the door. This definitely isn't a good idea!

The inside of the house is packed. People are dancing in a certain area with the music blaring next to them. Others have drinks in their hands and are talking to their friends. Laughter is everywhere.

I notice a small blonde girl at the top of a staircase with a drink in her hands. She sways and laughs at something a guy told her. She hands her drink over to him and nods. That's when she lifts her shirt and exposes her chest to everyone in view.

I turn away and shake my head. She'd regret that tomorrow when she finds out it's all over the internet.

Kelly looks at me and grins. "You want a drink?"

"Are you going to drink alcohol?" I ask her, raising my eyebrow. "You're only sixteen."

She rolls her eyes. "Are you going to act like my mother all night? Or are you actually going to let loose and have fun?"

How is getting drunk and acting like a moron fun? "I'll get one later. You go ahead," I tell her so she wouldn't get mad at me. Of course, I won't actually get a drink.

She goes off with some other girl in a different direction and I sigh. Well, now what do I do?

I walk towards a wall where no one is standing. I stand out of the way of everyone and try to make myself invisible. I have a feeling I am *not* going to enjoy tonight.

A guy with short brown hair walks up to me. I notice his green eyes right away. He offers me a smile. "Hey."

I frown a bit. "Hey." I look in another direction, hoping he'd get the hint that I don't want to talk to him. But he doesn't.

"Do you want a drink?" he asked.

I don't look at him. "My friend went to get me one." I lie.

"Are you sure?" he asks.

I squint my eyes at him. "Yes, I'm sure."

"So what's your name, cutie?"

Oh God, please help me.

"Riley," I answer simply.

He holds out his hand. "I'm Lucas."

I stare at his hand before reluctantly taking it.

"So, are you having a good time?" he asks me. Trying to make conversation, are we?

"Oh yeah. I'm having a *great* time," I say sarcastically. I suddenly have a boost of confidence in me, and I turn my whole body towards him.

He chuckles. "You're not like most girls, are you?"

"What do you mean?" I ask, getting caught off guard.

"You aren't drinking anything. You aren't dressed like a slut, and you are definitely trying to get rid of me right now," he says, smiling at the end of his sentence.

I turn my head and take in his appearance. He has on a dark green t-shirt, dark jeans, and black shoes.

"Checking me out now, are we?" he asks me, smirking.

"Cocky, are we?" I mimic him. Where did this boost of confidence come from?

Lucas nods. "Nope. Definitely not like most girls."

We fall into an awkward silence. I won't say it is completely silent, though, with the music and people trying to shout over the music.

"What did you say your last name was?" Lucas asks me after a while.

"I didn't say." I look at him. "But it's Summers."

He raises his eyebrows. "Is Carol Summers your mom?"

"Yeah, she is," I say slowly. How does he know my mom? "Why?"

"Your mom works with my mom, Catherine Thompson," he says matter-of-factly.

I can remember my mom mentioning a friend from work named Catherine. They go out for drinks along with Anna sometimes.

"I heard your mom saying something about you one time and she said your name." Lucas shrugs. Then he smiles. "I promise I'm not a stalker or anything."

I chuckle. "Well, thanks for letting me know." Talking to him isn't as bad now.

"Hey, your mom is friends with Anna Dixon, right?" he asks me. I nod. "Are you going to her wedding that's coming up pretty soon?"

I roll my eyes. "Yeah. I'm actually a bridesmaid."

"No shit." Lucas grins. "Anna actually asked me yesterday to be a groomsman since some other dude got kicked out of the wedding."

Wait, is he talking about Aiden?

"Riley!" someone shouts behind me. I turn and see Kelly making her way towards me. She is giggling with a red cup in her hands. "Riley, where have you been? I've been looking for you!"

She is obviously tipsy already.

"I've been standing right here the whole time," I tell her, rolling my eyes. I'm going to end up babysitting her tonight.

Her eyes drift towards Lucas. "Hey! I know you!" She points at him. Then she looks at me. "Have you been talking to him?"

I nod. "Um, yeah?"

She grins from ear to ear. "Way to go, Riley! You're actually socializing with a guy! I'm so proud of you!" she yells. "And with an attractive guy too! I'll leave you two to continue talking." She giggles then walks away.

I smack my forehead and groan. "Oh my gosh."

"That wasn't Anna's daughter...was it?" Lucas asks slowly.

I nod. "Yeah, it was. I'll probably end up taking care of her later on tonight."

"Isn't she only like, sixteen?"

Once again, I nod.

"She does know her brother is here, right?"

"Well, if Ryan sees her, she's dead meat," I say to him.

"You know Ryan?"

"Vaguely."

Lucas looks around and then back at me. "You wanna dance?"

"Not really."

He smiles at me. "You know you do."

I shake my head. "I'm fine right here. But if you want to go dance, then don't let me stop you."

He shakes his head. "Nah, I'll be okay. Besides, I kind of like your company."

Is this flirting?

"You're funny." I scoff. I wonder if Aiden cares that this guy is replacing him. "So, you're going to be in Anna's wedding too?"

He nods. "Yeah. Apparently, the groom's son got kicked out of the wedding and Ryan is now the best man."

Ryan didn't tell me that when we talked. "Interesting," I say simply.

***

It's close to midnight and I decide to look around for Kelly. I have no idea how we will get home since one of her friends drove us here. We really should have thought this through a little better.

Lucas has stayed by my side this whole time. I even let him get me a drink, but I had to watch him do it. I told him no alcohol, and he followed through with it. He's now helping me look for her.

"I have no idea where she is, or how we'll get home…" I am already frustrated.

Lucas puts his arm around me. "We'll find her soon. Don't worry."

I wiggle out from his grasp and look around. If something happens to Kelly, I'll never forgive myself.

"Led Zeppelin girl?"

I whirl around and find Aiden leaning against the wall with a red cup in his hands. He eyes me suspiciously. "What the hell are you doing here? This definitely isn't your scene."

"Maybe I wanted a change of scenery." I snap at him. I still remember when he was very rude to me when we talked on the phone that one time.

He smirks, then his eyes land on Lucas. "And who's this? Your boyfriend?"

"He is not my boyfriend. He is a friend." I frown at Aiden. "What are you doing here? I thought you were cowering away from your dad." Once I say that, I instantly regret it. I didn't mean for it to come out as harshly as it did.

"Cowering?" he asked, taking a step towards me. "Princess, I am not a coward. I'm fucking amazing."

That makes no sense.

"Aiden? What are you doing here?" Ryan asks. I look at him and he acknowledges me.

"I'm here to party." Aiden puts his hands up. "Seems to be the only thing I can do nowadays."

"Your dad has been worried about you," Ryan tells Aiden.

"I told him," I say to Ryan. "He doesn't want to listen to anybody."

Aiden looks angrily at me. "How about you mind your own fucking business?"

"Hey, man, she didn't do anything to you." Lucas comes to my defense, even though I don't need his input.

Aiden looks at Lucas. "Was I talking to you, bitch?"

Ryan steps in front of Aiden. "Aiden, you need to calm down."

"No! This piece of shit needs to keep his fucking mouth shut!" Aiden exclaims.

"Do you have to be so dramatic?" I ask Aiden as I roll my eyes.

"Shut the fuck up, Riley." Aiden snaps at me.

Lucas steps in front of me this time. "I suggest you back off, man. You don't need to be talking like that in front of a girl."

Aiden shoves Ryan out of the way and swings at Lucas. Before I can register what is going on, Lucas and Aiden are punching each other right and left on the floor. Ryan and another guy try to pry them off each other.

I feel someone tug on my arm and find that it's Kelly. She looks seriously drunk.

Ryan finally manages to get Lucas off Aiden, and he puts some distance between them. Once Kelly sees Ryan, she hides behind me. But I know that won't work. Ryan yells at Aiden, who has a black eye, a cut above his eyebrow, and red knuckles. As for Lucas, he only has a small cut under his eye.

"Aiden, you're coming with me," Ryan says with authority in his voice. He notices Kelly standing behind me. "Kelly, I can see you."

"No, you can't," she mutters into my shirt.

Ryan rolls his eyes then looks at me. "You two are coming with me too."

Lucas speaks up. "I can take them home."

"You've done enough for tonight," Ryan says to Lucas. "I'll take them."

***

It's decided that Ryan will take Kelly home so she won't get into any more trouble and I must take Aiden in. I am completely against the idea, but I lose in the end. My mom texts me saying that I probably won't see her until about eight in the morning.

And that is how we end up here with Aiden holding ice to his face while I argue with him.

"This is your fault," I say to him angrily. "We were all doing fine until you decided to show up and ruin things by getting into a petty fight." I was actually enjoying myself with Lucas. He wasn't trying too hard to flirt with me, and when he did, it was mild. He was good company.

"Seems like the story of my life right now. Life is a party for me until I go and fuck things up." He shakes his head.

I sigh. "I understand that you're going through a rough time right now, but you don't need to—"

"To what? Mess everything up for everyone?" he asks angrily. "Somehow I always do. And I don't need your sympathy. How do you know I'm going through a rough time right now?"

"Why else would you run away from home?" I ask him. "In all honesty, Aiden, that is a cowardly thing to do. You're basically running from whatever it is that is upsetting you instead of facing it."

He gives me a cold, hard stare. I know I am right and he knows it too. "This is how I deal with it," he says lowly. "I'm not a coward."

"Whatever," I say, getting up from the couch. I walk to our linen closet and grab two blankets and a pillow. I set them down on the couch next to him. "Here. Just so you know, my mom will be here about eight in the morning. And if you need any Band-Aids for your injuries, they're in the hall bathroom right there. There's a box on the counter of them."

I run upstairs and change into my pajamas. Once my head hits the pillow, I fall into a deep sleep.

***

I wake up with a start the next morning. I repeatedly blink until I can read the time on the clock near my bed.

It's seven thirty in the morning.

I yawn then stretch and sit up in bed. I definitely need more sleep considering I didn't go to sleep until about one in the morning.

Events from last night come rushing back into my mind and I get out of bed. I walk to my dresser and find a small folded white piece of paper sitting by my brush. I grab the paper and open it slowly.

Thanks for the help last night. —A

A small smile breaks out on my lips when I read this and what is also below it.

P.S. you look cute when you sleep.

Chapter 8

Saturday morning, my mom and I are sitting on the couch watching *Steel Magnolias*. We each have a bowl of cereal in our hands.

"I don't know why we watch this movie. It always makes me cry in the end," my mom says as she eats her cereal.

I smile. "That's what makes it a good movie."

Personally, I'm not paying attention. I'm a little worried about Kelly. I wonder if her mom knows she got drunk last night at the party. Ryan probably got a hold of her.

"So I thought you were going to stay at Kelly's house," my mom spoke up. "What happened?"

Oh! I haven't thought this through yet! "Um…Kelly got sick and you know how I am around sick people." Seriously? That's all I could think of?

"Oh," she says. "Poor Kelly. I wonder how she's doing this morning."

My mom is actually buying it. Victory dance! "Yeah. I'm going to go call her real quick." I stand up. I walk into the kitchen and put my empty cereal bowl in the sink. I run upstairs to my room, grab my phone, and call Kelly.

"Hello?" she answers sleepily.

"Did I wake you up?" I ask.

"Kind of." She groans. "My head feels like it weighs a ton."

I smirk. If I drank as much as she did last night, I would feel the same way. But I was smarter. "I bet it does."

"And I got an earful from Ryan last night. He promised not to tell Mom though."

"That's good," I say. I don't want her to get into too much trouble.

She sighs. "Yeah. I'll talk to you later Riley. I need medicine."

I hang up with her and sit on my bed for a minute. My thoughts drift to Aiden then. Did he go back home to see his dad after he left this morning?

There's a knock at my door, then it opens. My mom walks in and smiles at me.

"Riley, Anna just called me—"

"And she wants us all to meet at her house." I finish for her.

She nods. "They want everyone there by ten o'clock to discuss some things."

"Okay." I look at the clock by my bed. It's going to be nine thirty.

My mom leaves my room to let me get ready. I gather up some clothes and take a shower.

***

"How is everything going?" my mom asks me as she drives.

"With what?"

She glances at me then back at the road. "With the wedding, Riley. How's it going?"

"Oh," I say. "It's going fine I guess."

I know she isn't satisfied with my answer. But she knows I don't give her details even when she wants them. My mom and I talk to each other, but we aren't very close. Like I've said before, she wanted a peppy, popular cheerleader for a daughter but she got me instead.

We pull up to Anna's house right at ten o'clock, and I open the passenger door.

"Behave, Riley. And have fun," my mom says to me as I get out.

"Will do." I nod. I walk up to the front door, and before I can ring the doorbell, someone opens it.

That someone is Kelly.

She smiles at me and opens her arms. "There you are." She gives me a hug.

I walk inside and Kelly shuts the door behind me. We walk into the living room and I see the girls sitting there with a few other guys I'm assuming are the groomsmen. A few look older than me. Ryan gives me a small wave, which I return.

Not too long after I get there, two other guys walk in. One of which is Lucas. He sits down with the guy he came with, and Anna enters the room with Robert at her side.

She smiles at all of us. "I'm glad everyone could make it today. We just have to discuss a few matters that need to be taken care of."

I happen to glance at Lucas and he looks in my direction also. He smiles at me and I smile back. The cut he had gotten last night is still slightly visible on his cheek.

"With less than two weeks left until the wedding, our first rehearsal will be next Thursday at six o'clock in the evening. It will be held at the church down the road. We will let you know when the next rehearsal after that will be later on," Anna says to all of us. Then she starts talking to one of the other groomsmen personally.

Lucas stands up from his seat and makes his way in my direction. Kelly elbows me, and when I turn to scowl at her, she just winks at me.

"Hey, Riley," Lucas greets.

"Lucas," I acknowledge him. "How's your face?"

He chuckles. "It's doing alright. How's your friend's face?"

"Aiden is not my friend. But he seemed fine," I tell him.

"Okay!" Anna exclaims. "I almost forgot to mention this, but we will be taking pictures next Friday. So I want all of you to have your dresses and tuxes by Thursday. Maybe before the rehearsal, you can all get those," she suggests. "And the rehearsal *dinner* will be held sometime not next week, but the week after."

Someone asks Anna something and she walks over to them real quick.

"So you're the only brunette out of all five bridesmaids?" Lucas asks me.

I nod. "Which means I'm going to stand out in front of everyone."

"Isn't that a good thing?" he asks.

"No." I shake my head. "I prefer to stay invisible, if that's possible."

Lucas laughs a bit. "Well, good luck with that."

"One more thing, ladies and gentlemen!" Anna says. "When we take the pictures, we will have one group picture, one of myself and Robert, singles of the bridesmaids and groomsmen, and also the couple pictures of the groomsmen and bridesmaids. Which means I have to assign you to a partner." She says something to Robert and he leaves her side for a moment.

Robert comes back with a small notepad and a pen, which he hands to her. "Okay. Jenna and Ryan will be partners since they are the maid of honor and the best man." She writes it down on the notepad. "Then we will have Kelly with Drew, Halle with Max, Holly with Lucas, and Riley with Steven."

"Hey, Mom," Kelly speaks up. "Don't you think Riley and Lucas should be paired together, since they're closer in age?"

What is Kelly doing?

Anna hesitates for a moment. "I suppose you're right. Riley will be paired with Lucas, and Holly will be paired with Steven."

Lucas grins at me when Anna finishes talking.

"Okay," Anna says as she finishes writing. "Now that's done and over with—" she hands the notepad and pen back to Robert "—Robert is going to be making lunch soon, so you're all welcome to stay and eat." She smiles at us.

Well, I have nothing else to do today, so might as well stay.

A door slams somewhere in the house and we all look around confused. My eyes widen a bit when I see Aiden walking in with his leather jacket hanging off his shoulder.

"Sorry I'm late, everyone. Just wasn't in a hurry to get here," he says as he plops himself onto a chair. He notices me and offers me a smile and a wave.

Robert walks up to him and crosses his arms. "Aiden, I need to talk to you outside."

Aiden crosses his arms as well. "Nah, I think I'm good."

"That wasn't a question, Aiden," Robert says lowly.

"I think I'm just going to hang out with my dear friend Riley for a minute," Aiden says, standing up. He walks towards me and sits right between Lucas and me.

His dear friend Riley? Where did that come from?

"Hey, Riley," he says to me. He glances at Lucas and holds out his hand. "Hey, man. Sorry about your face."

Once everyone sees that the drama is over, they make their way towards the kitchen. Robert and Anna talk quietly to each other. No doubt talking about Aiden and what they will do with him.

Lucas shakes Aiden's hand. "No harm done."

Aiden looks at me seriously. "Thanks for last night, even though I was a complete jerk to you most of the time."

"I don't know if I should forgive you." I raise my eyebrow. He thinks he can just come over here and pretend we're best friends? No, I don't think so.

"I think you should," he says to me. "You're practically the only person who I can tolerate talking to right now."

"And that's why I should forgive you?"

"Yes." He nods.

I sigh. "Whatever. Just know I'm not going to put up with your crap anymore." I point at him.

He grins. "Okay."

I look over his shoulder and notice Lucas is no longer sitting next to him. "When did Lucas leave?" I ask, looking around for him.

"Who? The guy I punched last night?" Aiden asks.

"His name is Lucas, Aiden." I roll my eyes. I spot Lucas talking to Kelly near the kitchen door.

Aiden smirks. "So Kelly got wasted?" he asks quietly.

I nod. "She said she got an earful from Ryan."

He shakes his head and laughs. "I bet she didn't even drink that much. She probably just acted like she did."

How can you tell if someone is just pretending to be drunk?

I hear laughter come from the kitchen and sigh. Aiden and I are the only ones in the living room. Everyone else is enjoying themselves. They are basically all family or are close. I just got thrown in with the bunch and am expected to fit in.

Well, that's how I see it at least.

I look at Aiden then. "How did we end up sitting in here by ourselves?"

Aiden shrugs. "Hell if I know. Well, I'm not exactly welcome here anyways."

"Honestly, Aiden," I start. "You are scary and intimidating and frightening, and I don't understand why you're around me. We are not the same." I look him straight in the eye.

He stares at me before answering. "And you are innocent, nerdy, awkward, and not easy to converse with. But we are the same. We are both outcasts."

I guess he has a point there. I don't fit in because I *am* nerdy. I'm not like all these other girls who giggle every five seconds.

Then there's Aiden who everyone is kind of afraid to talk to.

"Do you have any close friends?" I ask him out of the blue.

"Define *close friend*," he says, leaning back.

I think for a minute. "Someone who you can talk to about anything. Someone who knows the real you and doesn't care. Someone who will always be there for you."

He hesitates but eventually answers. "No."

"Neither do I," I say as I think about it. Sure, Kelly is a friend, but she hardly knows anything about me.

"So, you think I'm scary?" he asks, sounding amused.

I nod. "Yes. Yes, I do."

He chuckles. "I'm not that bad."

"You just keep telling yourself that," I tell him. "Do you want to go into the kitchen?"

"I told you, I'm not exactly welcome," Aiden says sourly. "I'm fine right here."

I stay put and sigh.

"Aren't you going to go inside?" he asks me after a while.

"Aren't outcasts supposed to stick together?" I ask him.

A smile plays at his lips. "I guess we are."

Chapter 9

Later in the evening, I am at home alone again. Mom said something about going out with some friends and won't be home until late tonight. So here I am, sitting on the couch with a bowl of popcorn and watching my favorite movies.

Currently, I am watching *Star Wars Episode II: Attack of the Clones*. I had already watched the first one, *The Phantom Menace*. And I intend to watch the rest of them tonight.

The sound of the doorbell surprises me while watching the movie. I never have company this late, so I cautiously stand up from the couch. I grab the remote, pause the movie and slowly walk towards the door. There isn't a window near our front door, so I can't peek out and see who it is.

"Who is it?" I call out. There is no answer though.

I reach out and grasp the doorknob. I take a deep breath, raise the remote in my hand, and swing open the door.

Standing there with surprised faces are Kelly and Aiden.

"Riley?" Kelly questions me.

Jeez. I probably look ridiculous holding this remote in my hand. I find myself blushing. "Oh. Hey."

Aiden starts to laugh at me, making my face grow even hotter. "What the hell were you going to do with a remote? I don't think you can kill anyone with that thing."

Kelly chuckles along with him. "Seriously, Riley. Just let us in. We're not killers."

I stay quiet and open the door wider for them. They walk into my house and I shut the door behind them. I still feel embarrassed.

"So what are you guys doing here again?" I ask them.

Kelly looks at me. "I was bored at home and recruited Aiden to come here with me."

"I had nothing to do either." He shrugs.

"Well, I'm not really doing anything either. Just watching movies," I answer.

Kelly starts to walk into the living room, so Aiden and I follow.

"What are you watching?" Kelly asks me.

"*Star Wars*." I smile, easing up a bit.

Aiden chuckles. "Nerd."

Kelly sits on the big chair and makes herself comfortable. "I've never seen this movie."

She did not just say that. "You've never seen *Star Wars*?" I ask her immediately. "Have you been living under a rock your whole life?"

"Oh, the irony," Aiden says as he sits down on the couch. That is the spot where I had been sitting this whole time.

I shake my head. "You can't sit there. I basically claimed that spot."

Kelly laughs. "You sound like Sheldon from *The Big Bang Theory*."

Well, at least she's seen that show. "It's decided then. You must stay and watch *Star Wars*," I tell her, smiling.

She shrugs. "Okay."

I find the first movie and put it back on. When I walk back to the couch, Aiden is still sitting in my spot. "Sorry, but you're going to have to move." I cross my arms.

"And what'll happen if I don't?" he asks. Amusement fills his eyes.

"Then I will sit on you."

He grins. "Go ahead. I don't think I would have a problem with that."

Oh goodness. "Never mind." I roll my eyes. I sit next to him instead of fighting with him. I press play on the remote and sit back.

"Is this popcorn?" Aiden reaches for the bowl. He grabs a handful of popcorn and stuffs it into his mouth.

Sometime during the movie, Aiden finishes the popcorn himself and starts to complain how he wants more. Kelly repeatedly tells him to shut up, but he continues to whine.

I finally grab the bowl and stand up. "Fine. I'll go make some more." I stalk off towards the kitchen.

I stick a bag of popcorn into the microwave and wait. I cross my arms and I notice it's quite dark in the kitchen. Feeling a little uneasy, I turn to flip the switch. But a tall figure blocks me from it. I jump back, not expecting anyone to be in here with me.

Aiden chuckles at me. "Jumpy, are we?"

"Just a little bit." I lie. "What are you doing in here?"

"Waiting for the popcorn of course," he answers as he takes a step towards me. I feel how close he is to me and swallow.

I take a deep breath. "Um, can you turn on the light switch behind you?" I ask nicely.

"Why? I kind of like it like this," he replies.

I turn back towards the microwave and sigh. Just twenty more seconds.

If Aiden wasn't standing close to me before, he sure is now. I feel his presence directly behind me and it's a little unsettling. He doesn't say anything for a moment. The microwave beeps and I open the small door. I grab the bag, shake it and listen for any loose kernels. When I hear none, I start to open the bag. Suddenly, Aiden's hands cover mine.

"Careful there. Wouldn't want to burn yourself, would you?" he whispers into my ear, sending shivers up my spine.

"I'm fine," I say, sounding a bit shaky. I open the bag and pour the popcorn into the bowl in front of me.

His hands trail up my arms, making me freeze. They rest on my shoulders for a moment before they pull my hair back, exposing my neck. I close my eyes when I feel him breathing. "Are you sure about that?" he asks quietly. As he speaks, his lips brush against my skin.

I involuntarily sigh and nod, not trusting my voice.

His lips press against the skin on my neck. My heart is beating so loudly, I'm sure he can hear it. He places small kisses from my neck to my jawline as his hands rest on my hips, holding me in place. His hands put a bit of pressure on my sides. My shirt rides up a bit, and his fingers brush my skin. His touch feels like fire.

"Let's get back. Wouldn't want Kelly to make any assumptions, do we?" I feel his lips touching my ear as he speaks to me.

Aiden grabs the bowl and steps away from me. I look at him incredulously and he just winks at me.

When we reenter the living room, Kelly's eyes are glued to the screen. She pays no attention to us as we sit on the opposite ends of the couch.

I don't pay attention to the rest of the movie. My head is still trying to process what just happened in my kitchen. What was going through Aiden's mind during all of that?

"Riley."

What on earth possessed him to do such a thing? I couldn't even do anything either. I just stood there and let him do as he pleased.

"Riley?"

How helpless I felt. How did he make me feel that way? I have never been touched like that. Knowing I let Aiden do that to me feels unnerving, but then it feels okay.

"Riley!"

I blink and look at Kelly. She frowns at me once I look at her. "Were you zoned out or something?" she asks. "The movie is over. I thought we could watch the second one now."

I nod. "Oh. Okay." I stand up and look for the second movie. Once I find it, I pop it in and go back to the couch.

Aiden glances at me as I sit down. "Are you okay, Riley? You seem…distracted." A smile plays at his lips.

He is toying with me.

"I'm fine. Not distracted at all," I tell him confidently.

"Can we watch the movie now? You two can flirt some other time," Kelly says.

Aiden chuckles while my cheeks burn with embarrassment for about the millionth time tonight. I have never been accused of flirting with someone. Hearing that come from Kelly feels weird.

I press play on the remote and let myself get zoned into the world of *Star Wars* and not the world of Aiden.

Chapter 10

The next few days go by pretty quickly. There's nothing like spending eight hours surrounded by people who you can't stand. Seriously, I'm just ready to graduate already and leave this stupid school. I don't know why, but lately, it seems like I'm always on edge. I snapped at my mother on Tuesday morning because she didn't buy the right jelly for my toast.

Ridiculous, I know.

It's now Thursday, and I'm stressing over a test I have in my Principles of Democracy class. I really haven't studied for it and I'm worried about getting a bad grade. I try studying during lunch in the library but my brain is just not functioning today. So that puts me in a bad mood.

I'm making my way to class when someone bumps my shoulder as they pass by. I end up dropping my binder, causing a few papers to fly out.

"Great," I say sarcastically. I get down and start to pick up the papers. I think I have them all until someone hands me two more papers. I look up and see that it's Ryan handing them to me.

He smiles at me. "Losing your papers?"

I grab the papers and stuff them into my binder. I stand up and look at him. "More like losing my mind." I sigh.

"Is something wrong?" he asks.

I shrug. "I'm just in a bad mood and I don't want to deal with people."

"Then you shouldn't come to school if you don't want to deal with people." Ryan chuckles. "Or any public place for that matter."

I roll my eyes at him. "Well, thanks for that wonderful advice."

"So are you ready to take pictures tomorrow?" he asks me.

Pictures? What is he talking about? "What?" I ask, confused.

His eyebrow rises. "The pictures for the wedding. Remember? We're supposed to have our outfits by today."

"Oh crap." I close my eyes. As if I don't have enough to deal with. Now I have to get that stupid dress so we can take stupid pictures tomorrow.

"You forgot," Ryan says, sounding amused.

I nod.

"If it makes you feel any better, I'm barely getting my tux this afternoon."

"I can't believe I forgot about my dress," I say then sigh. "Well, if you'll excuse me, I have to go make a phone call to my mother," I say as I start to walk around him. I feel his arm wrap around mine and pull me back in front of him.

"I could take you with me this afternoon. I can get my tux and you can get your dress," he suggests.

I purse my lips. It will save me from getting yelled at by my mom. She will probably get all peeved off about me not telling her until the last minute. "Okay." I nod. "I'll go with you."

Ryan smiles. "Great. I'll meet you at the front entrance of the school when the bell rings."

***

Good news: I passed my Principles of Democracy test with an 89. It isn't an A, but it's close enough.

Bad news: I forgot to finish the homework that's due today and I got scolded by my teacher.

Once the bell rings, I make my way out of the classroom and start to walk towards the front entrance. Honestly, all this wedding stuff is the least of my worries right now. But if I forget to get my dress in time for the pictures, that will be so disrespectful and I will be letting Anna down.

I notice Ryan leaning against the wall near the front doors. He sees me walking towards him and pushes himself off the wall.

"Ready?" he asks.

I nod.

"Let's go then."

We walk out of the school and into the parking lot. Ryan says hi to numerous people as we walk. Most of them give me weird looks. They are probably wondering what I am doing walking with Ryan.

Leaning against Ryan's car is Nicole. Once she spots me, her eyes turn to slits. "And what do you think you're doing?" she asks me once we are close enough.

I'm about to answer, but Ryan cuts me off. "We're going to get some stuff for the wedding."

"Why does this involve her?" Nicole asks him. More like *demands*.

He crosses his arms. "She's a bridesmaid."

"So your mom asked her to be a bridesmaid and not me?" She sounds offended. "I'm your girlfriend, Ryan!"

He holds his hands up in defense. "I have no control over who she picks." He takes a step closer to her and kisses her cheek. "We have to go now. I'll call you later."

She puts her hands on her hips. "We're not done talking about this."

"It sounds like you are," I say as Ryan unlocks his car. I rush by Nicole and get on the passenger side. Ryan chuckles as he gets on the driver's side.

He pulls out of the school's parking lot. "What's with the sudden burst of confidence?"

"I said I wasn't going to deal with people." I give him a small smile. "So, where to first?" I ask him.

"If it's alright with you, I'd like to get my tux first. Then we can get your dress," he says as he stares at the road.

"I don't mind. You're the one driving," I tell him.

We fall into a comfortable silence for a while. I stare out the window and watch cars as we pass them.

"I'm sorry about Nicole." Ryan's voice interrupts the silence. "She can be really cool, I promise."

I smirk. "I'm sure she's 'cool' to half the guys in the school." I instantly slap my hand over my mouth once I realize what I said. I basically just called his girlfriend a slut in front of him. "I'm sorry. I didn't mean that. That was totally out of line. You can kick me out of the car right now if you want to. I won't be offended—"

His hand covers my mouth and he chuckles. "No worries, Riley. Calm down." He uncovers my mouth. "I know she was like that last year before we started dating, but I know she's changed."

That's what he thinks. But I'm not going to say anything.

"She just gets kind of jealous when I'm talking to another girl."

"Doesn't any girl get jealous when she sees her boyfriend talking to another girl?" I ask him.

He raises his eyebrow. "Are you defending her?"

"No. I'm just asking." I cross my arms.

"Why? Do *you* get jealous when you see the guy you like talking to some other girl?" he asks, sounding entertained.

I scoff. "I do not like anybody. All the guys at our school are idiots."

"Well, thanks." He rolls his eyes. "C'mon, Riley, you can tell me who you like. We're basically best friends."

"Best friends my ass."

Ryan laughs. "That is the first time I've heard you swear, Riley."

"I can promise you that I don't like anyone," I tell him. It's true though. All guys are idiots, but especially the ones who go to Fairfield.

"You like Aiden, don't you?"

My eyes widen and I glare at him. "I do not like Aiden. We're just acquaintances."

Ryan laughs some more. "It's okay, Riley. I won't tell him."

"Oh my goodness. There is nothing to tell," I say, hitting his arm. "I would threaten to spill embarrassing things to the girl you liked, but you already have a girlfriend and I have nothing on you, so that wouldn't work."

"And you will never find out the embarrassing things about me." He smiles. "Can I be honest with you, Riley?"

"Well, I would hope that aren't lying to me."

He smirks. "Seriously."

"Okay. Be honest with me," I say to him.

He takes a deep breath. "I sort of liked you before I found out that you'd be in my mom's wedding."

My jaw drops a little. "You liked...*me*? *Why*?"

Ryan smiles. "I don't know. You were different," he says. "Well, you still are."

"Wait. You say *liked*, as in past tense. What happened?"

He shrugs. "I actually talked to you, and something changed. I see you more as a sisterly figure, if that makes sense."

I nod. "It makes sense."

"Good." He grins. "So are we best friends now?"

I laugh at him. "I guess we can be. I don't know how that would affect my social status," I say snobbishly.

He puts his hand over his heart. "That hurts, Riley. You'd put your reputation before our friendship."

"Please." I waved my hand. "I should be concerned about that, not you."

"What's that supposed to mean?" he asks, frowning a bit.

I sigh. "You're Ryan Dixon. You're the star football player with the perfect girlfriend. And I'm Riley the nerd girl who no one talks to." I play with my fingers. "It would probably look weird if I started to hang out with you."

"Wow," he says. "Listen, I could care less what people would think. If you want me to, I could shout out that you're my best friend now." He nudges me. "And sure, you're a nerd, but who's going to be making fun of you when you're making ten times more money than the rest of us in five years?"

If you told me last year that Ryan Dixon would ask me to be his best friend and would say that being a nerd is okay, I would have thought you had serious issues and ask you to bring yourself to a mental hospital.

I grin. "You sure know how to make a girl feel a little better about herself."

"That's what I'm here for," he says. He parks the car and pulls the keys out of the ignition. "Now let's get my tux."

***

After getting his tux and my dress, Ryan drives me home. Somehow talking to him is a bit easier than talking to Kelly. It feels more natural.

He pulls up to my house and parks. "Well, this afternoon was fun, Riley."

"It was." I agree as I unbuckle. I grab my dress, which is in a full-length bag, and open the passenger door. "Thanks so much, Ryan. This was really nice of you."

"That's what friends are for, right?" he asks.

I nod. "Right." I get out of the car. "See you tomorrow," I say before shutting the door. I walk up to the front door and unlock it. Ryan drives off right as I shut and lock the door.

"Mom! I'm home!" I call out. I lay my dress on the dining table and look around. "Mom?"

"In the kitchen!"

I walk into the kitchen and find my mom cutting up some watermelon. She looks up at me and smiles. "Hey, Riley."

I sit down on a chair at the island. "Hey."

"How was school?" she questions.

"Same." I shrug. "How was work?"

She smiles. "Pretty good." She hands me a slice of watermelon and I gladly accept it. "You seem like you're in a pretty good mood."

"Yeah," I answer plainly. "I have my bridesmaid dress with me. A friend drove me to go get it for pictures tomorrow."

"What friend?" she asks as she puts the knife in the sink. She sits near me at the island.

"Ryan. Anna's son," I say, taking a bite of the watermelon in my hand.

My mom raises her eyebrow. "Is that why you're in such a good mood?"

"Please, Mom." I roll my eyes. "Ryan and I are just friends. I don't like him like that and he has a girlfriend."

"Alright fine." She sighs.

I finish eating the watermelon then walk in the dining room and grab my dress. I run up to my room and shut my door behind me. I set my dress on my bed and stare at it. It's a pretty dress; don't get me wrong. But it just isn't...my taste.

The more I think about my dress, the more it occurs to me how the wedding is not too far in the future. We have about a week until the wedding and it's going to go by fast. From what I've seen on TV, everyone starts to stress out during the last week.

I grab the dress and put it in my closet. I don't want to look at it until tomorrow.

My phone starts to buzz in my back pocket, so I pull it out. I look at the screen and notice it's a text from an unknown number.

Are you doing anything right now? —A

I forgot I had given Aiden my number when we were at Anna's house. I told him to text me that day, so I had his number, but he never did. So I guess I have it now.

No. Why?

It's not every day he just asks questions like that.

—Can you meet me at the park?

—Sure.

I grab Sassy's leash and pick her up. I might as well take her out for a walk if I'm going to the park.

"Mom, I'm taking Sassy out," I call out as soon as I reach the bottom of the stairs.

"Okay! Be careful, Riley!" she calls back.

I hook Sassy's leash on and walk out the door.

Chapter 11

Sassy only walks halfway to the park. The rest of the way I hold her in my arms. She is one spoiled dog. I must really love this dog if I'm willing to hold her like this.

The park comes into view and I sigh. I wonder what Aiden wants.

We get to the grass and I put Sassy back down on the ground. But once her paws hit the grass, she lays down on her stomach. I tug on her leash. "C'mon Sassy."

Did she budge? Not even a centimeter.

"Sassy, you lazy dog, I'm not going to hold you the whole time." I scold her. "We need to start walking."

She looks up at me and tilts her head to the side. Sometimes I wish I know what she thinks of me. She probably thinks of me as her maid or something. I tug on her leash again. She looks like she is about to stand up but she lies back down.

"Sassy, I will leave you here," I tell her. "I mean it."

"Are you really threatening a dog?"

I whirl around and find Aiden standing behind me. "I'm not threatening her. I'm scolding her."

Aiden rolls his eyes and bends down. Once Sassy sees him, she gets up and goes straight into his arms.

"It seems like she likes you," I say to him.

He chuckles. "Don't be jealous because she likes me better than you."

"I am not jealous," I argue. "Why did you want me to come here in the first place?" I demand from him.

He stands up with Sassy in his arms. "I wanted to talk to you."

"About?" I cross my arms.

"The wedding," he says, turning serious. "Let's go sit on that bench," he says as he starts to walk away. I follow him silently.

We reach the bench and set Sassy down on the ground. Aiden sits down on the bench and pats the spot next to him. "Sit down. I won't bite." He winks.

I sit down next to him and sigh. "So, why do you want to talk about the wedding?"

"Why do you ask so many questions?" He raises his eyebrow. I stare at him until he speaks again. "Just kidding. Jeez. But anyways, you seem like the only person who understands where I'm coming from right now. I thought I had Kelly on my side, but she thinks she's the shit now because she got wasted at that party."

Is that why she hasn't talked to me?

He takes a deep breath and looks at the ground below him. "My mom died when I was seven." I realize then that he's opening up to me. He's going to tell me his life story. "I remember her perfectly. She always curled her hair then would put it up in a ponytail. She always told my dad how lucky she was to find a guy like him. And she made a killer cheesecake." He smiles slightly.

"Then she got sick." His smile falters. "I didn't understand it then, but she had gotten cancer. I always wondered why she would tell me she's going to the doctor. I asked her what was wrong, but she told me she must have gotten a stomach bug or some shit like that."

"She knew you wouldn't understand," I comment.

He nods. "She made it seem like nothing was wrong. But I started to really wonder when she ended up in the hospital. I caught my dad crying every now and then, and it scared me. I remember the last conversation I had with my mom. We were visiting her in the hospital and I was sitting next to her bed. She held my hand and told me to always be a strong boy. No matter what." He purses his lips. I almost thought he's going to cry, but when he looks up, his face holds no emotion. "Things were harder after she died. Dad was working two jobs, so I hardly saw him. My dad and I had a pretty good relationship while Mom was still alive. But that changed."

He looks at Sassy in front of him and starts petting her. "I was in the seventh grade when he met Anna," he says, his voice sounding a bit bitter. "Each time she was around, he always said she was just a friend. She was constantly around and kept trying to be my friend. He eventually told me that they were dating. Seeing him with her when she was first around didn't settle with me. She was not my mom and she would never be my mom. I told my dad that when he told me they were dating. In a way, I hated my dad for doing that to my mom. How could he ever love another woman, you know?"

I nod. I can relate to Aiden in a way. I know my mom will start dating eventually. But none of those guys will be my dad.

"Our relationship has never been the same. I found out a year after they started dating that she had three kids of her own. Turns out she had divorced her husband because he cheated on her. My dad started to hang out with her kids more and more while I just sat back and watched him. He helped Ryan get into football. Did you know that? And me? I just got the talk on how I should have been in football or soccer or something. Ryan was the son he always wanted," Aiden rants. "I've never liked Ryan. I don't know if I ever will."

"Are you mad that Ryan's the best man now?" I ask him cautiously.

He shakes his head. "Fuck no. I don't even want to be in this stupid wedding. I told my dad straight up that I wasn't going to go. I think that was the day I left you and Kelly at the park."

I remember that day. I had heard Aiden yelling profanities at his dad while walking back home. I remember telling myself it wasn't my business.

"Do you hate Anna?" I ask curiously.

He hesitates for a moment. "I don't hate her. But I don't particularly like her." He makes a face. "She just always tried to be my friend and wanted to know everything about me. When I was in the eighth grade, I told her to fuck off because she wasn't my mom and I would never like her."

"You told her that?" I gasp.

He smiles slightly. "Well, not exactly like that, but it was something along those lines."

"Do you miss your mom?" I ask him quietly.

He nods slowly. "More now than usual. I see Ryan, Kelly, and Jenna with Anna and it makes me think of what my mom would have been like if she were still alive. Would she go to all my football games if Dad had helped me get on the team? Would she put up with the shit I pull every day?"

"I wonder things like that sometimes," I say out loud. "Would I have been different if my dad decided to stick with us? Would I be a normal teenage girl? Would he be impressed with my 4.0 GPA?"

"Has your mom seen other people?" he asks me.

I shake my head. "I know she wants to. I think she's worried about how I'd react."

"How would you react?"

I shrug. "I don't know. It depends on how the guy treats my mom. If he treats her well, then I will probably like him for making my mom happy. If he treats her like crap, then I'll probably give him hell."

Aiden chuckles lightly. "Yeah, I'd like to see you on a rampage."

"Watch it. You never know when I could snap," I tell him.

He stays quiet for a minute before speaking up again. "Do you think I'm taking this too far?"

"Taking what too far, exactly?"

"Acting out and being the bad guy of the whole situation?" he asks me.

I slowly shake my head. "I think you have every right to be upset. You miss your mom and you don't want Anna to replace her. That's all there is to it," I tell him. "But you're kind of hurting your dad with all of this. Even though it may not seem like it, he might really want your approval about this whole thing. And saying that you're not going to the wedding basically means you don't approve any of this."

He shakes his head and looks at me. "Way to make me feel guilty."

I put my hands up in defense. "Sorry. It might not be what you want to hear, but it is the truth. I'm not saying you should ask to be at the wedding again. But you should be there to support him. I bet it would mean a lot."

He narrows his eyes at me and smirks. "Maybe you should become a psychologist or something."

"I'll think about it." I offer him a smile.

"Well, that's my sob story," Aiden says, leaning back against the bench. "You're the first person I've told about how I'm feeling right now."

"I feel honored," I say, smiling. "But let me ask you this, Aiden. Do you think your mom would be happy with your attitude right now?"

He frowns. "I ask myself that a lot. And the answer is no. I don't think she would be happy with it right now. It's just hard going from seeing my mom and dad acting like the perfect couple to seeing him like that with Anna. Then not feeling wanted is only adding on to it."

I nod. "Then it's decided. You're going to the wedding in support of your dad."

He inhales. "Fine. If any shit goes down before then, I'm not going."

"Just try to work things out with him. And try to make an effort with Anna," I tell him.

"I'll try." He rolls his eyes. "What about you? Do you have a sob story?"

I think about it. "Not really. My dad left us when I was three, so I don't really remember him. And sure, I'm not the perfect daughter my mom wanted but that doesn't bother me too much."

"So everything in your life is perfect?" he questions.

I shrug. "It's not perfect, but it's not like I'm unhappy with my life."

He chuckles and shakes his head. "You are so boring, you know that?"

"I don't think I'm boring," I tell him, frowning. "I can be fun."

"Oh really?" he asks, sounding amused. "What's your idea of fun? Staying home and watching *Star Wars*?"

That sounded like an insult. And he just had to throw in *Star Wars*. "Listen, buddy, so what if my idea of fun is different from yours? We're all different."

"Yeah, but you haven't actually lived," he tells me. "Don't tell me that party was the first one you've been to." When I don't say anything, he grins. "It was, wasn't it?"

"So what?"

He stands up and looks down at me. "Get up."

I stand up also and look at him skeptically. "What are we doing?"

"Since you helped me with this whole situation, I'm going to help you now. And we're going to have fun." He beams.

Chapter 12

Aiden makes me drop Sassy off at home before we go anywhere. I kind of want my dog with me, but Aiden won't let me.

We are now walking down the sidewalk in the opposite direction of our houses. It's about sunset, which makes me a bit nervous. I don't want to stay out too long especially on a school night. And I have those stupid pictures to do for the wedding tomorrow too.

"You seem worried," Aiden says, sounding amused.

I wring my hands together. "I'm not worried. Why would I be worried? I'm just walking here with you when it's almost dark. And not to mention you can be scary. And I'm here alone with you. No, I'm not worried at all. I'm not even worried that a killer could be around and murder us. Or that we can get kidnapped at any given moment—"

Aiden's hand shoots out and covers my mouth suddenly. I look over at him with wide eyes.

He sighs. "Do I have to do this every time I'm with you?"

I shake my head.

"Okay, good. I'm going to remove my hand and you are not going to continue talking nervously, okay?"

I nod. He removes his hand from my mouth and I take a deep breath.

He looks at me with a questioning look. "What is wrong with you?"

"Did you not hear me rambling two minutes ago?" I ask. "I'm nervous, Aiden."

"Because you think I'm scary and you can be murdered at any moment." He rolls his eyes. "Yes, I was listening, Riley. But seriously, you shouldn't be worried."

"Maybe I should just go back home. It's already dark out and we have school tomorrow—"

Aiden covers my mouth again and sighs with frustration. "I thought I wasn't going to do this again," he says. "Now, listen to me. I'll have you home no later than nine thirty. That gives us about two hours to do something fun, on my terms."

Nine thirty? That's about the time I go to bed.

"Fine," I say. "It can't be anything dangerous or life-threatening though."

"Really? Because I was going to take you to juggle guns and stuff, but I guess that's out of the question," he says sarcastically.

"You know, your sarcasm is not appreciated." I snap at him.

Aiden rubs his face with his hands. "Maybe this wasn't a good idea. You're already pissing me off."

"Let's just turn around. This isn't going to work," I say. Aiden is annoying me now and I just want to go home. I turn around and start to walk away.

My eyes widen when two arms wrap around me and lift me up. Aiden throws me over his shoulder and continues to walk.

"Aiden!" I shriek. "Put me down now!" I yell as I hit his back.

Two people walk past us and give us weird looks.

"Sorry. She's not all there right now," Aiden says to them.

I smack him again. "You are mean and careless and rude and...and mean!"

"You said that twice, Riley."

"I don't care. Put me back down this instant."

I hear him sigh. He sets me down carefully and chuckles when I cross my arms over my chest. I'm not happy with him right now and I'm not going to take this.

"You aren't scary when you're mad, you know." Aiden continues to laugh at me.

"Aiden, I'm going home," I say to him.

Aiden purses his lips. "Okay, okay, just calm down," he says. "Maybe we can do this another time. You're obviously not going to cooperate with me right now, so let's go back."

I start walking ahead of him with my arms still crossed. I hear him chuckle behind me. "Are you mad at me, Riley?"

"You aren't my favorite person right now." I huff.

"You aren't my favorite person either, if that makes you feel any better."

I frown and turn towards him. "How is that supposed to make me feel better?" I ask him. "Don't answer that. I don't care if I'm your favorite person." I notice my house come into view and I sigh in relief.

"Well, I'm going to show you my idea of fun one way or another Led Zeppelin girl." He smiles.

"It'll have to be another day," I say as we walk.

We end up at the end of my driveway and I face him. "Well, this was an interesting attempt at having fun."

Aiden grins. "Just wait for the real fun."

"Can't wait," I say sarcastically. I start walking backwards.

"Hey, before you go," Aiden starts to say. "You're going to that photo shoot crap tomorrow for the wedding, right?"

I really wish we don't have to. I'm not like these other girls who are photogenic. I tend to look awkward in every picture I'm in. Especially school pictures, which are the worst. "Yes, I am. Why?"

Aiden looks down and kicks a rock by his foot. "My dad said I could go if I wanted to. I told him no though…"

"And your point is?" I ask, not seeing where he's going with this. He shouldn't just trail off like that and assume I know what he's talking about.

"I'll be there if you're there," he finally says.

"Oh," I say, sounding surprised. "Okay."

He takes a few steps towards me and I take a few steps back. But he's faster than me, so I almost trip on his foot. He grasps my waist. He starts leaning towards me, and my breath catches in my throat. His eyes sparkle when he glances at me. He leans closer and my eyes involuntarily shut. I feel his cheek touch mine as he speaks into my ear. "Goodnight, Riley. And watch where you step."

It's suddenly cold as he pulls away from me with an evident smirk on his face. He gives me a small wave and starts to walk down the sidewalk.

Dammit, he did it again!

I told myself not to let that happen again. That incident in the kitchen had left me feeling weak and powerless, and I hate the feeling. And here I am in the same position, letting the same thing happen.

Damn Aiden.

I turn and trudge towards my front door. I pull out my house key and unlock the door. I feel on edge again, so I slam the door as I walk inside.

"Who was that?" My mother's voice nearly makes me jump out of my skin. I whirl around and see her smiling at me.

"Jeez, Mom." I put my hand over my heart. "Way to give me a heart attack."

She rolls her eyes. "You're such a drama queen, Riley, I swear."

"Well, don't scare me like that," I say, walking around her. I head off to the kitchen to get a water bottled water. My throat is dry and I need something cold.

"I was just asking who that was with you outside." I hear her behind me.

I open the fridge and grab a water bottle. "Aiden Callaway," I answer. I take a big drink from the water bottle.

"Callaway?" She frowns. "As in Anna's fiancé's son?"

I nod. "Yeah."

"I haven't heard many good things about that boy." She continues to frown.

"Mom"—I rolled my eyes—"haven't you always told me not to judge someone until you actually know them?"

She shrug. "Yeah. But I don't know about you hanging around him."

"He's just going through a hard time," I say. Whoa, am I defending Aiden Callaway? "This wedding isn't settling well with him."

"Why? He should be happy."

"That's what I told him," I mutter. "It's not exactly my place to tell you his personal stuff, but it's been rough for him."

"I just don't want you being with the wrong crowd, Riley."

"Oh please." I roll my eyes at her again. "When have I ever hung with the wrong crowd? When have I ever even hung out with a crowd? If I knew he was someone I shouldn't be friends with, then I wouldn't be talking to him." I snap.

She looks slightly taken aback by my outburst. I'm stunned too. I don't think I've ever snapped like that at my mom and it's clear that she's a bit hurt over it.

I sigh. "I'm sorry. Today was just a long day, and I'm tired and I'm ready to go to bed now."

She nods. "I'll see you in the morning."

I take that opportunity to run up the stairs to my room. I shut my door behind me and squeeze my eyes shut.

Why am I acting like this?

I quickly change into my pajamas and get into bed. But I'm having trouble falling asleep. My heart is pounding in my chest and it isn't stopping. I sit up in bed and rub my face.

It's that whole thing with Aiden. I hate that I felt weak when he came close to me. I hate that he has that effect on me.

I hate not knowing why I'm acting like this.

***

I have to say, sometimes sitting in the library during lunch gets boring after a while. Of course, I can help our librarian, but she never wants to put me to work. So here I am sitting at a table by myself, with absolutely nothing to do. And obviously, I have no one else to hang out with.

Maybe I should start socializing more.

Ha! Like that will ever happen. I hate everyone in this school.

I put my head on the table and sigh. There are about twenty minutes left of lunch and I know I'm not going to last. I hear someone sit in front of me and I look up immediately.

Ryan smiles at me. "Hello."

"Hi," I say, sitting up. I look around then look back at him. "What are you doing here?"

"I can't visit my best friend?" he asks me.

I roll my eyes. "I know that's not the reason you're here."

"You are right about that." He points at me. "You're leaving with me today."

When was this decided? "Can I ask why?"

"We're doing that photo shoot remember?" he says. "Anyways, we're going to have to miss our last class so we can get ready and take the pictures. Don't worry. Your mom already knows."

"Okay then," I say. As much as I don't want to take these stupid pictures, it's all for Anna and the wedding. I have to repeat that to myself because I can be selfish sometimes.

He stares at me for a moment. "You don't want to be in the wedding, do you?"

Where had that question come from? "What makes you assume that?" I ask him.

"You never look happy when someone mentions the wedding," he tells me. "Like right now when I mentioned the pictures."

I shrug. "That doesn't mean I don't want to be in the wedding. I'll admit that I didn't want to do it in the first place, but then I met all of you guys…"

Ryan smiles. "And then you fell in love with all of us."

I laugh. "I wouldn't say I fell in love. I guess you guys kind of grew on me."

He laughs too. "Oh please. You did fall in love." He leans forward in his chair. "You love Aiden."

My smile drops as soon as he says that. "Excuse me?" I ask him. If I had heard him correctly, I think he said I love Aiden.

"Don't deny it, Riley," he says as he grins.

"I am going to deny it!" I exclaim. "Aiden and I are barely friends. How can I possibly love him?"

"Fine," he says as he leans back in his chair. He crosses his arms over his chest. "Then he loves you."

I laugh at that. "You're either delusional or just plain stupid. Why are you even suggesting these things?"

He chuckles. "I'm a very observant person and I've noticed that you've been spending some time with Aiden lately."

"So?"

"So, what I'm saying is that he doesn't hang with a lot of people and he told me himself he doesn't go around hanging out with girls like you—" He stopped suddenly.

I narrow my eyes at him. "Go ahead and say it, Ryan." I snap, feeling angry. "Guys like you and Aiden don't 'hang out' with nerds like me. Guys like you and Aiden only make us nerds feel invisible and use us to do your homework." I stand up and grab my bag. "Which is fine with me. I don't need friends like you. I've been fine on my own." I walk away from him.

"Riley! Come back!" I hear Ryan call out. I ignore him though. I don't know why I'm so upset. I know I'm a nerd.

You know why you're mad. Ryan just said that Aiden said he especially doesn't hang with nerds like you.

I walk out of the library, shove my hands into my pockets, and start down the hallway. I need to move as quickly as possible, or Ryan will catch up with me. I decide to head towards my locker, since lunch is almost over anyways. I look down at the floor as I walk. A few people give me weird looks as I pass by them, but I just continue to look at the ground.

I round a corner and run right into someone. "Sorry," I mutter, not bothering to look up.

"Led Zeppelin girl?"

I glance up and see Aiden standing in front of me.

"Hey." He smiles. "Do you always run into people in the hall?"

I disregard his comment and start to saunter around him. But he grabs my arm and pulls me back in front of him.

"Is everything okay?" he asks slowly.

I squint at him. "Oh yeah. Everything is just great. Don't worry about a nerd like me. Sorry for running into you. Next time, I'll just make myself invisible," I say as I walk around him.

"Riley!" I hear Ryan behind me. He approaches Aiden and me. "I didn't mean what I said back there, I swear."

"What did you do?" Aiden asks Ryan.

I step away from them. "You know what? Just stop pretending to care about me. I'm nobody compared to you guys. I'm fine with no friends. I always have been."

"What the hell are you talking about?" Aiden asks incredulously. He reaches out to touch my arm, but I flinch.

"Just leave me alone." I snap at him. I turn and make a run for the girls' restroom. Once I'm in, I walk into a cubicle and start to cry.

I feel so angry right now and I can't keep it bottled in any longer. So many emotions run through me before I finally calm down. I take a deep breath and wipe my eyes with the backs of my hands.

I open the door to the stall and walk towards the sink. I look at myself in the mirror and sigh. I look like I just got hit by a train. The restroom door opens and I see Nicole and one of her blonde friends walk in.

Nicole smirks when she sees me. "Aren't you the one who's in Anna's wedding?" I don't respond to her. "You are, aren't you?" She walks closer to me. "You know, because of this stupid wedding, I haven't had much time with Ryan."

And that's my problem how?

"I should have been in the wedding," Nicole states. "Not a pathetic loser like you. I mean, look at yourself." Her blonde friend snickers. "And I bet you've been spending a lot of time with Ryan, haven't you?"

Don't let her get to you, Riley.

She now stands next to me and looks down at me. She's a few inches taller than me in those heels she's wearing. "You better stay away from him, *bitch*. He's my boyfriend, not yours."

"Why would he go for her anyways, Nicole?" the blonde asks. "Like you said, she's a pathetic loser."

They both chuckle and I sigh.

Nicole raises her eyebrows. "No comments? Not so confident now that Ryan isn't here, are we?"

Say something, dammit. Don't let them talk like this to you.

"Let's go to the other restrooms," Nicole tells her friend. "I don't want to be in here with this waste of space."

And with that, they leave.

Now I really have an excuse to stay away from Ryan and Aiden. Before I talked to any of them, I had been fine. Nicole never acknowledged me; I didn't feel so on edge, and people left me alone. Which is exactly how I like it.

Chapter 13

I convince my mom to pick me up from school instead of leaving with Ryan. I'm not ready to talk to him quite yet. My mom doesn't ask any questions as to why I'm not going with Ryan, and I'm thankful for that.

She tells me that we are going to Anna's house so all the girls can get ready. Which is okay with me. As long as I don't have to see Ryan or Aiden, I will be fine.

We drive into Anna's driveway and I sigh. "Do I have to do this?" I ask my mom.

"Yes, you do," she answers. "Now, go on. I don't want you running behind."

I groan and get out of the car with my dress in my hands. Why do we have to do the pictures now? Don't normal people do them right before the wedding so everyone is already dressed up?

Whatever. This isn't my wedding so I can't go around telling people what I do and don't like about it.

I walk up to the front door and ring the doorbell. It opens a few moments later, revealing Kelly. She smiles at me.

"Hey, Riley. Long time no talk," she says as she opens the door wider for me.

I walk in and smile in return. "I've been busy."

"So, the girls are getting ready here and the guys are going to get ready at Robert's house," she explains as I follow her into the living room. The other girls are already here. I also notice three different girls sitting on one of the couches.

Anna sees me and grins. "Now we have everyone here!" she exclaims. "Okay, so three of you will get your makeup done while the other two are getting their hair done, then you'll switch. Understood?" We all nod. "Okay, so Jenna, Halle, and Riley, you girls get your makeup done first. Just follow Lynn and Sarah to the other room," she says, also referring to two of the other girls. She turns towards Holly and Kelly. "You two follow Gabby to get your hair done."

And we are off. It all goes by in a blur. I actually start dozing off while my hair is being curled. We aren't allowed to look in a mirror until we're completely finished getting ready, which is kind of frustrating. I've never curled my hair before and I want to know what it looks like.

After slipping on our dresses, everyone is finished getting ready. That's when we can look in the mirror at ourselves.

"Riley," Kelly says, "you look amazing!"

I glance at myself in the mirror and my eyes widen. "Holy crap..."

I look like an entirely different person. I actually have makeup on, but it isn't caked on. My hair is in soft curls that fall past my shoulders. I actually look like…a girl.

Jenna smiles at me. "You look great, Riley."

"I'm so jealous of your hair!" Holly exclaims.

I feel myself blushing from all the attention everyone is giving me. "Thanks," I mumble as I look down.

Anna walks in and she just looks stunning. Her dress is…different. It's a knee-length white dress. I expected an actual dress.

"Before anyone freaks out," Anna starts. "My real wedding dress is being saved for the wedding day. I don't want Robert to see it yet, so I've decided on wearing a replacement for right now."

That's smart.

"Now, let's get going. The boys are already making their way to the park," she tells us. We all shuffle out of the front door and get into Anna's Expedition.

We arrive at Apodaca Park, which is a huge park filled with big trees. The grass is green and some trees have small white flowers covering them. It's a nice park. Nicer than the one I live near.

Everyone gets out of the vehicles and I notice Lucas right away. He smiles at me and approaches. "Hey," he says.

"Hey yourself," I tell him.

He looks down at my feet, then his gaze meets my eyes again. "You look great. I didn't recognize you at first."

I shrug. "This is the only time I've actually dressed up."

"Well, I like this look on you." He grins.

I see Ryan talking to Jenna off to the side. I instantly remember Nicole's words from earlier. She actually thinks I'm going after Ryan when we're just friends. I tell myself not to let her words get to me, but being called a pathetic loser and a waste of space isn't exactly comforting.

At the corner of my eye, I see Aiden standing near Kelly. She's talking to him with her hands and he's just standing there looking uninterested.

"Okay, let's go, everyone! The photographer is here!" Anna exclaims.

We all make our way to where the photographer is. I'm walking along when someone grabs my arm and holds me back.

"What the—" I turn and see Aiden standing next to me. "Oh. It's *you*."

"What do you mean it's *me*?" he asks. "I just wanted to ask you what the hell your problem is."

I shrug and look away from him. "I don't have a problem." I lie.

He scoffs. "Please. You can't just all of a sudden act like a bitch to me and say nothing is wrong."

He did not just call me... "Well, now I definitely have a problem. I don't appreciate the name-calling." I snap at him. I try catching up with the rest of the group, but Aiden catches my arm again.

"Look, I really don't understand why you're giving me the cold shoulder," he says. "I have no idea why you're pissed off."

"Are you pretending to be my friend?" I ask him suddenly.

"No?" It sounds more like a question than an answer. "Who said I was pretending?"

"Ryan and I were talking and—"

"Riley!" someone calls out behind me. "C'mon, the girls are taking the pictures now!"

Aiden looks at me. "Can we talk about this after you're finished?"

I just nod and walk away from him.

***

Taking the pictures isn't as bad as I thought it would be. The couple pictures are a little awkward for me though. Lucas holds my waist a little tighter than I want.

I'm talking with Kelly when Ryan approaches us and starts to talk to her about something. But she soon leaves, leaving us alone.

"Riley," Ryan says as he stands next to me, "are you still mad at me?"

I glance over at him. He has his lip sticking out like a puppy and his eyes are wide. I smirk. "You look ridiculous like that."

"You didn't answer my question," he says.

I sigh. "I guess I forgive you."

He grins and wraps his arms around me. "I feel so much better now that we're cool."

"You might want to let go. We wouldn't want your girlfriend to get the wrong idea, would we?" I ask him.

"Nicole is just going to have to accept the fact that you are now my best friend," he says. He frowns then. "Why are you worried about her anyways? Did she say something?"

I look at the ground. "It's okay, Ryan—"

"She told you something, didn't she?" he asks. "Don't listen to anything she says, Riley. When Nicole gets jealous, she says a lot of stupid stuff."

"I don't understand why she's jealous." I shake my head. "I've never done anything to her, so why am I all of a sudden a waste of space?"

Ryan frowns. "What?"

"It's nothing," I tell him.

"She called you a waste of space?" he aks me. I don't answer. "I can talk to her—"

I shook my head. "Just leave it alone. Don't make this situation worse than it actually is."

He sighs. "Fine."

"You have no respect for anyone! All you care about is yourself, Aiden, and frankly, I'm sick and tired of this attitude of yours!" we hear someone shouting.

Mine and Ryan's attention turn to Robert who is currently yelling at Aiden. But Aiden is just standing there with a cigarette between his fingers and staring at his dad.

"I've had it up to here with this crap, Aiden," Robert says. "I don't want you at the wedding if you're going to act like this. If I so much as hear of you being at the wedding, I swear I will—"

"You'll what?" Aiden asks, challenging him. "I'm eighteen, *Dad*. I can do whatever the fuck I want. And I don't even want to come to this fucking wedding anyways."

He and Robert have a stare down before Aiden chuckles bitterly. He throws the cigarette onto the ground and stomps on it. He then starts walking in our direction.

Aiden looks at me angrily. "You can't say I didn't try." I nod and look at the ground as he walks away from everyone.

Everyone just watches Aiden as he walks down the sidewalk. Part of me wants to go after him, but another part of me tells me to give him some space. He'll talk when he wants to talk.

Anna walks up to Robert and says something to him that I can't hear. Robert just sighs and runs a hand through his hair.

Ryan whistles next to me. "Well, that was quite a scene."

I nod in agreement. "It was." I look to my left and notice Robert making his way to me.

He offers me a small smile. "My son is just a ray of sunshine, isn't he?"

I don't know what to say.

"It's, Riley. Am I correct?" he asks me and I nod. "From what I've heard, I understand that you and Aiden have been talking these past few days."

Who cares about Aiden and me? And why is it a topic of conversation now?

"We have," I say slowly.

"Has he told you anything? I mean, has he talked to you at all about the wedding?" Robert asks me, frowning.

"He has," I tell him. "I had convinced him to come here and to the wedding..." Aiden is obviously not welcome at the wedding anymore.

Robert sighs. "I see. Well, I'm glad he listens to someone around here."

He walks away to Anna and the rest of the bridal party. Ryan glances at me and raises his eyebrows. I shrug.

When Aiden wants to talk, he will.

Chapter 14

Our first wedding rehearsal will be this coming Tuesday. It was supposed to be last week, but Anna changed it because of pictures getting in the way.

It's now Sunday morning. My mom leaves to go grocery shopping. She claims we need more healthy food instead of buying junk food. Which is a load of bull crap to me. We do have enough healthy food. I think she wants me to eat healthier so I don't gain weight and not fit into my dress.

I am currently sitting on my couch, eating a Hershey's bar, and watching *The Big Bang Theory*. Oh how I love Sheldon. He is, hands down, my favorite character.

My phone buzzes next to me and I groan. *It's probably Mom,* I think. I pick up my phone and glance at it. It's a text from Lucas. He and I had exchanged numbers sometime during the photo shoot on Thursday.

Hey Riley, wanna hang out today?

I frown. Lucas is nice and all, but I'm watching *The Big Bang Theory*. Wow, I am pathetic, blowing someone off to watch a show on TV.

C'mon, Riley.

My thumbs roam over the keyboard on my phone before I actually start typing my message back.

Sure. What do you wanna do?

I smile to myself. See? I can go out and socialize with people. My phone buzzes again and I look down at it.

We could see a movie.

A movie will be fine. I agree and Lucas tells me he'll pick me up around four. It's almost three now, so I have plenty of time to get ready.

***

"So what movie are we seeing?" I wonder out loud. I'm sitting next to Lucas in his car and he's driving us to the theater.

He shrugs. "Whatever is fine with me."

"What do *you* want to see?" I ask instead. I hate it when people say they don't care what movie we see. We all want to see a certain movie.

"I wanted to see *Fast & Furious*," he says, smiling. "What about you?"

I don't want to see *Fast & Furious*. But I'm not going to tell him what I'm thinking. "I haven't really paid attention to the movie trailers lately, so I don't know what's out."

"We can decide when we get there then," he says.

We fall into an awkward silence. I stare out the window and watch as we pass different stores and neighborhoods.

"Are you excited for the wedding?" Lucas asks, breaking the silence.

I look at him and shake my head. "Not really."

"You're not?"

"No. I didn't want to be in the wedding in the first place, but my mom made me do it," I tell him. I notice we are pulling into the parking lot at the theater and my eyes scan over the movie posters.

"*The Great Gatsby*," I whisper excitedly. The book was absolutely amazing to read. When I saw the previews of the movie, I promised myself I would see it. I completely forgot that it's out.

Lucas parks and we both get out. "So, *The Great Gatsby*?" Lucas asks me.

I blush. "You heard me?"

"It wasn't exactly a whisper." He laughs. "I wouldn't mind seeing it. It actually looked pretty interesting."

"Then off to buy tickets!" I exclaim. We walk towards the building and make our way inside.

I had only been to the theater a few times. Lame, I know. I almost forgot what it looks like in here. I glance up and around to take in the surroundings. A group of girls pass by me and give me weird looks.

Just because they're in booty shorts and small tank tops doesn't make them better than me.

I'm in my jeans, a Red Hot Chili Peppers shirt, and my old beat up Converse. I'm comfortable, so that's all that mattered. I feel someone's arm on my shoulders and I look up at Lucas giving me a goofy smile in return. He holds up two tickets in front of my face.

"I've got the tickets already, so let's get snacks," he suggests. I nod and we start walking. It feels odd with his arm around me though. I need an excuse to get away from his grasp.

"I'm going to go to the bathroom before we go in." I lie. I pull myself away and look around for the restrooms. I see the sign not too far away.

Right as I'm about to enter the ladies' room, I hear someone giggle and squeal. "Aiden, stop!"

My head snaps in the direction where I hear the voice. Near the restroom doors, Aiden has some brunette against the wall and is kissing her neck. She is giggling like crazy and he has a slight smirk on his face.

I frown and push the door open to the ladies' room. Well, I have to say that Aiden is the last person I would have expected to see here. And that's the first time I've seen him with a girl. Is that his girlfriend? Are they on a date?

Why do you even care, Riley?

After I go to the restroom and wash my hands, I walk out of the bathroom and accidentally hit someone with the door. It isn't a hard hit, but I definitely hit someone.

It's the brunette Aiden was just with. She scowls at me when she sees me walk out. "Watch where you're going, bitch."

I hold up my hands. "It wasn't me. It was that door." I point to it. "Evil door, I tell you."

She stares at me like I have three heads. "Was that supposed to be an insult?"

What an airhead.

"No," I say slowly. "I'm going to leave now."

When I try making my way around her, Aiden appears at her side, and he raises his eyebrows when he sees me.

"Led Zeppelin girl," he says, sounding surprised. "What're you doing here?"

"I'm going to see a movie, obviously," I say, rolling my eyes.

He rolls his eyes too. "Well, no shit. Who are you here with?"

"Lucas."

"The one from the party?"

I cross my arms. "The one you punched at the party? Yes, that Lucas."

"Hold on." The brunette interrupts us. "How do you know my boyfriend?" she asks me. So she is his girlfriend.

"I'm in his dad's wedding," I tell her.

"I'm not your boyfriend, Molly," Aiden says, sounding annoyed.

So she isn't his girlfriend? I'm confused.

She takes a step away from him. She looks at him with big puppy eyes. "But you said the other day—"

"I say a lot of shit, Molly. But I don't recall saying you were my girlfriend," Aiden says to her.

I duck my head and slowly start to walk away. Well, that was awkward.

Lucas sees me and approaches me. "Hey, what took so long?"

"Ran into some people." I wave it off. "Now, let's go watch the movie."

***

The Great Gatsby totally lives up to my expectations. It's truly amazing and I feel like watching it over and over again until I can no longer stand it.

I don't think Lucas enjoyed it as much as I did, but I don't care.

We walk out of the theater and I toss the popcorn bag into a nearby trash can. I sigh happily and look at Lucas. "Thanks for bringing me here. It was actually kind of fun."

Lucas smiles. "Anytime."

We walk out of the building and I notice the sun is just about to set. I stretch and instantly feel lazy.

Someone suddenly grabs hold of my arm, making me jump. With wide eyes, I look over and I see Aiden standing next to me, smiling.

"You scared me!" I pull my arm away and smack his arm. He just chuckles as I hit him.

"You should be more aware of your surroundings," he says, smirking. "I could have easily picked you up and ran off with you. Especially since you weigh nothing."

I do not weigh nothing! I weigh...well, I don't know how much I weigh, but it's not nothing! I squint my eyes at him. "What do you want?"

"Are you still mad at me or something? It's been like three days," he says.

I'm not mad at him. He didn't really do anything to me in the first place. I was madder at Ryan than anyone, but I forgave him right away. "No. I'm not mad."

He smiles. "Great." He glances over at Lucas. "Hey, man, is it okay if I steal her away? I'll take her home."

Steal me away?

Lucas looks at me. "Are you going with him?"

I look at him, then at Aiden, then back at Lucas. "Yeah," I finally answer.

Lucas looks slightly disappointed. "Okay. I'll talk to you later then."

I give him a smile. "Okay." He walks to his car and I watch him leave.

"*I'll talk to you later then,*" Aiden mimics Lucas. "Please."

I frown at Aiden. "You're being rude right now. Maybe I should have gone with Lucas." I cross my arms.

"I'm glad you didn't though." Aiden smiles brightly. "Because we're going to have fun right now."

Oh no. I was wondering when we'll try this again. "What are we going to do?"

"It's a surprise," he says. "C'mon, let's go before it gets too dark."

I follow him to the parking lot. We approach a silver car. I feel like I've seen this car before.

"Is this your car?" I ask curiously. I don't remember Aiden having a car.

Aiden shakes his head. "No. It's my friend Alex's."

Alex? I think about the name and the car for a second. Then it hit me. This is the same car I had gotten in with Aiden when he basically kidnapped me. And Alex was the guy driving.

We get into the car and I buckle my seatbelt. "Why do you have his car?"

"He lets me borrow it every now and then." Aiden shrugs. He starts it and then we are off.

"Wait, what happened to that one girl you were with?" I ask, remembering the brunette.

Aiden smirks. "I left during our movie and told her I was going to the restroom. But I never went back."

That's actually quite hilarious but mean at the same time. "You are an evil person, Aiden Callaway."

"I wouldn't say that," he says. "I'd say I have a different personality than others."

"But doesn't everyone have a different personality than others?"

Aiden sighs in frustration. "Don't make me drop you off on the side of the road."

We say nothing else after that. I glance out the window and see that we are pulling into the parking lot of the public library. I'm about to ask what we're doing here but Aiden gives me a look that makes me shut up. We both get out of the car and Aiden walks around the car and pops the trunk open. He grabs a black backpack and I immediately feel nauseous.

"Follow me," Aiden instructs.

Instead of arguing with him, I follow him like he told me to. We walk to the side of the building, which has me more curious as to what we will to do. We walk to the back of the library. Aiden takes a few more steps before stopping and setting the black backpack on the ground.

He holds his arms out and gestures to the library. "We have reached our destination."

I glance at the library and my eyes widen. There's graffiti all over the wall and even on a separate wall that hides the dumpster. I stare in awe at the wall covered in art. It isn't all that gang crap either. It's graffiti art.

Aiden crouches down next to the black backpack and reaches inside. Whatever he pulls out, he tosses it to me. "Think fast."

I catch the object and look down at it. It's a spray can. I'm about to ask what it's for, but then the answer occurs to me.

"Aiden, I can't graffiti a wall!" I exclaim.

"Don't talk so loud!" he whispered. "It's fine as long as we don't get caught." He assures me.

I roll my eyes. "Oh, that makes it so much better."

Aiden ignores my last comment and walks up to the wall. He takes the spray can and starts to spell something out on the wall:

Riley.

"Don't put *my* name!" I say angrily. My name is in a bright blue color, making it stand out.

"Maybe I should put your last name too," Aiden smirks.

I open the spray can in my hand and I start to spray the wall too. I finish and take a step back.

Aiden.

The color I used was a bright pink. I smile and look at Aiden. He nods. "Not bad, Summers, not bad at all."

He grabs another spray can from the back and opens it. He starts to spray something again. I just stand there and watch what he's writing. I smile when he finishes.

Fuck what they think.

It's exactly what Aiden would say. Bet he lives by that motto too. He looks at me and motions to the wall. "Go ahead, Summers. Have a go at it."

"I don't know what to write," I say, staring up at the wall. There are so many pictures and quotes.

"Just write whatever comes to mind," he says, shrugging.

I frown and bite my lip. I think about it then smile. I start to spray once again.

"Don't put 'Vandalism is bad' either," Aiden tells me.

I chuckle as I continue to spray. It's just one word. Nothing too crazy.

Outcasts.

Aiden grins when he sees the word. He sprays on two arrows that go from our names to the word *outcasts*. Aiden looks at me and smiles. "I believe I have turned you into a rebel, Ms. Summers."

"Rebel is my middle name," I say seriously. We both start laughing. We then put the spray cans back into the bag and walk back to the car.

Aiden starts to drive to my house. "I hope you know that that wasn't it for the fun." He grins. "That was just the beginning."

"That wasn't so bad." I shrug. I think it will be something a little more dangerous. But Aiden can be a little bit unpredictable, so I don't know what to expect the next time we have his idea of fun.

Chapter 15

Aiden drives into my driveway and parks. He turns his body and looks at me. But he doesn't say anything.

I feel awkward with him staring at me. "Is there a reason you're staring at me like that?" I ask as I grab my bag.

He shrugs. "There might be a reason."

I raise my eyebrow. "You're talking in riddles, Aiden." I don't understand why he has to be so confusing. It's really frustrating.

He chuckles. "Well, I hope you had as much fun as I did."

"I'll admit that it was fun," I assure him.

"Possibly more fun than staying home and watching *Star Wars*?" he questions.

"I don't think we're there yet." I shake my head. I mean, what can top *Star Wars*??

"Damn," he says. "Well, that just means that there will be more fun activities for us to do in the future." He has a slightly evil glint in his eye.

I nod. "Sounds appealing."

"Oh, it will be." He grins.

Silence fall between us. For some reason, I find myself not wanting to leave the car just yet. I let my mind wander for a few seconds before I look back at him. "Aiden?"

"Yeah?" He glances at me.

"Are you staying at home?" I ask him curiously. He and his dad have been bickering a lot, so I'm curious to see if he's currently living under the same roof as his dad.

Aiden shakes his head. "I'm staying with Alex for a while. I think my dad knows that's where I'm staying though." I nod. "Why, do you want me to stay over here at your house?" he asks, smirking suggestively. "I'm sure we'd have a lot of fun—"

"I am *not* asking you to stay over!" I exclaim. I feel myself blushing at his innuendo as he laughs.

He gives me a cheeky smile. "I'm just kidding, Riley. No need to freak out." He laughs some more. "It's okay if you're having dirty thoughts about me—"

"I'm getting out of the car now," I say as I grab the door handle.

Aiden's hand shoots out and grabs my own hand. "Wait."

My heart is pounding as I look down at our hands. "What?"

Realizing that he had grabbed my hand, he let go and scratches the back of his neck. "So, you wanna meet up again tomorrow after school? We can have more of my kind of fun." He smiles.

I don't know if I have anything planned for tomorrow afternoon. "I'll think about it," I answer him. I get out of the car and shut the door behind me.

I walk up to my front door and pull out my key. Someone's hand covers mine and pulls the key from my grasp. I turn around and see that I am face to face with Aiden. How did he get out of the car without me hearing him?

"You'll think about it?" he asks me.

I nod slowly. "Yes." I lean against the door and cross my arms. He has my key in his hand still.

"What could be more important than spending an afternoon with me?" he inquires.

I laugh slightly. "A lot of things."

"Oh yeah?" He takes a step towards me. "Like what?" His face is only a few inches away from my own. My breath catches in my throat.

"Th-things." I stutter. His eyes bore into mine, and all I can do is stare back at him. I notice his eyes are a nice brown color. Almost like chocolate.

The door opens behind me, causing me to fall back due to me leaning against it. My arms flail around, but there's nothing I can grasp onto. So I fall right on my butt.

"Riley!" I hear my mom exclaim. I look up at her, and she holds out a hand to me. I take it, and she yanks me back up to my feet.

I dust myself off and feel myself blushing. I had just embarrassed myself by falling. Great.

I look at Aiden, who is smirking at me, then at my mom, who is looking at me. "I thought I heard you out here," she starts to say. "I was just wondering what was taking so long."

"Oh," I say.

My mom's eyes flicker to Aiden then back at me.

"Right." I nod. "Um, Mom, this is Aiden. Aiden, this is my mom." I introduce them.

Aiden holds out his hand. "It's nice to meet you, ma'am." He offers her a smile.

"It's nice to meet you, Aiden." She shakes his hand. "Please, call me Carol."

My gaze flashes to Aiden, and he looks at me, continuing to smile. "I'll see you tomorrow, Riley."

"Okay." I nod. He walks away and opens the driver's door on the car.

I follow my mom inside and shut the door behind us. I sigh and run a hand through my hair. My mom looks at me expectantly while I frown at her. "What?" I ask.

"He seems like a nice boy." She muses.

"I guess," I say as I make my way towards the kitchen. I feel like having a snack.

My mom follows me. "So, is that the boy you went to the movies with?"

I shake my head as I grab a banana. I start to unpeel it. "No. I went to the movies with Lucas."

She smiles at me. "I knew you'd make more friends this year, Riley. I just didn't think they would be boys."

"Well, I still don't fit in with most girls, Mom," I say to her.

"That's okay," she says, grinning. "As long as you're having fun and staying out of trouble, I don't care who you become friends with."

Staying out of trouble. I wonder what my mom will do if she ever finds out that I had spray painted on the back wall of the library with Aiden. That's a secret I will keep from her. "Okay." I nod. "I'm going up to my room now."

I run up the stairs and lock myself in my room. I walk over to my dresser and start to empty my pockets. I frown when I don't find my house key. I smack my forehead when the realization hits me.

Aiden still has my house key.

***

I walk through the halls on Monday morning looking for Aiden. I need my key back. I had convinced my mom that I had left it in Aiden's car rather than telling her that he deliberately took it from my hands.

I have no idea where his locker is. So now I'm just roaming the halls, hoping I'd find him somewhere. Then the thought of calling or texting him hits me.

Why didn't I think of that earlier?

After pulling my phone out, I call Aiden. I don't want to wait for him to text back. It will be faster if I call him.

"You just can't wait to talk to me, can you?" he answers arrogantly.

I roll my eyes. "Please. The only reason I called is that you still have my house key and I want it back."

"Do I now?" he asks. I can almost see him smirking. He knows what he was doing when he took my key yesterday. "I didn't even realize."

"You're a liar," I tell him. "I need it to get into my house this afternoon, Aiden."

"You won't need it right away," he says. "We're leaving right after school to have fun, remember?"

I sigh. I almost forgot about that. "I said I'd think about it. I didn't say yes to this." I walk up to my locker and open it.

"Well, you're going to have to agree if you want your key back," he replies. I don't have to see him to know that he's wearing an evil smile as he says that.

I groan. "Fine. But I better get my key back."

He chuckles. "Turn around, Led Zeppelin girl."

I frown and slowly turn my body. I see Aiden walking through the front entrance and making his way in my direction. Once he's close enough, I end the call. I point at him. "You took my key on purpose."

He put his hand over his heart. "How dare you accuse me of such a thing?"

I roll my eyes. "You're being dramatic."

He looks down at his phone and sighs. "Well, I have to go to my locker now."

I start walking backward. "Okay."

"I'll see you after school," he says to me. He then turns around and starts walking away.

I continue to walk in the direction of my locker. I don't know if I feel okay or angry still. I mean, I'm angry at

Aiden for taking my key, but then I think about the time I've been spending with him, I don't feel angry anymore.

Someone's shoulder brushes against mine and I look to my left and see Nicole and her blonde friend walking next to me. I stop and frown at her. She flashes me a fake smile.

"Oh, look, Stacey. I had no idea I was walking next to a slut." Nicole smirks at me.

"Excuse me?" I ask her. Now there's a new one. I've *never* been called a slut. "What are you talking about?"

She looks at me and glares. "I never would have thought you were like that." She steps closer to me. "Trying to steal my boyfriend and sleeping with Aiden Callaway? Wow, nerd girl. You've really come out of your shell."

Whoa, whoa. Stealing her boyfriend? Sleeping with Aiden? Nicole has officially gone off the deep end. "You have no idea what you're talking about," I tell her calmly. Truthfully, I'm fuming right now. How can she accuse me of those things?

"Oh, I'm pretty sure I do know what I'm talking about." She snarls. "Why don't you just do us all a favor and go rot in a hole or something? No one enjoys being around a nerdy slut like you."

People start to gather around us and my cheeks burn from embarrassment. Nicole is drawing attention towards us both and she loves it. My heart is pounding in my chest from nervousness and fury. I stare at her then glance around at the crowd around us. Everyone has an amused face on. No one cares that I'm basically being bullied right now by Nicole. My eyes start to water.

"Go ahead and cry, you little bitch." Nicole scowls at me. "Nobody cares about you and nobody ever will."

Tears start to spill from my eyes. I've never been more humiliated in my life.

Nicole smirks at me and waves her hand. "Go. Run off, you whore."

And I do. I run down the hallway, pushing past people, and into the girl's bathroom. I walk into one of the stalls and cry my eyes out. Nicole embarrassed me in front of everyone in the hallway. And she accused me of being a slut.

I wipe my tears away and pull out my phone. I'm not going to humiliate myself more by going to class. I call my mom and ask her to pick me up because I'm not feeling good.

I'm not telling her the truth.

***

My mom questions me if I really am sick. I don't think I've convinced her that I am, but she takes me home anyways.

After taking a shower, I plop myself on my bed and stare at the ceiling. My eyes are still red and puffy from crying. I'm not leaving my room for the rest of the day. I'm fine right here.

Once again, Nicole had gotten to me and embarrassed me. And once again I'm starting to think about how speaking to Ryan and Aiden plays a significant role in my situation. I was always left alone, and I like it that way. I had no drama going on. Now that Ryan and Aiden have entered my life, things aren't the same. I'm not the same person, and I'm doing things I didn't use to do.

I guess it's a good and a bad thing.

I grab my iPod and plug in my earphones. I turn off my phone and drown out all sounds with my music. I close my eyes and drum my fingers to the beat of a few songs. I find myself getting sleepy. Glancing at the clock, I notice that it's barely going to be ten in the morning.

I curl myself into a ball and fall asleep on my bed.

***

Something tickles my nose while I'm sleeping. I frown in my sleep and crinkle my nose. But the tickling continues, and it's getting very irritating. I finally just bury my face in my pillow.

I then feel something poking my side repeatedly. I squirm and turn on my other side. But the poking continues still.

What the hell is going on?

My eyes open and I immediately shut them. It's way too bright outside. I slowly open them again and blink a few times. My face is inches away from someone else's.

So I scream.

I scramble around on my bed, trying to sit up and get away from the person in my room. I end up getting too close to the edge of the bed, and I fall back. Whoever is in my room starts to laugh at me. Not just a small chuckle either. It's a full-on, belly-aching laugh.

I quickly sit up and look around, trying to locate the laugh. I see *him* standing in the corner of my room, bent over, still laughing. I frown when I see him.

"What the hell are you doing in my house?" I demand from him.

Aiden stands upright and chuckles. "Well, you weren't at school during lunch, so I came to find you."

"How did you get inside?"

He pulls out my key and smiles. "I still have this, remember?"

I groan and stand up. "Well, as you can see, I'm fine. So leave my key on my dresser and *get out*."

He jumps and lands on my bed. He puts his hands behind his head and stretches out his legs. "I think I'll stick around for a while." He looks down at my outfit. "And by the looks of it, I would say that you don't plan on going back to school." I'm in my maroon sweats with my gray Beatles shirt on.

I cross my arms. "No, I'm not." I just want a day to myself. Is that too much to ask for?

We stay quiet until he speaks up again. "I know what happened this morning," he says as he looks down and plays with his hands.

When he says *morning*, I look at my clock and see that it's twelve thirty. Then I think about what had occurred this morning and sigh. "I'm sure everyone knows what happened." I snap at him. I'm not in the best mood now, especially since he had disturbed my sleep.

"Not everyone." He shrugs. "Anyways, that's why I came over."

"Is it now?" I ask him. "To make sure the bullied nerd girl hasn't gone suicidal and tried cutting herself? Then to go and tell everyone so they can just continue to think about how weird she is and how she will never be accepted by anyone?" I rant. My heart is racing in my chest. I take a deep breath to try and calm myself down.

Aiden sits up on my bed. "First of all, I don't think of you as the 'bullied nerd girl.' Never have, and never will," he says seriously. "Second, I don't fucking talk to anyone at school, so why would I tell them something that isn't my business? And third, I really hope you haven't cut yourself and gone suicidal."

I manage to calm myself down. I sigh and run a hand through my hair. "I'm fine."

"I didn't ask if you were fine," he says. "And don't lie to me. I know you're not fine."

Dammit. "Why would being called a slut and a whore bother me?" I ask sarcastically. "Why would being accused of trying to steal Ryan from Nicole upset me? Or the fact that she told everyone I slept with you and embarrassed me in front of everyone? Hmm, why wouldn't I be fine?"

Aiden sits there silently as I ramble on. I'm fuming, and I clench my hands into fists. I'm not done with this. "I was all right. I was okay with being left alone at school and eating lunch in the library every day." I pace in my room. "I didn't care that while everyone talked during class, I was sitting in my seat reading. Then I had to be in this stupid wedding and actually socialize with people. Then I met you, Ryan, and Kelly. I actually thought that it wouldn't be so bad if I had at least a friend by my side. But I was wrong. Being with you guys only made my life harder. I never had this kind of drama in my life before. I'm a different person now. I'm not as quiet as I used to be and I don't know if that's a good thing or a bad thing. I want my old life back, but then I don't." I'm breathing heavily.

Aiden raises his eyebrows. "Well, damn."

"That's all you can say after I just spilled all that out to you?" I demand, still feeling outraged.

Aiden pats the spot next to him on my bed. "Sit."

"I'm fine right here."

"Just get over here, Riley. Don't you trust me?" he asks.

I narrow my eyes at him. I slowly make my way around the bed and sit down next to him.

"Good." He nods. "Now, I'm kind of glad that you exploded like that. I didn't know you had it in you." He gives me a small smile. "Whenever you're around me, I get this quiet, sometimes annoying girl who holds up her guard with sarcastic comments. It's like you don't trust anyone. I trusted you with my sob story, and you still didn't let me inside. But now," he says, "I just saw this completely different side of you. It was the side that showed your real feelings."

I look down at my hands.

"I know being talked about sucks. Everyone thinks I go and get arrested every weekend, which is not true. But you just have to ignore it. They don't know the real you, so they make assumptions. It's what people with no lives do. They talk about other people," he tells me.

I sigh and look up at him. "When did you start giving good advice?" I tease him to lighten the mood.

He chuckles. "I guess you brought out the Dr. Phil in me."

"I'm sorry," I say suddenly.

"Sorry for what?" he asks.

"Now everyone thinks you slept with a nerdy girl like me," I say, looking down again.

He sighs. "I told you. I ignore things like that that aren't true." He scoots closer to me. "Unless you want that rumor, in particular, to be true…"

I stand up quickly. "I am not going to sleep with you." He starts to laugh. "It's not funny Aiden."

"It kind of is," he says. "Though, I'm kind of hurt that you wouldn't want to do it with me. I mean, every girl wants me."

I roll my eyes. "Wow, Aiden. I had no idea you could be so cocky," I say to him.

He shrugs. "Not all the time. But I do have my moments."

"So, it's been great talking to you, but you need to leave now," I say.

"Why?"

"Because you have to go back to school."

He crosses his arms. "If you get to stay home from school, then so do I."

I groan. "You can't stay here Aiden."

"Give me a good reason why I can't stay here," he says, leaning back on my bed.

"You could be missing a valuable lesson at school," I say. We both stare at each other, and I shake my head. "Never mind. That was a terrible reason."

He clasps his hands together. "Cool. Looks like I'm staying here for a while."

I have no idea how this afternoon is going to go. But I guess I'll find out.

Chapter 16

"I'm bored," Aiden says for about the thousandth time since he got here.

I rub my face. "I told you, you don't have to stay here."

Aiden is sprawled out on the couch in the living room. We have been watching TV, but Aiden keeps on complaining how boring it is just sitting here. For the record, *The Big Bang Theory* is *not* boring.

Aiden sits up suddenly with a huge grin on his face. "I know what we can do."

I squint at him. "What?"

"Get dressed. We're going out," he says, standing up.

"Whoa, whoa." I stand up too. "Tell me what we're doing first."

He smiles. "It's a surprise. Just go get dressed, but not in anything fancy."

I roll my eyes as I make my way to the stairs. "Oh yeah, because I dress fancy all the time."

I run up to my room and shut my door, locking it of course. I bring out a pair of jeans and my black *Metallica* shirt. I quickly put those on then grab my old Converse. I brush my teeth in the bathroom then run a brush through my hair. I pick up my phone from my bed and make my way back downstairs.

Aiden is sitting by the door and is on his phone. He looks up at me. "I'm glad you're not one of those girls who take forever getting ready." He stands up. "Nice shirt."

"Thanks," I say. I look down at my phone. "Are we going to leave now? Because my mom gets off at five and I want to be home before her."

"It's only two o'clock, Riley." Aiden chuckles. "We have plenty of time." He opens the front door, and we both walk out. Aiden hands me my key, and I lock the door. I put the key in my pocket as we walk towards Alex's car.

We get in and are on our way to wherever Aiden is taking me.

"We'll need to stop at the dollar store for some things," Aiden says. "It won't be a lot."

I'm really curious to see where we're going and also, why we need things for this idea of his.

Soon enough, we pull into the parking lot of the nearest dollar store. I start unbuckling when Aiden puts his hand over mine. I look at him, confused.

"I'm going in by myself," he says to me. "I'll be right back."

I sit back in my chair as Aiden opens his door. "This is so unfair."

"Life is unfair!" he exclaims as he shuts the door.

About five agonizing minutes later, he comes out of the store with two bags in his hands. He opens the driver's door and sets the bags on my lap. I peek in the two bags then look at Aiden skeptically. "Aiden," I say calmly, "why are there two boxes of condoms in one bag and three bottles of paint in the other bag?"

He starts to laugh. "Well, the paint is for us. The condoms are for my use."

"Aiden!" I exclaim.

"I'm just kidding!" He continues to laugh. "We're going to use the condoms also. But not for the purpose you think."

Condoms and paint. I don't have any idea what he wants to do with all of this.

"You should have seen the lady's face when I put the condoms on the counter." He smirks. "I just told her it was an emergency."

I start to laugh at him. I can only imagine what her face looked like. "That might've been the wrong thing to say."

He shrugs. "I don't know her, so why should I care what she thinks?" He has a point.

"So, now do you mind telling me what we're doing with condoms and paint?"

"Okay," he says, smiling. "I was originally planning on using water balloons instead. But there weren't any water balloons, so I had to settle for the condoms. So what we'll do is fill the condoms with paint and drop them on people's heads from the top of a building."

My jaw drops. "I can't do that! Do you have any idea how mad people will be when they get covered in paint?"

Aiden sighs. "If we don't do that, then our other option is to throw the paint filled condoms at each other in the park."

I think about this. "But I already showered today."

"It's one or the other."

I bite my lip. Maybe I should be more spontaneous. "Um, why don't we do both?" I suggest, still a little bit unsure.

Aiden's smile grows. "Okay. We have to drop two paint filled condoms each on someone. Then we'll head to the park and throw them at each other. Deal?" He holds out his hand.

I stare at it for a moment. I cover my eyes with one hand and shake his hand with the other. "Deal."

***

We walk through the entrance of an old building. I glance around once we're inside.

"Where are we exactly?" I ask Aiden slowly.

"We are in my uncle's old store. He died a few years ago and now this building just kind of sits here. I usually go up to the rooftop and hang out," Aiden says matter-of-factly.

I look around nervously. My hands shake as we make our way up the stairs. I take each step carefully, making sure I don't trip and fall. We make it to the top, which holds a door that says "EXIT." Aiden opens the door, letting the cool air hit us. We step onto the rooftop, and I let out a sigh. I have to say, the view up here is pretty nice.

Aiden sets the two grocery bags on a small table nearby and takes out the boxes of condoms and bottles of paint. "Let's take out the condoms and start filling them with the paint," he tells me.

I grab a box of condoms and a blue paint bottle. "Two each, right?"

"Well, I might throw more than two. But yeah." He nods.

I open one of the condom packages and shake my head. I can't believe I'm going through with this. I start to fill the first condom with the blue paint. I can't help but laugh while filling it up. "This is absolutely ridiculous."

"But it will be ridiculously hilarious." Aiden chuckles.

We both finish filling up our first ones, and I look at Aiden. He has an evil grin spread across his face. "Let's do this."

We walk to the edge of the building. I glance down at the ground below us and notice a few people walking along the sidewalk.

"So are we going to aim or—"

Aiden tosses the first one over the ledge and leans over before I can finish asking him my question. We hear a splatter then an angry voice saying, "What the hell?"

Aiden leans back and starts laughing. I peek over the edge and see the guy covered in the red paint Aiden has filled his up with. I giggle at the sight below me. Aiden looks at me then. "Your turn, Summers."

I take a deep breath and launch mine over the edge without aiming. We hear another splatter. I peer over the ledge and see a kid covered in my blue paint. He looks up and sees me. "Hey!" he screams.

I lean back, and Aiden and I start to laugh. I didn't think this was going to be fun, but it actually is.

That's how we spend our time on the roof. We end up throwing about five each over the edge of the building. We're now on our way to the park with our already paint-filled condoms to have our war.

"You look nervous." Aiden chuckles at me.

I rub my hands together. "I'm just not sure how I feel about getting condoms filled with paint thrown at me."

"It'll be fun. I promise."

Aiden parks the car in the small parking lot, and we both get out. We had packed a bag with the condoms, so Aiden grabs that bag from the backseat. We walk towards a small secluded area. Aiden gently sets down the bag and looks at me.

"Ready?" he asks, grinning from ear to ear.

"Sure." I nod.

Aiden grabs a few from the bag and sets them on his side. I then reach inside and start to grab a few.

Something hits me, and my arm instantly feels wet and sticky.

I gasp and look at my arm, which is covered in red paint. I look at Aiden who has an evil smirk on his face. I reach down and grab the nearest one to me and throw it at Aiden. I hit him right in his stomach, turning his shirt blue.

"Remind me to never use this brand of condoms. They break easily." Aiden chuckles. I roll my eyes then throw another at him.

And so our war begins.

***

We arrive at my house at exactly four-thirty. The paint had dried on mine and Aiden's skin, making me feel all stiff. We're covered in red, blue, and green paint, which when combined makes the ugliest color I've ever seen.

Aiden sighs next to me. "Well, this was a fun afternoon."

"I agree." I nod. I open the car door and start to get out.

"I'll walk you to the door," Aiden says suddenly.

We make our way up to my front door, and I pull out my key. "Don't even try to take my key, Aiden. I will hurt you if you do." I threaten him.

"I'm not afraid of you, Riley," he says, sounding amused. He stands directly behind me as I try to insert the key into the lock. "You should be afraid of me," he whispers into my ear.

My breath catches in my throat from how close he is to me. I feel his hands settle on my waist, giving me goosebumps. He turns me around so I'm facing him. Instead of focusing on the paint covering his face, I just stare into his eyes. "Do I scare you?" he asks quietly.

"Sometimes," I say.

He smirks and leans closer to me. My back presses against the door while both his hands rest on the door beside my head. I'm trapped between his arms. He leans a little closer and my eyes flutter close. His lips gently press against my cheek and linger there for a minute. My eyes pop open to see him smirking still.

He pulls away and gives me a smile. "See you tomorrow, Riley."

I feel my face heat up from what just happened. I quickly turn around and unlock my front door. Once I make it inside, I lean against the door and touch my cheek.

He kissed my cheek.

Once again, I let him get close to me, and I let my guard down. That's the third time he's done it. I feel weak and defenseless.

I stomp up to my room to take another shower. I have to hide the evidence that I ever left the house. Otherwise, I will hear it from my mother.

***

I'm hesitant when I walk into the school's main building. I keep my head down as I weave my way around everyone. No one's really paying attention to me, so I take this as a good sign. I walk to my locker with no problem.

As I open my locker, I feel a presence near me. I look over and see Ryan standing next to me with his arms crossed.

"Yes?" I ask because he's not saying anything.

"So you left yesterday?" he questions.

I look back at my locker. "Obviously."

"And it was because of Nicole, right?"

"Listen, Ryan, it's okay—"

He steps closer to me. "No, it isn't okay. I had no idea she hurt your feelings until I heard her talking about you after school. I was going to break up with her right there, but I figured I'd wait."

I face him. "Why? This doesn't concern you, Ryan. I can handle myself."

"Oh really?" he asks. "If you could handle it, then you wouldn't have left yesterday."

"So what are you going to do? Just break up with her?" I ask him. I don't need his help. I'm fine.

He runs a hand through his hair. "Yes. But I'm going to do it in front of everyone at lunch."

"Well, let me know how that goes. I'll be in the library during that time," I say as I shut my locker.

"So what did you do yesterday? I know Aiden left, but did he go see you?"

I nod. "Yes."

"What did you guys do?"

"Um…we played with paint."

He raises his eyebrow. "You…played with paint."

I sigh. "Ask Aiden. I'm sure he'll tell you the whole story."

"Hey, are you ready for the rehearsal tonight at the church?" he questions.

Oh crap. I keep forgetting about this wedding stuff that I need to go to. I should be more responsible about this. "Uh, sure I am." I give him a small smile.

He chuckles. He probably knows that I'm lying about that. "Well, just wear a nice dress or something. We're just going to go over how everything will play out. Okay?"

"Okay." I nod.

Ryan gives me a smile before walking away. I take a deep breath as I start to walk in the opposite direction to my first class. I internally groan when I remember that I'll have a ton of makeup work to complete since I missed yesterday.

What a fun afternoon I'll have!

Not.

Chapter 17

After lunch, everyone is buzzing in the hallway. They're probably talking about Ryan breaking up with Nicole earlier. I hear a girl talking about it in the bathroom, and it sounds like Ryan embarrassed her pretty badly. I'm trying really hard to stay away from her since she might be on a rampage.

As I walk to my next class, I feel someone's presence next to me. I smile when I look over and see who it is. "Can I help you, Aiden?"

"Yes, you can actually." He nods. "Wanna hang out again after school?"

I'm about to agree when I remember I have the rehearsal tonight. "I would like to, but there's the wedding rehearsal tonight..."

His expression darkens. "Right. Somehow I keep forgetting you're in the wedding also."

"So do I," I mutter. "Maybe tomorrow?"

He shrugs. "Maybe." Then with that being said, he goes his separate way.

I frown but then brush it off.

***

"No, Max, you stand here next to Halle. Drew, stop messing around! This is serious!" Anna exclaims at them. She seems stressed out, which is understandable. From what I've seen on TV, brides tend to turn into *bridezillas* when their wedding is in less than a week. "There. Nobody move! This is where you're all going to stand while I'm walking down the aisle."

So far we have covered the order that each couple will come out. Lucas and I are last. Then Anna shows us the speed in which we need to be walking. It can't be too fast, and it can't be too slow. I have a huge headache and hearing all of this isn't helping me at all. I didn't know weddings can be so complicated.

Anna stands in front of us all and crosses her arms. "I do not want anyone messing around while you're up here. People's attention will not only be on Robert and me but on the bridesmaids and the groomsmen. So please act professional," she says. "Okay. Since the wedding is on Saturday, I want all the bridesmaids at my house by nine in the morning. You all need plenty of time to prepare since the actual wedding starts at three. And all the groomsmen need to be at Robert's house at ten. Please don't be late. I do not want a rough start."

I sigh silently and look down at the dress I'm wearing. I thought I was going to look silly, but Kelly and Jenna convinced me that this dress looked amazing on me.

So that boosted my confidence a little bit. It's a dark blue dress that stops at my knees. The bottom half has lace flowers. It isn't too girly, and I actually kind of like it.

"Our rehearsal dinner is going to be Friday at six in the evening at my house. Everyone is invited." Anna gives us a smile.

After the rehearsal is over, I wait outside of the church for my mom. I sit on the curb rubbing my head with my hands. Once I get home, I am so taking Tylenol.

I see Ryan walking towards me. He sits down with me on the curb and sighs. "My mom is turning into a bridezilla."

I chuckle. "She's just stressed."

"She's been going on a rampage at home, and it's getting crazy." He shakes his head. "I just want this wedding to be over with."

You and me both.

"So do you need a ride? Or are you just going to sit on this curb all night?" he asks me.

"My mom is picking me up," I say. "Thanks for the offer though."

We stay quiet for a moment before I speak up. "How did the break up go?"

Ryan groans. "I thought I could just end things with no problem. I decided that embarrassing her wasn't right. But she brought attention to herself like she always does."

"I heard she embarrassed herself," I comment.

Ryan nods and chuckles. "She did. It was annoying and entertaining at the same time." I chuckle too. "The only downside is that she and her parents are going to the wedding."

Crap. I will probably be harassed by her once she sees me at the wedding on Saturday. "That'll be fun," I say sarcastically.

"Oh yeah. Loads of fun."

"What do you think Aiden will do during the wedding?" I ask him. I was going to ask Aiden earlier, but I didn't see him for the rest of the day.

Ryan shrugs. "I have no idea. I haven't had a conversation with him for a while now."

Aiden is shutting everyone out. I don't blame him for being so upset, but he is only hurting himself more. "Oh," I say, looking down. I hear a car pull up and see that it's my mom.

Ryan stands up and holds his hand out to me. I take it, and he pulls me up with ease. "I'll see you tomorrow, Ryan." I wave to him.

"Bye, Riley." He gives me a small smile.

I get into my mother's car, and we drive back to our house.

***

I haven't heard from Aiden in two and a half days. The last time I talked to him was in the hall on Tuesday. It is now Friday, and I still haven't spoken to him.

I'm now at home, getting ready for the rehearsal dinner. My mom had bought me another dress for this evening. She's going with me too since she and Anna are good friends.

My dress is a little girlier than I like it, but I'm not going to complain out loud. My mom pins my hair up in a side bun, leaving a few pieces loose. She claps when we finish getting ready and claims that I should always wear makeup and dress like this.

I think otherwise.

As I'm in my room, my phone starts buzzing on my dresser. I glance down at the screen and see that Aiden is calling me.

Frowning, I answer, "Yes?"

"Hello to you too, Summers." Aiden's voice rings through my ears. "It's always a pleasure hearing you sound so cheery."

I roll my eyes. "Oh yes, I'm feeling very cheery right now."

"I'm going to ask you something, and you have to give me a good answer," he tells me.

"Okay," I say slowly. "What's your question?"

I hear him take a deep breath. "Black or red?"

"Are you serious right now?" I demand. "Why are you asking that?"

"Dead serious. Just choose now because I'm kind of in a hurry," he says.

I sigh in frustration. "Black."

"I'm glad you said that," he says then hangs up. Aiden is so weird. And that's not okay for me to say since I'm kind of weird myself.

My mom calls my name from downstairs, and I glance at the clock. It's about ten 'til six. I hurry out of my room and go downstairs. I'm glad I convinced my mom to let me wear flats instead of heels. I probably would have broken my ankle running down the stairs.

***

I stand next to Kelly while she talks to one of her friends. They're talking about another girl from their school. This is really boring, but I have no one else to talk to. It's about five after six, and Ryan has yet to show his face, so I can't speak to him.

My mom and some other ladies are surrounding Anna and talking away about the wedding. Or they can be gossiping. Or both.

I thought Anna's house is huge, but her backyard seems bigger and nicely landscaped. There's a good-sized patio right when you walk outside.

The patio door opens, and Ryan steps out. He's dressed in a button-up shirt and black pants. Then after him, Robert steps outside. What surprises me is the one standing behind Robert.

It's Aiden.

He's dressed in a white button-up shirt that's untucked. A tie hangs loosely around his neck, and he has on black pants. In one hand is his black leather jacket.

Strangely, I find myself not wanting to look away from him. My stomach does this weird thing, and I feel like I'm going to pass out. He's facing Robert who's saying a few words to him. Aiden nods then turns around and starts walking away. I quickly turn away and act like I wasn't just staring at him.

Someone taps my shoulder, and I slowly turn. Aiden smirks at me. "Hello, Ms. Summers."

"Mr. Callaway," I say, feeling like I'm in *Pride & Prejudice*. "What are you doing here?" I ask curiously.

He shrugs. "Nothing better to do on a Friday night. Not one party is being thrown." He shakes his head disapprovingly.

I chuckle. "What a shame."

He gives me a once-over then looks back at my face. "You look...different."

"I know," I say, frowning at the dress. "You look different also. Why did you ask me black or red?"

"The tie color," he says, grabbing his tie. "I had a red one and a black one, but I wasn't sure which one I should pick."

"So you called me," I say slowly.

He nods. "Very few people's opinion matter to me." He winks.

"Aiden, what are you doing here?" Kelly asks next to me.

"I had nothing better to do," he tells her.

Kelly smirks. "Mmhmm. Sure..." She waves to us before leaving.

I look back at Aiden. "So it's been a while," I tell him.

"Since what?" He frowns.

"Since we last talked."

He smirks. "You missed me, didn't you?"

"I did not." I cross my arms. "I'm just saying we haven't talked in two days."

"You missed me." He nods. "It's okay, though, because I missed you too." He nudges my arm.

Before I can even react to his comment, Anna grabs everyone's attention. "The food is ready everyone! Form a line right here and come grab a plate!"

My stomach growls. I didn't snack on anything when I got home from school, and I'm really regretting that decision. I make my way to where the line is forming and stand.

Once I get my plate of food, I sit at one of the empty tables and quickly start eating. I'm starving.

Aiden pulls a chair next to me and sits down. "I hope you're not mad at me anymore for ignoring you for two days," he says.

"I guess I'm not mad." I shrug as I continue to eat.

"Oh and guess what?" he asks me. I look at him. "I had to take three showers in a row just to get that fucking blue paint out of my hair."

"I only had to take two showers." That paint was hard to get off. I won't be using that brand of paint anymore. Once it's on, it never comes off.

"Can I get everyone's attention please?" Anna's voice rings out. "Thank you! Okay, so there are a few people who want to make a speech. So whoever wants to go first can go ahead!" Anna smiles as she sits back down next to Robert.

One of Anna's sisters stands up and makes a speech about Robert and Anna. Aiden becomes a bit edgy next to me. I know he doesn't like what she's saying about fate bringing them together.

I don't know what possessed me to do it, but I grab Aiden's left hand. He looks at me incredulously, obviously shocked that I'm now holding his hand. I squeeze it to let him know that it's okay. He turns back to Anna's sister and continues to hold my hand.

The next person to talk is Jenna, along with Kelly. Their speech is short but beautiful. It doesn't drag on.

After Jenna and Kelly's speech, Ryan stands up and clears his throat. He starts off by congratulating Anna and Robert. Then he moves on to something that no one else mentioned. "Personally, I wasn't sure about you guys getting married. But then I actually got to know Robert, who is kind of cool." He smiles. "I also got to know Aiden, Robert's son."

Aiden leans forward in his chair and focuses on Ryan.

"In a way, I admire Aiden," Ryan says to everyone. "He's been through a lot, and he's managed to stay strong. He may look like your everyday troublesome kid, but he's not. Once you get to know him, he can be a real chill guy. And I'm glad that after tomorrow, I can call him my stepbrother."

I look at Anna and Robert to see their reactions. Anna looks shocked but somewhat proud. Robert's expression is hard to read. He looks like he's about to cry, but he stays calm.

"I've got a great family, and I know it'll be even greater having Robert and Aiden around." Everyone claps as Ryan sits down.

I glance at Aiden who has his jaw clenched. "Are you...okay?" I ask hesitantly.

He exhales. "I don't know if I should be happy, or fucking pissed right now."

"Why?" I ask him.

"Well, I know he lied when he said he admired me," Aiden says. "But I shouldn't be so mad because he basically just praised me in front of everybody."

I look at Ryan who's smiling at me. I smile back at him then look at Aiden. "You shouldn't dislike Ryan so much. I bet he has somewhat the same feelings as you do."

"How?" he asks me.

"Their dad chose to leave them Aiden," I tell him, remembering Kelly's words when I asked her about her dad. "Your mom didn't decide to leave you, but their dad did. He left them to have another life with another woman. I bet Ryan's hurting too."

Aiden sighs. "How did *you* become the person who understands everything in my life?"

I shrug. "I don't know. Why? Do you want me *not* to understand?" I ask him, feeling a little bit hurt.

He smirks and squeezes my hand. "I do want you to understand because no one else will," he tells me.

At that moment, I realize why my stomach felt weird when I saw Aiden walk earlier. I know why I always let my guard down around him. I know why I missed him over these two days that I didn't see him.

I have a crush on Aiden Callaway.

Chapter 18

Today is the day.

Today is the day of the wedding, and I'm freaking out. I keep worrying about my dress being ruined, my hair looking like crap, and my makeup being done by a clown. I've never acted like this before, and it scares me.

I'm turning into a *girl*.

I'm totally kidding. I'm already a girl. But I am freaking out a bit.

I am sitting in a chair at a local hair salon, and I keep cringing every time the lady working on my hair gets close to my ear with the curling iron. Holly sits in the chair next to mine, and she wears a huge grin on her face. She's ready for today. I'm not.

Anna chats with Jenna on the other side of the salon. Jenna is probably trying to calm her mom down. Anna's acting like a crazy person this morning. I think everyone just wants to get this wedding over with.

After our hair gets done, we all go to the church where we will get our dresses then get our makeup done.

I have to admit that I'm pretty nervous. What if I trip while walking down the aisle? I take a deep breath to calm myself down. I don't do well in situations where I have to stand in front of everyone, even if I'm not speaking.

The lady working on me finishes the last touches on my makeup. I sigh and get up from my chair to put my dress on. I open the bag that holds my dress and pulls it out. I step into a small room and slip it on.

When I step back out of the room, Anna has on her dress already and is walking around talking to people. I smile when I see her. She looks beautiful.

I sit down on one of the small couches nearby and slip on the treacherous heels we have to wear. Someone sits next to me, so I look over and find Anna sitting there.

"Are you ready, Riley?" she asks me with a bright smile.

I nod. "Sure."

"You'll do great." She puts her hand on my arm.

Let's hope she's right.

Aiden

I pace in my room, rubbing my chin. Well, it isn't exactly my room. I'm staying in one of the guest bedrooms in Alex's house. And I keep thinking about this stupid wedding today.

I'm still uninvited. But I don't give a shit. I don't want to go to that fucking wedding anyways. Nothing can make me go. Not Ryan, not Kelly, not my dad, and not even Riley.

There's a soft knock on the bedroom door. "Come in," I say as I sit on my bed.

Alex walks in and crosses his arms. "Why aren't you ready?"

"Ready for what?" I demand.

"Ready for the wedding," he says. I glare at him and he busts up laughing. "I'm just kidding, bro. I know you're not going."

I shake my head. "You're an ass, Alex."

"I know." He smirks. "I thought you were *thinking* about going."

"I'm not fucking going, Alex. Nothing is going to get me over there." I cross my arms.

He leans against the doorframe. "Not even that girl you were talking about yesterday?"

Of course, he will bring her into this. "Not even Riley can make me go," I tell him.

Alex grins. "C'mon, Aiden," he says to me. "Just admit that you might actually like this girl. You've been hanging out with her and constantly talking to her. Not to mention that little hand holding thing you told me about."

I do *not* like Riley. Sure, she's fun to hang out with, but…I don't know. She will never go out with me anyways. Not that I have ever thought about going out with her.

It's just kinda nice talking to her about all this bad shit going on. She doesn't judge me, and she doesn't tell me that I'm a screw-up. And I forget everything that is going on when I'm with her. That's part of why I keep asking her to hang out. Once I'm with her, I don't think about anything else.

"You're whipped." Alex shakes his head and chuckles. He walks out of my room and continues down the hall.

"Shut the fuck up, Alex!" I yell after him.

I lean back on my bed and sigh. I'm extremely bored right now, and I can't even call Riley since she's in the wedding.

I bet she spent all day with the girls getting ready. I bet they covered her face in makeup, put a shitload of hairspray in her hair, and made her walk in dangerously high heels.

I shudder at the fact that girls do all of this crap to look *pretty*.

Looking at the clock, I notice that the wedding has started already. I frown and close my eyes. As soon as I do, an image of my mom enters my mind. She smiles at me. She looks healthy. She looks like she did before she was diagnosed with cancer.

My eyes spring open before I can get emotional. I can't believe my fucking dad is marrying another woman. If

Dad really loves Mom, he won't be marrying Anna right now.

I rub my face and try to calm down. Will I ever speak to my dad after the wedding?

I stand up from my bed and walk to my closet. I throw on the nearest pair of jeans and t-shirt I can find. I grab my leather jacket off my bed and walk out of the room. I find Alex in the kitchen eating cereal.

"Going somewhere?" he asks with a mouth full of Frosted Flakes.

I grab the keys off the counter. "Yup." And with that, I walk out of the house.

If Riley can't be here to make me forget about everything, I'm sure Jack Daniels can be of assistance.

Riley

We all clap as Robert dips Anna and pecks her lips on the dance floor. Seeing them together is really heartwarming. You can tell that they really love each other.

Here I am, sitting at a table watching more couples go out on the dance floor. Lucas comes up to me and asks me to dance, but I tell him my feet are hurting from the heels. So Kelly takes my place.

My mind wanders as I glance around the room. I wonder what Aiden is doing right now. I have a bad feeling in my stomach that he isn't doing so good right now. But the reception just started. I can't leave yet.

As evening turns to night, people are still on the dance floor, moving their bodies to the rhythm. Robert and Anna are sitting at a table by themselves, talking to one another. I'm fine sitting by myself, just watching everyone else have a good time like I always do.

I hear some shuffling next to me, and I glance to the side. My eyes widen when I see Aiden sitting in a chair next to me. I'm about to smile at him until I see the bottle of liquor in his hands. His eyes are half-closed, and he leans against the table.

"Riley." He reaches out and pinches my cheek.

I frown at him. "You're drunk," I say, looking away from him. How can I have ever developed feelings for someone like Aiden? Sure, he can be a little sweet at times, but he has no idea how to deal with things.

He nods. "Fuck yeah, I am." He slurs. He takes another drink from the bottle. "Where's my dad?" he asks me.

"He's over there." I nod in Robert and Anna's direction. "Maybe you should go home before he sees you like this. It would be for the best Aiden."

Aiden scowls at me. "You mean before he sees that his own son is turning into a screw-up?" He slurs again. "I don't give a fuck what he thinks anymore. I am never going to speak to him again after tonight anyways." He stands up abruptly, knocking over his chair. He turns to start walking, but he trips on the chair and grabs onto the table.

I quickly stand up and grab his arm. "Let's take you home, Aiden," I tell him softly.

He pulls his arm away from me. "Not yet." He continues to walk in the direction of Robert and Anna. I follow him to the table to make sure he doesn't fall on his face.

Robert glances at Aiden, and his eyes widen like mine had. "Aiden..."

I stand by Aiden awkwardly and hold onto his arm to prevent him from falling.

"Don't talk to me," Aiden growls. "I don't want to hear anything from you. I don't want to hear about how perfect your life is now that you're with *her*." He points at Anna. "I don't want to hear from you about how I'm fucking up my life."

Robert stands up and walks around the table. "Aiden, go back home, and we'll discuss this later."

"I don't want to fucking talk about this later!" Aiden yells in Robert's face. As he raises his voice, a few people take notice of his presence and frown at the profanities he's using. "I'm getting my stuff from the house, and I'm leaving," Aiden says. His speech improves a little bit, making the slurring less noticeable.

"No, you aren't." Robert shakes his head. "How are you going to take care of yourself, Aiden? Look at you. You can't even stand on your own two feet without someone holding you up," he says, gesturing to me.

Don't bring me into this, please.

"I will be fine on my own." Aiden snaps. "I've been on my own for a while now. Ever since you gave all of your fucking attention to their family." He points at Anna again.

At this point, I'm sure everyone in the room is watching the argument between Robert and Aiden. I see Ryan making his way over to us, and I mentally groan. Does Aiden really have to make a scene?

Ryan walks up to Aiden and sighs. "C'mon, Aiden. I'll take you home," he speaks softly.

Aiden shoves him away, making him lose his balance a bit. I hold onto his arm, holding him in place. "Get the fuck away from me, Ryan. I want nothing to do with you."

Okay. Maybe I should step in *now*. "Aiden"—I tugged on his arm—"I'll take you home," I say to him.

Aiden glances at me then back at Robert. "I'm done talking to all of you." He grits his teeth.

I sneak towards my mom at another table. When I'm close enough, I speak to her, "I need the keys."

My mom frowns. "I don't think you should—"

"Give me the keys, Mom," I say, losing my patience. "He needs to get home safely."

"Riley, just go sit back down. I'm sure someone—"

I grab her small bag from the table and reach inside.

"Riley!" she exclaims.

I pull out the keys and look at her. "I'm doing what I think is right mom." I snap at her. I turn around and don't see Aiden anywhere. I jog to the entrance of the building.

I find Aiden leaning against the wall outside, rubbing his face. I slowly approach him, hesitant on how he'll react. "Aiden?" I ask quietly.

He looks up, and his eyes are red-rimmed. "Riley...I..."

"Let's go," I tell him.

He pushes himself off the wall and walks towards me, stumbling a bit. I walk him to my mom's car and help him get in on the passenger side. I get in on the driver's side and yank my heels off. I throw them in the backseat.

"So, where to?" I ask Aiden hesitantly.

"Alex's house," he mumbles.

"Mind telling me where his house is?" I ask.

He gives me an address, and I instantly know where the street is. I always see it when my mom and I go to Wal-Mart.

We drive in silence. Aiden has his arms crossed as he stares out the window. He doesn't speak until I drive down Alex's street and ask him which house it is.

He looks up. "It's that one with the chain-link fence." He points to it. I pull into the house's driveway and park. "Wanna come inside?" Aiden asks me.

I raise my eyebrows but shake my head. "No thanks. I have to get back..."

"Right," he mutters. "Thanks for the ride, Riley." He opens the passenger door and steps out of the car. I wait until he's inside to leave.

***

Saturday morning, I don't wake up until about ten. My mom and I got home kind of late. Then she scolded me for taking her keys. Which was totally unnecessary because I made it back safe without a scratch on her car.

I go downstairs and greet my mom. She makes us some pancakes, so we sit down at the kitchen table and eat in silence. After finishing what's on my plate, I stand up awkwardly and put it in the sink.

I run back upstairs to my room and shut my door. I throw myself on my bed and sigh. I'm incredibly bored right now. I reach over to the small table by my bed and grab my phone. I have two messages. I open the first one and find that it's from Aiden.

Wanna hang out today?

I read the next one, which is also from him.

Unless I made myself look like an ass last night and you never want to speak to me again.

I smile slightly and text him back:

I wouldn't say that. What did you have planned today?

He doesn't waste any time texting me back.

You wanna meet at the park?

I agree to meet him there and start getting ready. I put on some jeans and my old Pink Floyd shirt. I throw on my shoes and run a brush through my hair. Luckily for me, I showered last night and my hair dried pretty straight.

I go back downstairs and walk into the kitchen again where I find my mom. "I'm going to the park," I inform her.

"Are you taking Sassy?" she asks.

"No. I was just going to meet someone there," I say.

She eyes me suspiciously but sighs. "Okay. Keep your phone on and let me know when you're on your way back."

I nod. "Will do."

***

When I arrive at the park, Aiden is already waiting. He is leaning against a tree and has his phone in his hand. His dark brown hair is up in his usual messy fashion. He has on his black leather jacket. He also has a pair of Ray Bans covering his eyes.

He hears me approaching him and looks up. "You made it," he comments.

"Yup. I didn't get kidnapped or anything." I joke.

He smirks. "What's with you and thinking you're going to get kidnapped?"

"You never know." I shrug. "It could happen at any time."

He shakes his head. "You are too much."

We walk to a bench and sit down. I lean back and sigh. "So what's up?" I finally ask him.

He leans forward and rubs his temples. "Well, I have a killer headache right now. But I'm pretty sure you know why."

He's hung over.

I nod. "Yes. I do."

"I'm just..." He looks up and stares at the grass. I guess he's trying to find the right words. "Disappointed."

"Disappointed?" I question.

"Disappointed in myself, to be more specific," he tells me. "I embarrassed myself last night in front of everyone in that damn room."

I remember all the horrified faces when people took a look at Aiden, especially Anna's side of the family. I'm curious about what was going through their mind at that time.

I stare at Aiden as he speaks. I can tell the change in mood in him. Before the wedding, he was very negative towards everything and was totally resentful. Now, he seems drained and not as full of life as he used to be. And I'm not going to blame that on the hangover.

"Have you talked to your dad or Ryan this morning?" I ask curiously.

He shakes his head. "No. You're the only person I've talked to besides Alex."

I feel something warm inside of me. At this moment, I can't help but feel good about myself. I'm actually helping someone that I never thought I would be talking to in the first place.

He groans. "I'm such a screw-up, Riley. I don't even know what to do with myself."

I genuinely feel bad for him. "Aiden, you're not a screw-up. You're just a bit...misguided is all," I speak softly. "How about we talk about this later? It's not good to start off a day all depressed."

Aiden smirks. "Are we going to have your idea of fun now?"

I think about it. I smile, knowing what we can do. "Yes, we are."

Chapter 19

Aiden

"What the fuck, Riley. This isn't fun." I groan. I rub my face and sigh. Why did I agree to this? I should have known better.

"Don't be so loud! And it is fun!" she exclaims quietly. "I told you we were going to have my idea of fun. And my idea of fun is coming to the library and finding a good book."

I've never actually been inside the library. I've only spray painted the wall behind it.

"I don't even read, Riley," I say in my normal voice. A guy sitting at a table nearby looks up and shushes me. I glare at the guy before turning back to Riley. She's looking at the shelf in front of her. She stares intently at the books until she finally grabs one. She looks up at me.

"You don't have to stand here with me. You can look around for something interesting," she says, glancing back down at the book.

I watch her for a moment. Her eyes scan the paragraph in the book. She chews on her lip before putting the book back on the shelf.

"I don't even know where anything is," I say to her. "What section are we in anyway?"

She smiles. "Teen fiction."

"How many books do you usually get when you come here?" I ask curiously as I stare at the shelf next to me.

"About two or three," she says. "You better lower your voice or the librarian is going to kick us out."

I scoff. "It's not the first place I've been kicked out of."

I notice a small couch near us so I walk over to it and plop myself down. I don't know how long Riley is going to take, so might as well make myself comfortable.

About five minutes later, Riley approaches me with three books in her hands. "I'm going to check these out then we can leave."

"Cool," I say as I yawn. I stand up and follow her. She weaves around different tables and shelves.

A lady sitting at a tall desk with a computer on it glances in our direction. She smiles. "Riley, it's been a while since you've come here," she tells Riley.

Riley sets the books on the desk. "I've been busy, I guess." She looks at me then. "Are you sure you don't want to get a book?"

"I'm sure," I smirk. I'm not the type of person to read for fun.

"This book again, Riley?" the lady asks her as she holds up the book. The book is called *The Fault in Our Stars*.

Riley smiles at the lady. "It's my weakness."

After Riley and the librarian finish talking, we leave the library. I sigh once we're outside.

"Wow, Riley. You sure know how to have fun," I say sarcastically. "It was almost too crazy for me."

She rolls her eyes. "Shut up, Aiden."

I grab the books from her hands and glance down at one of them. "*The Fault in Our Stars*," I read out loud. "How many times have you read it?"

She shrugs. "I have no idea. But I reread it all the time."

"It must be a good book then." I read the summary. I look at Riley. "It sounds like it would be a sad book."

She nods. "It is."

"So what else do you have planned for us?" I ask her as I take the other two books from her. We approach my car, and we both get inside.

Riley takes back her books once we're seated. "Nothing. What do you want to do?"

I think about it. "We can make out in the backseat," I suggest, smiling.

"Aiden!" she exclaims. I notice her cheeks turn pink, which makes me laugh. It's fun messing with her like that. She's too innocent, and she blushes easily.

"I'm just kidding," I say as I pull out of the parking lot. "But I'm pretty hungry. Do you want to stop and get something to eat?"

Riley nods. "Sure."

I know of a small diner outside of town that has great food. I like to go there sometimes by myself.

"So, did you trip or anything walking down the aisle?" I ask Riley, teasing her. It's too quiet, so I decide to make conversation.

"No," she mumbles. "I'm glad I didn't. I was so nervous I thought I was going to mess something up."

"But you didn't?"

She shakes her head. "No, thank God. Lucas gave me a pep talk before we started walking, so that helped a bit."

I don't know why but hearing her talk about that guy doesn't settle with me. It's probably because we fought at that party. "You and Lucas, huh?" I ask, trying to get more information.

She glances at me, clearly confused. "What do you mean?"

"I mean," I start. "Do you like each other?"

"Of course I like him. That's why I talk to him," she says.

I smack my forehead. "I mean, do you like him more than a friend?"

"Oh." She looks out the window. "No. I don't like him like that."

I feel a slight wave of relief in me, but I ignore it. "He's into you, you know," I tell her.

"Well, that's too bad for him because I don't need a boyfriend." She continues to stare out the window.

I smirk. "You're right. You only need me." I nudge her arm teasingly.

She rolls her eyes. "Please. I don't *need* you. I can stop talking to you anytime I wanted."

"This is a side of you I've never seen," I say, sounding amused. "Cocky Riley. I like it." I wink at her.

Her cheeks tint pink, and I laugh at her. "I'm not as cocky as you are, Aiden Callaway. You think every girl likes you? Well, you're wrong. There's one girl who doesn't think you walk on water."

"That girl can't be you." I scoff. "You're always flirting with me."

She laughs at me. "Me flirting with you? In your dreams, Callaway."

"Hey, only I can call you by your last name."

"Things are changing around here." She shrugs.

I pull into the parking lot of the diner and we both get out. I can't help but think that Riley is finally opening up to me. I'm seeing the real Riley instead of the quiet one.

"I've never been here," Riley says, looking at the building.

"You'll like it. Trust me," I tell her.

We both walk in and sit in a booth. I sit directly across from her. I grab two menus and hand one to her. A waitress comes by and greets us then asks what we want to drink. Riley asks for lemonade. I can barely hear her when she speaks. I ask for water, then the waitress leaves us.

"You remind me of a little mouse," I say, laughing. "You're too shy and innocent."

She crosses her arms. "Leave me alone. I'm not as shy and innocent as I used to be."

"Really?" I ask, not believing her. "I find that hard to believe."

"Well, it's true," she says as she glances out the window near us. I notice she doesn't like to keep eye contact. I don't know if she does that with me only, or with everybody she talks to.

"You blush at everything I say to you. And you don't keep eye contact," I tell her.

"That doesn't make me shy and innocent." She snaps at me.

I'm a little taken aback. She's obviously upset about something now. "What's up with you all of a sudden? Was it something I said?" I ask cautiously. There is nothing more dangerous than an angry woman.

I remember when my mom would come home in a bad mood and didn't really talk to anybody; my dad would make her sit down while he cooked and cleaned for her. He would also tell her repeatedly that she was the love of his life until she laughed at him for being so cheesy.

I almost smile until I remember that he's already married to Anna. Will he do the same thing to her?

"I'm just feeling tired." Riley shrugs. She looks up at me and frowns. "Are you okay? You look like you're going to punch someone."

Shaking my head, I sigh. "Just remembering times when my mom was alive and healthy," I say nonchalantly.

Riley tilts her head to the side. "Can I ask what your mom was like?"

I'm about to respond but the waitress comes back with our drinks and asks us what we want to eat. I don't have to look at the menu to know what I want. But Riley quickly looks down at hers and asks for a small hamburger with fries.

When the waitress leaves, I glance at Riley who's looking at me expectantly. I've never noticed how her eyes look green in the sunlight. I blink and speak. "My mom was the sweetest person. She wasn't one of those moms who overdid everything and wanted everything perfect. She was pretty laid back." I smile softly. "She always told my dad she loved him and he always said it back. She was an elementary school teacher. She taught first grade."

"What was your favorite thing about her?" Riley asks as she leans forward.

I smile at the fact that she's so interested in hearing about my mom. "My favorite thing would be her baking. She loved to cook, but baking was her calling. She always made me the best birthday cakes and best cupcakes for me to bring to class. Whenever we had a bake sale at school, she volunteered."

"Did you pick up her talent for cooking and baking?" Riley asks.

I shrug. "I know how to cook some things. Baking isn't my thing though. Can you imagine me in an apron? That would totally mess up my reputation." I joke.

"Right." She nods. "You're the *supposed badass*."

"Supposed?" I raise my eyebrow. "Summers, I *am* a badass."

She laughs. "You just keep telling yourself that."

For some reason, I like hearing her laugh, especially when it's me who's making her laugh.

Listen to yourself, you wuss. You're turning into a girl.

"So, I've noticed something," I say, changing the subject.

"What's that?"

"You haven't worn your Led Zeppelin shirt since I ran into you that one time," I tell her. She's usually wearing a band t-shirt, but she has been wearing a Led Zeppelin shirt that day, and the name *Led Zeppelin Girl* kind of stuck with me.

She frowns. "I haven't even seen that shirt. I have a lot of band t-shirts, and I can't keep track of all of them."

The waitress comes back and hands us our food. I'm starving. I sneak a glance at Riley in front of me and watch her eat. In a non-creepy way of course.

She takes a small bite of her hamburger and glances out the window. I wonder what's going through her mind. She looks like she's lost in thought.

"Do you want to go back to Alex's house with me?" I blurt out. I surprise myself with the question I ask.

Her eyes widen. "Um...I don't know..."

I realize what I asked her and how it sounded. "I thought we could hang out there and you can meet Alex..." I'm suddenly nervous, and I don't even know why.

"Um—" she bites her lip "—sure."

All the nervousness leaves, and I find myself grinning.

Chapter 20

Riley

I play with my hands as I sit in the car with Aiden. He's driving us to his friend Alex's house, and I have to say, I'm pretty nervous.

I don't even know why I'm so nervous. I've been alone with Aiden before. I know Aiden won't try anything with me, but still.

"You look scared," Aiden says, sounding amused.

"I'm not." I lie.

"Sure," he says, smirking. "Just relax, Riley."

I take a deep breath then sigh. It's been a long day, and I'm already tired. I rest my chin on my hand as I stare out the window.

A few minutes later, I notice we're entering a familiar neighborhood and I know we're close to Alex's house.

"Does Alex live with anyone?" I ask curiously.

Aiden shakes his head. "He used to have a roommate, but that guy got himself a girlfriend and they eventually moved in together. I'm just staying for the time being."

"How old is he?" I ask.

Aiden taps his chin. "I believe he is going to be twenty-one next month."

We pull into the familiar driveway and park. We open our doors and get out of the car. Aiden walks a little ahead of me and pulls out a key. He unlocks the front door and holds it open for me.

"After you." He smirks.

I slowly walk forward and into the house. I don't know what to expect when I walk in. The outside of the house looks decent, but does the inside look the same?

I glance around and see that the inside is actually pretty nice. There aren't many decorations, but the place isn't trashed.

Aiden walks past me and I follow close behind. We walk into what I assume is the living room, where a guy is sitting on the couch watching TV. He looks in our direction and raises his eyebrows.

"Holy shit, I didn't even hear you guys come in," he says. He stands up and walks towards us.

Aiden looks at the guy. "Alex, this is Riley. Riley, this is Alex."

Alex smiles at me and holds out his hand. "Nice to meet you, Miss Riley."

I shake his hand gently. "You too."

Alex glances at Aiden then back at me. "I would have cleaned up a little bit if I had known you were coming back with Aiden."

"It's fine," I say shyly. I don't really do well with meeting new people.

"I'm going to show her around if that's fine," Aiden says to Alex.

"Go ahead. Just don't take her into my room. It's not exactly clean." Alex smirks.

Aiden's hand finds the small of my back and leads me out of the living room. I feel butterflies in my stomach when Aiden's hand touches me.

We walk into the hallway again and make our way into another room, which is the kitchen.

"My favorite place besides my room." Aiden smiles. "Where all the food is."

"Of course." I laugh.

We walk out and Aiden shows me a small game room with a pool table and an air hockey table, a bathroom, and a small dining room. We then walk down a different hallway where Aiden presents me with Alex's bedroom door, another smaller bathroom, and last but not least, his bedroom for the time being.

He opens the door and walks in. His room isn't anything fancy. His bed pushes up against the wall and is composed of a dark blue comforter with white pillows. There's a small desk in the corner of the room where his backpack is thrown. A door off to the side is slightly open and I can see that it's a closet. The walls are a plain white, making the room look bright.

"What do you think?" Aiden asks me

I think about it for a minute. "It's…clean," I tell him.

He chuckles. "For now it is. My bedroom back at my house is trashed."

"Good to know," I say sarcastically but smile at him. I find myself walking towards his bed. I sit down and discover it's soft. *Really* soft.

I lay back and sigh. "Your bed is so soft."

Aiden laughs at me. "It is. I sleep like a baby at night."

I close my eyes for a minute and instantly feel tired. I wish my bed is this comfortable. I'll probably get a better night's sleep.

I feel the bed dip and my eyes spring open. My eyes widen when I come face to face with Aiden. I'm lying on my back on his bed while he hovers over me.

My face instantly heats up.

"Wha-what are you doing?" I stutter.

"Seeing your reaction—" Aiden smirks "—and it's pretty…adorable. You know you blush easily?"

That only makes my face grow redder than it already is. "You know this is really awkward?" I find myself asking him.

He chuckles. "I don't know. I kind of like this."

"Hey, guys, I'm going to order a pizza, do you…" Alex says.

Aiden stands up straight and I immediately sit up. My cheeks are still burning from embarrassment.

Alex raises his eyebrows. "Um, should I come back in a minute?"

"No." Aiden shakes his head. "You were going to order a pizza?" He changes the subject.

"I was wondering if pepperoni was fine with you guys," Alex says, looking back and forth between Aiden and me.

I nod mutely and Aiden agrees. Alex walks out of the room with a smirk on his face. I close my eyes and exhale.

"That was awkward," Aiden says.

"No," I start. "That was embarrassing." I stand up and walk around him. "I think we should go back into the living room—"

I stop when Aiden grabs my wrist. I turn to look at him and he pushes me up against the wall. My eyes widen in surprise. He smirks as his face draws closer to mine.

"Do you like me, Riley?" he asks as he smirks.

"Of course, I like you, Aiden—"

"More than a friend?" He tilts his head.

My brain is frying as I try to come up with an answer. I can't tell him that I develop a silly crush on him. He probably doesn't see me in that way, so why tell him? "No." I keep my voice steady.

He raises his eyebrows. He opens his mouth to say something but closes it immediately. He pushes himself away from me and reaches into his pocket and fishes out his phone. He frowns at the screen but holds it to his ear.

"Hello?" he answers as he turns away from me.

I take this opportunity to slip out of the room. I make my way around and find myself in the kitchen where Alex is pouring a glass of milk. He looks up and smiles when he sees me.

"Hey, Riley," he says casually.

"Hi." I give him a small wave.

He closes the gallon of milk and puts it back in the fridge. "Where's Aiden?"

"He's on the phone," I answer.

Alex takes a drink from his cup. "Oh shit, I didn't even ask if you wanted anything to drink."

I chuckle. "I'm fine. No worries."

"Sorry I interrupted your little moment earlier. Aiden will probably kick my ass later on for it." Alex grins.

Great. He probably thinks Aiden and I are a thing. "It wasn't a *moment*," I tell him. "Aiden was just being weird."

Alex smirks. "Sure, he was."

I'm about to respond when Aiden walks in and grabs the car keys from the counter. Alex raises his eyebrow. "Going somewhere?"

Aiden ignores Alex and looks at me. "Sorry to cut your visit short, but we have to go."

"Okay..." I say.

"It was nice seeing you, Riley." Alex offers me a smile.

Aiden grabs my wrist and pulls me out of the kitchen before I can tell Alex goodbye. We walk out of the house and get into the car. Aiden quickly drives away.

"Why did we have to leave?" I ask him. He looks tense. I wonder who he spoke to on the phone.

"My dad is a fucking asshole." He grits his teeth. "He packed up all the stuff from my room at our old house and put it into a new room at Anna's place."

My eyes widen. I remember Kelly mentioning something about Robert and Aiden moving into Anna's house once the wedding was over with, but I completely forgot about that until now.

"What are you going to do?" I question.

"I'm going to get my fucking stuff and I'm moving in with Alex. I don't care what anyone tells me." He grips the steering wheel tightly. "I'm taking you home first though. I don't want to drag you into that bullshit."

I stay quiet throughout the car ride to my house. Aiden looks pretty scary when he's mad, so I decide to leave him alone.

Soon enough, he pulls into my driveway. I slowly open my door.

"Riley," Aiden says suddenly. I look at him. He scratches the back of his neck. "Do you wanna walk to school together tomorrow?"

Well, I definitely didn't expect him to ask that. I wonder where that came from. "Are you going to walk over here from Alex's house?" If he wants to do that, he can. But it'll be a pretty far walk.

He shakes his head. "I'll probably have Alex drop me off. Is that fine?"

I give him a small smile. "That's fine."

Once I'm inside the house, I'm ready to just lay down from the long day I had. But my mom calls me to the living room.

"Yes?" I ask as I sit down next to her.

She grabs the remote and turns the volume down on the TV. "I got the mail today."

"Okay…"

"And there was something for you. I didn't open it though," she says, sighing. I raise my eyebrow. "It's in the kitchen on the counter." She's acting kind of strange over whatever it is I have in the mail. I stand up and walk towards the kitchen.

I'm kind of nervous as I approach the counter. I see a white envelope sitting on the counter. I reach for it and grab it. My name is written on the back, but I don't recognize the handwriting. I open it carefully and pull out the paper that's inside. I unfold it and begin to read.

Riley,

It's been so long since I've seen you. The last time I saw you, you had just turned three. I know now that you are eighteen, and I'm sorry I didn't reach out to you on your birthday. I didn't know how you would react to me reaching out to you.

Please don't hate me, Riley. I know I haven't been the best father. I haven't even spoken to you until now. I couldn't bring myself to call you, so I decided to write this letter.

I'm not living in town anymore, and I assume you knew that already. But I do live an hour away from you. And I would like you to come visit me sometime. I have talked to your mother about this once, but she didn't think you would want to come. I have no way of knowing if you have discussed this with your mother.

If you don't want to visit, I understand. Just know that I would like to know the young lady my daughter has

become, and I do care. I always have. Please just consider it.
Give me a call when you make your decision.

Love,

Dad

I purse my lips as I finish reading the letter. My dad wants me to visit him? My mom walks into the kitchen and looks at me. "What was it?" she asks curiously.

I set the letter down. "It was a letter. From Dad."

Her eyebrows raise and she stares at me intently. "What did he say?"

"He wants me to visit him," I tell her as the information is still processing in my mind. Why is he reaching out to me now? After fifteen years of silence from him, he wants to see me now.

"I knew he would do this," she mutters, mostly to herself. "If you want to visit him, then you can. I'm not going to keep you away from him. He is your father after all. This is your choice, not mine."

I think about this. Do I want to see him? I don't even know what he's like. Does he have a new wife? Does he have another kid?

Instead of standing in the kitchen, I run up to my room so I can have some alone time. I'm not sure if I want to see him. I mean, I don't even remember him that much.

But will it hurt to see the dad I haven't seen in fifteen years?

Chapter 21

The doorbell rings as soon as I sit down to eat some cereal for breakfast. I look down and eat a spoonful real quick. I'm starving and nothing is going to come between me and my food. I take a few more bites then stand up from the chair. My bare feet slide across the carpet as I make my way to the door.

Once I open it, Aiden smirks. "Well, it took you long enough."

I give him a small smile. "I was eating." I open the door wider for him and let him inside the house. My mom left for work already, so it's just us, making me a little uneasy.

We walk into the kitchen and I sit down at the kitchen table where my cereal sits. "I would offer you some cereal, but I got the last bit of it," I tell him.

"I already ate anyways." He shrugs. He glances around the kitchen. "Nice house."

"Thanks," I mutter. I didn't really sleep well last night, so I feel grumpy. I kept thinking about the letter from my dad and was trying to decide if I want to meet up with him or not. I've never actually thought about this since I never really expected to hear from him after all this time. I want to think this through.

Aiden sits across from me at the kitchen table. "What are you thinking about?" he asks, slightly tilting his head to the side.

I take in his appearance. He looks different, I guess. His hair is the same, but his outfit is somewhat off. He's wearing a dark red plaid shirt with the sleeves rolled up to his elbows. He leaves it unbuttoned and wears a plain white t-shirt underneath. Along with that, he wears regular jeans and some old Converse. I notice he doesn't have his black leather jacket with him.

"Riley?" I hear him ask. I blink and see him staring at me. He wears an amused expression on his face. "Damn, if I didn't know any better, I would say you were checking me out."

The blood rushes to my cheeks. "I was not," I mumble. In a way, I guess, I was checking him out. But I will never admit that out loud.

He chuckles. "It's okay. I know I'm gorgeous."

"You tell yourself that," I say, continuing to eat my cereal.

"A lot of girls find me attractive, Riley. You're not the only one who thinks so." He grins.

I roll my eyes. "You're being exceptionally conceited today. I don't know if I want to walk with you to school today." I finish my cereal and stand up. I rinse the bowl and set it in the sink.

"Of course, you do," he says to me. "You could get kidnapped remember?"

I face him. "I could fight them off. I'm sure I would be fine." What a lie.

He smirks. "Oh yeah. I'm sure you would," he says sarcastically.

"Anyways," I say, changing the subject. "I'm going to go brush my teeth and get some shoes, then we can go."

Aiden is already walking towards the living room when I finish speaking. He grabs the remote and turns the TV on. I make my way up to my room and finish getting ready.

Today, my outfit consists of a Fleetwood Mac t-shirt with some jeans and my black Converse.

When I walk back downstairs with my bag on my shoulder, I find that Aiden is no longer watching TV in the living room. I slowly walk around and finally into the kitchen.

I find him leaning against the counter. He holds a paper in his hands and stares at it intently. I realize the paper he's reading is the letter from my dad.

I walk up to him and snatch the letter from his hands. "What do you think you're doing?" I demand from him.

He sighs and crosses his arms. But he doesn't say anything.

"Let's go," I say as I turn around. I fold the letter and stuff it into my backpack.

Once I lock the door, we start walking in the direction of the school. We walk in silence until Aiden decides to speak.

"So what are you going to do?" he asks.

I look at him. "What?"

"Are you going to visit your dad?" he asks instead.

"I don't know." I kick a rock on the sidewalk. "I don't know what to do." I look back at him and he has an unreadable expression. He stares at me, and I see something flash in his eyes. But it's gone before I can think any further about it.

Aiden clears his throat. "I think you should see him."

I shrug. "I think I should see him too. But then I think of why he wants to see me now after all these years. It just…it doesn't make sense."

My mind is trying to process everything still. Like I said, I can't just decide right now what I want to do.

"That's true." He nods. "I don't think it'd kill you to see him though. At least he wants to see you."

I look at him and narrow my eyes. "Why do you want me to see him so badly?"

"You might not get another chance like this," he says to me. "Don't you want to know what your dad is like?"

I do want to know what he's like. "Okay."

"Okay?" He raises his eyebrow.

"Okay, I'll tell him I want to see him," I say, hesitantly. I'm going to do this. I want to see him.

***

I pace in the hall by myself, holding my phone in my hand. It's lunch time, so there's hardly anyone in the hall. My mom had given me my dad's phone number and his work number so I can call him, but I'm extremely nervous. I take a deep breath and look down at the screen.

Just do it already.

I press the call button and hold the phone to my ear, waiting for him to answer. Maybe I should have called his cell number. He could be busy. I pace some more until the ringing stops.

"Lance Summers speaking." I hear him answer. I almost forget that I have his last name.

"Um, Dad?" I squeeze my eyes shut, waiting for him to respond.

After a few seconds, he replies, "Riley? Is it really you?"

"Yeah, uh, it is," I say awkwardly. I don't do well on the phone. I lean against the lockers behind me.

"I can't believe I'm speaking to you right now," he says. "I guess I'm still picturing you as a little girl. I'm assuming you're calling about my letter?"

"Yes, I am," I say to him. "And I would love to go and visit you sometime."

I hear him sigh. "That's great," he says happily. "I was afraid you would say no. I'm so glad you want to come down and visit," he tells me. "I'll call your mother later and sort all of the details out."

"Okay." I nod.

"I'll talk to you soon, Riley."

"Okay. Bye." We hang up and I exhale. Well, that went pretty good. It's settling in now that I'm actually going to see him.

"Boo," someone whispers behind me and pinches at my sides.

I whirl around, expecting to see Aiden. But I'm caught off guard when I see that it's Ryan. "You scared me." I place my hand over my heart. What is it with people scaring me?

He chuckles. "Sorry."

"So what's up?" I ask him casually. I haven't talked to Ryan in a few days.

He shrugs. "Not much. The usual."

I'm not sure what *the usual* is, but I go on with the conversation. "How's everything at home?"

"Good." We start walking down the hallway together. "Robert has been good to us. As for Aiden, he went to the house yesterday and argued with Robert. Aiden had taken a few boxes of his and left. Apparently, he won't be staying with us."

Because he's staying at Alex's. "I know," I say.

"I heard you spent the day with him yesterday." He nudges my arm.

I roll my eyes. "Maybe because that's what friends do? You know, hang out?"

He laughs. "So you finally admit that you two are friends?"

I nod. "Well, it seems like we're friends."

We stay quiet for a few seconds. "So, Nicole tried getting back together with me this morning," Ryan speaks.

I raise my eyebrows. "What did you do?"

"I told her it wasn't going to happen." He smirks. "I'm done with her. And if she talks shit to you again, let me know so I can deal with it."

I frown. "But shouldn't I fight my own battles? No offense, but I don't want a bodyguard."

He raises his eyebrow then smiles. He reaches out and pinches my cheek. "Awe, is Riley Bear finally growing up?"

I frown. *Riley Bear?* "That is the most awful pet name I have ever heard." I shiver.

He laughs at my reaction. "I don't care. It's going to stick."

This is just great. I have an awful pet name now. "I refuse to respond to *Riley Bear*," I tell him. I then start to walk away from him.

But he catches up with me and walks along beside me. He stays quiet for a moment, and that makes me a bit nervous. Ryan isn't one to stay quiet for too long.

"Do you like Aiden?" he blurts out.

I look at him with wide eyes. I definitely wasn't expecting that. "Why are you asking me that?" I question.

"Because I want to know." He presses on. "I won't tell him if you do. I'm just curious."

I'm *not* going to tell him about my silly crush. This reminds me of when Aiden had me pushed up against the wall in his room in Alex's house and I find myself blushing slightly at the memory. I lied to Aiden when he asked me if I liked him, so I'm going to lie to Ryan also. "I don't like him," I tell him.

He lifts his eyebrow. "Really?"

"Really."

He smiles and wears an amused face. "Interesting." Before I can ask him what is interesting, he starts to walk away. "I'll talk to you later, Riley."

I just watch him as he walks down the hallway. He greets many people as he walks the hall, reminding me that Ryan is *Mr. Popular*. He saunters down the hall with such confidence. Sometimes I wish I can hold my head high as I walk through the halls, but I keep my head low and hide my face with my hair.

The more I think about it, the more it seems impossible for me to have that kind of confidence.

***

"You did not," I say to Aiden as we walk along the sidewalk. He's telling me about his experience in his Biology class.

"I did." He nods happily. "Though I did drop the frog's internal organs on her purposely, I made it look like an accident so I wouldn't get into too much trouble."

I shake my head and chuckle. "Such a rebel you are."

He shrugs. "I can't help it. I was born to be a badass." He grins from ear to ear.

Once again, I find myself glancing down at his attire. "I meant to ask you this morning," I start. "But I forgot. So I'm going to ask now. Why do you look so…normal today?"

Glancing down at his clothes, he shrugs. His eyes meet mine, and he speaks. "Well, first of all, my leather jacket got dirty, so it needs to be cleaned. I've been too lazy to wash it though, so it's currently sitting on my floor in my room," he says. "And I don't know. I guess I just wanted to switch things up today. I think this is the only red shirt I own. Everything else is black, white, or gray."

I can't say that my wardrobe is colorful either. My band t-shirts are black, white, or dark blue. I think I have a purple tank top somewhere in my closet.

We approach my house, and I turn to him. "This is my stop. Where are you going?" I ask him.

"I'll give Alex a call so he can get his lazy ass up and come pick me up." He smiles.

I glance at my house then back at Aiden. I chew on my lip. "Um, you can come inside if you want. You know, so you don't have to wait out here," I suggest to him.

He raises his eyebrows. "Really?"

"Yeah," I say, feeling surer about it.

"Okay." He grins.

We both walk up to my house and I unlock the front door. My mom is still at work and probably won't be home until after five o'clock.

"I control the remote!" Aiden suddenly yells and takes off to the living room.

Wait—*what?*

"Oh no, you don't!" I say, running after him. He's not going to keep the remote from me.

Aiden dives for the couch and grabs the remote. I tackle him and reaches for the remote. He stretches his arm so I can't reach it at all. Damn, I hate having short arms.

Aiden chuckles at me. "Ha, you can't reach," he teases.

I jump on top of him and lean over. I realize that I'm now straddling him and my cheeks are flushed. But Aiden ends up falling onto the floor, taking me down with him. I land on the floor next to him.

We both start to laugh until Aiden holds up the remote. "I'm in control."

I try to snatch it away from him, but he yanks it away. I try again, and I grasp hard onto it. We are both pulling at it like two five-year-olds fighting over a toy.

I eventually pull it away from him, and I smile. "Victory is mine!"

Aiden sighs but crawls on top of me. My heartbeat speeds up and my cheeks burn. Aiden hovers over me and I have no idea what he's doing.

"Riley..." he whispers softly. He leans down and nuzzles his face into my neck. I'm frozen on the ground. He gently kisses the soft skin on my neck, and my eyes close involuntarily. His lips find their way up to my earlobe, which he nibbles on delicately as his hand rests on my waist. "You are so..." he says, making me open my eyes. He grins darkly. "Gullible." He pecks my cheek while his hand clutches the remote, which is still in my hand, and pulls it away from me.

Aiden pushes himself off me and I curse myself for falling for that. How many times has he done that to me? And I don't learn.

I sit down on the opposite end of the couch and cross my arms angrily as Aiden looks for something to watch on TV. I sit there silently and occasionally play with my phone.

He glances at me after a while and smirks. "C'mon, Riley. You can't be *that* mad at me."

I huff. "Manipulative asshole," I mumble under my breath.

"I'm sorry, what was that?" he asks, holding his hand to his ear.

I look at him and scowl. "I said you're a *manipulative asshole.*"

He chuckles and shakes his head. "I thought that's what you said." Suddenly, he lunges at me and I cover my face with my hands. I know he's above me and I refuse to pull my hands away from my face.

"Riley...look at me," I hear him say.

"No. You're going to kill me," I say into my hands.

I hear him laugh. "I'm not going to kill you. I promise."

I slowly remove my hands and come face to face with Aiden. He offers me a lopsided smile. "Don't think."

"Wha—"

I'm cut off by Aiden's lips meeting mine.

Chapter 22

I'm shocked, to say the least.

But I somehow manage to move my lips in sync with Aiden's. One of his hands comes up and cups my cheek softly. The kiss doesn't last too long, but it feels like it lasted an eternity.

Aiden eventually pulls away and just smiles at me. He goes back to his spot at the end of the couch and continues to watch TV with the remote in his hands. I stare at him.

How can he act so calm and collected after he just stole my first kiss?

My heart is leaping around in my chest, and I feel like my stomach is going to burst with butterflies coming out. Weird visual, but it literally feels like it. My breathing is ragged, and my face is red from blushing.

Aiden continues to stare at the TV and doesn't acknowledge me at all. I clear my throat, hoping to catch his attention, but that doesn't work.

I frown and stand up. I end up running up the stairs to my room and shutting the door behind me. I lock it then go into my bathroom. I pace inside and keep running my hands through my hair.

My first kiss. I just had my first kiss with the guy I'm crushing on and he's ignoring me.

There's a feeling of hurt in my chest and I keep taking deep breaths. Is it normal to act like this after your first kiss? I always thought I'd feel bubbly and giggly afterward, but this is not the case.

Why am I acting so ridiculous? I'm overthinking this whole thing. Aiden told me right before, "Don't think." What was that even supposed to mean? Don't think during the kiss? After the kiss? Both?

I rub my temples and feel a headache coming on.

After taking some Tylenol for my headache, I come out of the bathroom and unlock my bedroom door. I slowly walk down the stairs and hesitantly make my way into the living room, ready to face Aiden.

But when I enter, he's gone.

The TV is shut off and the remote is on the coffee table in front of the couch. Anger rises through me and I ball my hands into fists. He kisses me then takes off?

When did my life turn into a freaking soap opera?

Aiden

I'm sitting in the living room of Alex's house with my feet propped up on the small table in front of me. Alex and two of our buddies are all in the kitchen, mixing drinks. They try getting me to join in, but I ignore them and come in here to watch TV.

"Aiden!" Alex shouts. "C'mon, man! Just have one drink!"

I sigh in frustration and stride into the kitchen. They all have shot glasses in their hands. Alex shoves one into my hand. "What the hell is this?" I ask, looking in the glass. I take a whiff of it and scrunch my nose. Whatever it is, it sure is strong.

"Just drink it!" Jake exclaims.

Jake is the ideal party dude. If you want a *real* party, you call this guy. He stands a few inches taller than me and has blonde hair. I'm always slightly intimidated by him because he's bigger than me, but I will never admit that out loud.

"On the count of three," our other friend Isaiah says. "One...two...three!"

All three of them down their shots. I give in and lift the glass. The liquid slides down my throat and I cough a little. That's really strong.

Alex grins at me. "Was it bad?"

It actually wasn't. I shake my head. "No."

"Another round then!" Jake grins.

***

I don't remember how many shots I took. But I do remember drinking straight from bottles of unknown liquor.

Jake and Isaiah were supposed to go back home, but they both end up passing out on the couches.

I lean against the counter in the kitchen, holding myself up. The alcohol is running through me, giving me a nice buzz. I know I shouldn't have drunk that much because I have school in the morning.

But then I think, *Who gives a fuck about school?*

Alex comes in and smiles at me. He's stumbling around also. "Aiden!" he exclaims. "You should go to bed, little boy. You have school." He messes up my hair.

"Fuck off," I growl at him. "I'm not going to school."

He holds his hands up and laughs. "Whoa, calm down," he tells me. "What has you grouchy as fuck?"

I groan and hold my head in my hands. "Riley fucking Summers, that's what." I snap at him. I turn around and stagger my way into my room. I slam my door and pace around for a few minutes.

Why did I have to fucking kiss her? Why couldn't I have given her a kiss on the cheek or something?

She probably hates me because I ran out on her. That was probably her first kiss and I had to go and fuck everything up. That was a douchebag move of me.

After I left Riley's place, I went somewhere I really regret going to. I feel fucking weird and I'm not myself.

I yank my shirt off and change into some pajama pants. I then throw myself onto the bed and quickly fall asleep.

Riley

My mom had told me that I'm going to stay with my dad this weekend. I have to leave Friday morning and come back Sunday afternoon. This means I will miss a school day. But that doesn't bother me too much. I'm actually kind of excited to see him.

I stare out the window of Ryan's car and watch everything go by in a blur. Ryan had called me this morning and offered me a ride to school, which I gratefully accepted. I'm not exactly in the mood for walking today.

"Is there something wrong?" Ryan suddenly asks. I glance over at him and he's watching the road.

"No." I lie. "Why?"

He shrugs. "You don't seem like yourself today."

"Just tired." That part is true. I didn't sleep well the night before and now I feel like crap.

We pull into the school parking lot and I immediately see Nicole getting out of her car with some of her friends. She hasn't bothered me for the past couple of days, but I'm still uneasy about her. I feel like she can pop up anywhere and claw my eyes out with her perfectly manicured nails.

Ryan parks the car and we both get out. A few people stare at us as we walk towards the building. Everyone knows Ryan but no one cares about me. They're probably wondering why I'm walking into the building with him.

I catch Nicole's gaze right before we walk into the doors. She gives me a sickly-sweet smile, which I don't return. I just look away from her and duck my head.

"Will I see you at lunch?" Ryan asks. I catch him looking in Nicole's direction, but his attention turns back to me.

"I'll be in the library again," I tell him.

He grins. "I'll see you there then." He walks away from me and down the hall.

I sigh and walk in the direction of my locker. I quickly find it and open it. As I put a book in place, I feel a presence next to me. I look to the side and find Nicole standing there. I expected her blonde friend Stacey to be right behind her, but it's just her.

"Riley," she speaks.

"Nicole." I acknowledge her.

She crosses her arms. "What makes you think that you can just take Ryan away from me like that?" she asks.

I frown. "What are you talking about?"

"He broke up with me because of *you*." She takes a step towards me. "Well, guess what? You can have him."

Nicole has gone off the deep end. "What?" I ask, not understanding.

"I have my eyes on someone else now." She flashes me a smile. "I don't know why I didn't go after him in the first place."

"Who?" I inquire.

She smirks. "Aiden Callaway."

She can't be serious. She *can't* like Aiden. But why is she suddenly interested in him? As far as I know, she never really liked him. "Oh really?" I ask, raising my eyebrow.

Nicole grins and takes another step towards me. She's about an inch and a half taller than me so I have to look up slightly. "I'm going to ruin your relationship just like you ruined mine." She sneers.

"My relationship?" I scoff. She really is obviously delusional.

"You and Aiden have been getting pretty close, haven't you?" she asks. "Well, he's going to be mine and there's nothing you can do about it. I've practically got him wrapped around my finger already."

"I'm sure you do," I say, rolling my eyes. I'm not in the mood for dealing with her today. I'm pissed off and she's making it worse.

She pulls out her iPhone and unlocks it. She goes to her messages and shows me the screen. The name on top says *Aiden* with a kissing face next to it. My eyes roam down the screen and read a few of the messages shown.

Aiden: Can't wait to see you tonight

Nicole: Are you on your way yet?

Aiden: No. Still at Riley's. Don't worry, I just have to do something real quick then I'm out of here.

Nicole: You better hurry ;)

Aiden: Oh I will

Anger rises in me. "When were you guys texting?" I ask, keeping my voice steady.

"Yesterday afternoon. He was coming over for some *fun*." She smirks.

I slam my locker shut and walk away from her. If I stood there any longer, I probably would've punched her in the face because I'm so angry.

I can't believe Aiden would do that to me. I don't want to believe Nicole, but I have no idea where Aiden went after he left. He probably did go to her house. He probably thought I wasn't enough for him.

My mind is racing with different scenarios. I clench my fists as I walk into my first class.

***

I haven't seen Aiden all day. The only person I talked to was Ryan and that was for lunch. He tried getting me to talk about what happened, but I didn't want to. He doesn't know exactly what was going on and I don't intend to tell him.

I'm now at home, bundled in a blanket on my bed and listening to my iPod with Sassy curled up next to me. I have the volume turned up as high as I want it, and I close my eyes. My emotions swirl around, making me dizzy.

One of my earphones is pulled out of my ears suddenly and my eyes spring open.

My mom stands over me. She raises her eyebrow. "Is there a reason you're drowning out the world?"

I'm not talking to my mom about all this. "No. Just tired. I didn't sleep good last night."

"You and me both," she says. "I'm going to start dinner, so don't fall asleep unless you want to starve."

"Thanks," I say sarcastically.

***

Ryan and I walk through the building doors the next morning and I glance around. Everyone seems to be buzzing about something but I'm not sure what.

"Why is everyone all hyped up?" I ask Ryan.

He shrugs. "Who knows? But I really don't care. Let everyone gossip."

"I'm going to my locker," I tell him. We go our separate ways and I make my way down the hall. I find my locker and open it.

Someone leans against the locker next to mine and I stiffen when I see who it is in my peripheral vision.

"Good morning, Summers," Aiden greets.

I ignore him. I don't want to get sucked into all this drama.

"Riley…"

"What do you want?" I snap at him. It comes out harsher than I want, but I can't care less now.

He looks surprised. "What's got you in a grumpy mood this morning?"

I purse my lips and turn away from him. How can he act like he didn't steal my first kiss then run out to Nicole? That only makes me angrier.

"Okay, don't tell me then," he mutters. "Anyways, I was thinking we could go somewhere for lunch today. I have Alex's car." He gives me a small smile.

"Aiden! There you are!" Nicole's annoying high-pitched voice exclaims before I can tell Aiden no. Nicole basically throws herself at him. Her eyes flicker to me before they go back to him.

"Nicole, what are doing?" he asks her. But he doesn't try to push her off.

She flashes him a fake smile. "I was looking all over for you."

Aiden's eyes flash to me and I close my locker. "To answer your question, I'm saying no thanks. I'm having lunch with Ryan," I tell him.

Nicole smirks. "Well, he certainly downgraded. I, however, upgraded," she says as she looks up at Aiden.

I don't respond to that. I just walk away from them.

*****

Friday eventually comes and I can't be any happier. Not only am I missing school, but I get to see my dad. My mom will drive me there and pick me up on Sunday.

I had finished packing last night. My mom was being delusional and only let me pack two of my band t-shirts. The others she had bought for me and made me pack.

I don't understand why she was acting like that. I'm eighteen and I can wear whatever the hell I want to. But I didn't want to make her too upset, so I packed the shirts anyway.

Ryan and I spent more time together these past couple of days. I didn't see Nicole or Aiden at all, so that made school a little easier. I also went to the movies with Lucas again. I know he wants to be more than friends, but I just don't like him like that way and I hope he gets the hint.

Before I leave the house, Ryan texts me and wishes me a safe trip. I smile and send him a quick thank you.

I get into my mom's car and we're off. While I stare out the window, I feel my phone buzz in my hand. I look down and see that I have a message from Aiden. My heart races when I see his name. I open the message and read it.

Can I talk to you at lunch?

Seriously? I quickly replied, I'm not going to school today

Why? he responds hastily.

I scoff. Why does he care?

—Out of town, that's why

—Oh. Well can you call me around twelve?

I hesitate as I read his message. Do I really want to talk to Aiden? I slowly type my answer.

—I guess

—Awesome. Talk to you later Led Zeppelin Girl

I mentally sigh. How can he act like nothing is wrong? Am I being overdramatic with all of this? *No.* I have every right to be angry with him. He's been toying with me and I'm not going to take it anymore.

And I intend to get some answers from him when I call him later.

Chapter 23

I feel someone shaking my arm and my eyes spring open. I quickly rub them and yawn.

"Riley, wake up," I hear my mother tell me. "We're here."

I glance around and let my eyes adjust to the light. I look out the window and see that we're at an unfamiliar house. My dad's house, to be more specific. I sit up in my seat and sigh. "Okay." I nod. "Are you coming inside with me?"

She gives me a small smile. "I think it would be best if I just drop you off."

I understand. I open my door and open the backseat door to get my bag. Once I have it on my shoulder, my mom rolls down the passenger window. "Do you have everything?" she asks.

"Yup." I nod.

"Okay. Call me if anything happens and I'll be here in a heartbeat." She smiles.

I chuckle. "Sure thing, Mom."

"Have fun. I love you," she says.

"Love you too, Mom," I say, backing away from the car. I turn around and make my way up to the front door. I glance up at the house and notice that it's pretty nice. It's bigger than ours. My nerves kick in.

I hear my mom drive off as I ring the doorbell. I fidget with my shirt as I wait for someone to answer. The door slowly opens and reveals a tall man.

"Riley?" he asks. I recognize his voice from when I talk to him on the phone.

"Hi, Dad," I say awkwardly. It feels weird calling him Dad.

He grins. The first thing I notice about him is how tall he is. He isn't freakishly tall or anything, but he definitely is not average height. His dark brown hair has a few greys here and there. He wears a white pin-striped button up shirt with black dress pants. "I can't believe it's you." He smiles. "Come in." He opens the door wider for me.

I shuffle past him and grip onto my bag. I glimpse around the house before looking back at him.

"You can sit your bag on the couch." He gestures to it. "I'll take you into the kitchen to introduce you."

Introduce me? "Okay." I smile weakly.

We walk into a hallway then we approach another doorway. I take a deep breath when we walk into the kitchen. It's pretty nice in here. There's a big island in the middle with a sink. There are stainless steel appliances all around us.

"Honey, Riley is here," I heard my dad say.

Honey?

A lady with light brown hair comes into the kitchen. She looks about a year or two younger than my dad. She has big brown eyes and her makeup looks natural. She's really pretty, to say the least. She gives me a small smile then eyes me up and down as if she's scanning me. "Welcome to our home, Riley. I'm Alyssa."

I don't like the way she's looking at me. It almost looks like she doesn't approve of me or something. "Hello." I offer her a small smile.

"Would you like something to eat?" she asks me.

"No thank you. I'm still full from breakfast." I feel like if I eat anything right now, I'd probably throw it back up.

My dad looks at me. "Have a seat, Riley," he says, pointing to the stools by the island.

I slowly walk over and sit down. I play with my hands nervously.

"I can't believe you're eighteen already." He shakes his head. "It doesn't seem that long since I've seen you."

Well, it has been, I want to say. But I bite my tongue.

He snaps his fingers. "I'll be right back. I have something for you," he says, walking out of the room.

I sit there uncomfortably. Alyssa glances at me and clears her throat. "So, you're staying until Sunday, correct?" she asks me. I nod. She doesn't say anything after that though.

Soon enough, my dad comes back in with a gift bag. Tissue paper spills over the top as he sets it in front of me. "I know I didn't have to, but Alyssa insisted I get you something."

Alyssa gives me a small smile.

I pull the tissue paper out of the bag and peek inside. I reach inside the bag and fish out my gift. The first thing I grab is a book, which excites me. I look at the cover and read the title. *Great Expectations* by Charles Dickens. I look at my dad.

"I hope you like to read. If not, then I hope the other present makes up for it," he tells me.

I smile. "I love to read," I assure him. Once again, I reach inside and pull out a rectangular box. I take the top off and discover a silver heart-shaped locket. Even though I'm not a big fan of jewelry, the piece is very nice. "Thank you. It's beautiful," I tell them.

"I told you she'd like both." Alyssa smacks my dad's arm. She looks at me. "A man should always trust a woman's instincts."

I put the gifts back in the bag and set it down next to me. Alyssa takes a seat next across from me while my dad sits next to her.

"So tell us about yourself, Riley," Alyssa tells me. "I'd love to hear about my stepdaughter." She seems more interested in me. Though I mentally cringe when she calls me her stepdaughter. I don't think I want to hear those words.

"I want to assume you're a good student?" Dad asks.

I nod. "I've been getting straight As all through high school. I think I got a B once during my sophomore year, but that teacher never gave out As," I say, easing up a bit. I still remember that teacher. I never smiled at her when she saw me in the hallways.

"That's good." My dad smiles.

"What about friends?" Alyssa asks. "Do you have a lot of them?"

That sounds kind of offensive. I feel like I'm getting interviewed for something. "A few…"

"What about a boyfriend?" Alyssa smiles. "A pretty girl like you must have a boyfriend."

I scoff. Boy is she wrong on so many levels with that statement. "I don't have a boyfriend," I tell her. "I have guy friends, but no boyfriend."

"What are your friend's names?" my dad asks.

"Um, there's Kelly, Ryan, Lucas…" I mentally sigh. "And, uh, Aiden." I just add him to the list so it will sound like I have more friends than I actually have.

Alyssa stands up from her seat. "I'm getting quite hungry. I think I'll start lunch," she tells us. "We can talk some more later."

"I'll start lunch, honey. Why don't you show Riley her room for the weekend?" my dad suggests then looks at me. "Once you're settled in, we can all regroup at the kitchen table."

Alyssa and I both nod. I stand up from my seat and grab my gift bag. I then follow her out of the kitchen and seize my bag from the couch. Alyssa takes me through a different hallway and points out the bathrooms and bedrooms. I notice a room we pass by has small play toys and a little bed.

Do they have a kid?

Alyssa opens the door next to the room. She walks in and I follow her. She looks at me. "This will be your room this weekend. Make yourself comfortable."

"Okay. Thank you," I say to her.

I throw my bag on the bed as she walks out. I sigh and sit on my bed. I glance around the room and notice how plain it looks. The walls are white; the bed comforter is a beige color, and the pillows are white too. In front of the bed is a medium-sized dresser with three drawers to it. There is also a small table next to the bed with a lamp and a clock. I see that it's going to be twelve.

My stomach fills with butterflies once I remember Aiden wants me to call him at twelve.

I busy myself with settling in. Even though I only fill up one drawer in the dresser with my clothes, I keep finding something to do. It's ten minutes past twelve and I keep wanting to distract myself.

But my heart flips when I feel my phone buzzing in my back pocket. I slowly slide it out and see Aiden's name on the screen.

I sigh and answer, "Hello?"

"I knew you weren't going to call me," he automatically says.

I sit down on the bed. "I didn't notice the time. Plus, I was busy," I tell him, slightly lying.

"Busy visiting with your dad?" he asks.

I frown. "I don't remember telling you that information."

"It might've slipped out of Ryan."

I roll my eyes. "It slipped? Or you forced it out of him?"

"Slipped, forced, same difference," he says. "Why didn't you tell me you were visiting him this weekend?"

I scoff. "Why would I tell you when you've been ignoring me since Monday afternoon?" I snap at him. No more small talk. I want answers now.

"I tried talking to you on Tuesday." He defends himself. "You were the one ignoring me."

"I had a good reason to ignore you," I retort. He's not going to twist this around and make me look like the bad guy.

"And that reason is?" he asks.

I ball my fist, feeling angry again. "You kissed me. Then you just left. You can't just kiss someone then leave automatically."

"I had somewhere to be. Besides, you went upstairs after the kiss anyway," he tells me.

I'm fuming. "Oh yeah. Did you have fun screwing around with Nicole after you left my house?" I ask, remembering the messages Nicole showed me between them both.

He stays quiet for a minute. "Riley that was planned before I even thought about kissing you. Hell, I didn't expect you to invite me into your house, let alone let me kiss you. I thought I could just go over to her house after I walked you back home…"

"You make me sick," I say angrily. "Do you even care that Nicole is basically bullying me? I spilled my heart out to you, confessing that her words do get to me sometimes and you helped me through it. Now you're off messing around with Nicole and toying with me. Do you care at all?" I ramble. I'm now pacing in my room.

He lets out a frustrated sigh. "I do care, Riley." He sounds helpless. "I don't—I just—it's hard to explain."

"What's hard to explain?" I demand.

"That's the thing. I don't know what is hard to explain."

I sigh. "I'm done with this. You're making no sense and I'm not going to waste my time."

"Riley…You can't do this. You're the only person I can talk to about everything without being judged."

"Go talk to Nicole." I snap at him.

There's a knock at the door before it slowly opens. Alyssa comes in with a small smile on her face. "Lunch is ready."

"I'll be down in a minute," I say to her.

She frowns a bit. "Is everything okay?"

I nod. "Everything is fine. I just need to tell them something really quick." I gesture to my phone.

She nods and slowly walks out of the room.

"Who was that?" Aiden asks, sounding normal.

"None of your damn business," I tell him. "Stop acting so normal. It's pissing me off even more."

"Why don't you just hang up on me if you're so mad?" He taunts. "If I didn't know any better, I would say that you're using this opportunity to just talk to me."

I purse my lips. "Just leave me alone, Aiden."

"Sorry to burst your bubble, Summers, but I'm going to keep calling and texting you until you fully forgive me."

Are you kidding me right now?

I sigh in frustration. "I need to go."

"Then go." I can practically see him smirking.

"I will," I say then angrily hang up. I wish I have a flip phone at this moment because just tapping the screen isn't working for me.

I put my phone back in my pocket and I make my way back to the kitchen. I find it with ease and walk in.

Alyssa and my dad are already sitting at the kitchen table and I instantly feel guilty because they're waiting for me. I sit down quickly and give them both a small smile. "Sorry for making you wait," I say sheepishly.

"It's fine, dear." Alyssa smiles. She hands me a plate with a sandwich and some chips. I give her a quick thank you, and soon, we're all sitting together at the kitchen table.

"Um, so what do you guys do for a living?" I ask, making conversation. I feel my phone buzz in my back pocket. I grab it and put it in my front pocket.

My dad clears his throat. "A friend of mine and me own a law firm in town." I raise my eyebrows. I didn't know he's a lawyer. "I took the day off today so we could have some time together," he tells me.

"I stay here," Alyssa says, gesturing around us. "I'm in charge of keeping this place in order."

I nod, understanding.

Alyssa gives my dad a look and it looks like they're having a conversation in their heads. My dad finally clears his throat and looks at me. "Uh, Riley, there is another person we want you to meet."

"Okay," I say slowly. "Who?"

My dad seems to have trouble speaking at the moment, so Alyssa speaks instead. "Our little girl, Amanda."

I suspected that they have a kid, but hearing them say it feels weird. What I don't understand is why my dad left my mom and me to go get himself another wife and have another little girl. "Oh." I look down at my plate. My phone buzzes twice in my pocket but I ignore it. "How old is she?" I ask.

"Seven," Alyssa responds.

My phone vibrates like crazy in my pocket, so I finally take it out. I notice that my mom is calling me. "Um, I'll be right back. It's my mom," I say as I hop off the chair.

I walk to the doorway of the kitchen and answer, "Hello?"

"How's everything going down there?" she asks. I guarantee she's going to call me at least twice a day.

"Fine. I already got settled in," I tell her.

"How is...everyone?"

I bite my lip. "Good. Did you know about..." I remember that I'm still near my dad and Alyssa.

"Alyssa? And Amanda? Yes, I did," she says honestly.

"I wish you would've told me before I came," I say, feeling a bit hurt.

"I didn't want you to decide that you didn't want to go," she says. "I know it might be a little hard to take in, but promise me you'll try to have fun over there."

I sigh. "I promise."

"Okay. I'll talk to you later, Riley."

"Bye, Mom." I hang up with her and look at the messages I have. I have three of them from Aiden.

Led Zeppelin Girl

I'm going to keep texting you

*Please forgive me Summers. Believe it or not, I can't
handle knowing you're mad at me :(*

I roll my eyes. I'm not going to let him off the hook
that easy. I walk back into the kitchen and sit back down at
the table and set my phone next to my plate.

"So have you done anything exciting lately?" Alyssa
asks me.

I think about it. I've spray painted on the back of the
library; I've had a paint-filled-condom war..."I was in a
wedding recently."

"Oh really? Whose?" she asks.

"A friend of my mom's," I say then take a bite of my
sandwich.

Alyssa's eyes sparkle. "I love weddings. They
always fascinate me." She grins.

"They last too long." My dad frowns. "Sure, it's a
happy day, but they seem to drag on."

I chuckle. He isn't a big fan of weddings either.

Alyssa smacks his arm. "Oh hush. You don't know
what you're talking about."

Soon enough, we all finish and I help Alyssa clean
the kitchen. Around two thirty, Alyssa rushes my dad out the
door to go pick up Amanda from school.

I'm kind of nervous to meet her. I didn't even know
she exists until now.

I'm sitting in the kitchen with Alyssa when the front
door opens and I hear a small girl talking.

"What's my surprise, Daddy? Is it a dog?" I hear her
ask.

I am not a dog.

"No, honey. Why don't you go look in the kitchen?" I hear my dad tell her.

It kind of hurts to hear him say that. Why wasn't he there for me? I never got the chance to say Daddy.

A small girl walks through the doorway. She has big brown eyes, like Alyssa's. Her hair is dark brown and curled slightly at the ends. Her eyes land on me and she doesn't say anything.

"Who are you?" she asks me.

I give her a small smile. "I'm Riley."

"She's your half-sister, Amanda honey," my dad tells her.

She squints her eyes at me like she's analyzing me or something. It's similar to what Alyssa did earlier. She then looks up at my dad. "You said I was your princess." She crosses her arms.

Something tells me she doesn't like me.

He kneels down to her level. "Well, you can both be my princesses," he says, smiling. "Haven't you always wanted a big sister?"

Amanda looked back at me. "No."

"Amanda," Alyssa warns. "Behave yourself now. Riley is staying at our house this weekend and we want her to feel welcome."

"What's a half-sister?" Amanda asks my dad.

"That means Riley has a different mommy," Alyssa explains.

She raises her eyebrow. "But the same dad?"

They both nod.

"Why couldn't you get me a pretty big sister?" Amanda puts her hands on her hips.

Okay. That's rude. I already don't like this little girl.

"Amanda." My dad snaps.

I need to speak up or something. I'm not going to let some seven-year-old have the upper hand. "Well, I didn't want a younger sister anyway."

Amanda frowns and walks up to me. "My daddy is my daddy. I'm his princess and he loves me more."

I cross my arms. "You're probably right about that. That must be the reason why he hasn't talked to me in fifteen years." I shock myself with the words that just came out of my mouth. I notice my dad's eyes widen slightly and Alyssa looks shocked as well. "I'll be in my room," I say quickly as I grab my phone off the table. I walk past them and make my way to the hallway. I go into my room and shut the door.

I don't hear any footsteps behind the door, so they're probably giving me my space right now. I can't believe I can defend myself against a seven-year-old and not Nicole. Why can I never stick up for myself when Nicole was around?

I run my fingers through my hair and sigh in frustration. It's not fair. It's not fair that Amanda gets to have the relationship with my dad that I never got the chance to have. How could my dad leave my mom and me?

As I sit on my bed, I pull out my phone and am tempted to call my mom and tell her I want to go home. But I can't bring myself to do it. I think I want answers from my dad before I leave though. I'm not going to go on with my life without knowing why he left us. My mom told me it was because they didn't love each other anymore, but I find that a little hard to believe.

I debate with myself on whether or not I should call Ryan and talk with him about it. I decide against it. The thought of calling Aiden enters my mind, but that idea quickly leaves.

You're supposed to be mad at him, remember?

I lay back on my bed and sigh. I hold my phone up tightly so it won't fall on my face. I've dropped it on my face before, and it left me with a busted lip. Pathetic, I know. My thumb roams over the call button for Aiden. I close my eyes and tap the screen. I slowly hold it to my ear.

"I knew you couldn't stay mad at me," Aiden answers. I can practically see him grinning.

"You're not completely forgiven," I warn him. "But I just wanted to…I don't know…talk, I guess."

He stays quiet for a minute. "What's up?" he finally responds.

"All of this," I start as I look around my room. "Is a little overwhelming."

"What's your dad like?" he asks curiously.

I blow a piece of hair out of my face before answering. "He seems pretty cool. But he has a wife and a little girl."

"Oh," he says. "Is that what's bugging you?"

"Yes." I close my eyes. "I just don't understand why he would leave us, only to be put back in the position he was in before. It just doesn't make sense."

"Have you talked about it with him?" he asks.

"No." I sigh. "There was a small fallout a while ago and I came into my room."

He chuckles. "What did you do?"

I frown. Why does he assume it was my fault? "I didn't do anything. His daughter started it."

"How old is she?"

"Seven."

Aiden starts to laugh. I glare at the phone. "What are you laughing at?" I demand.

"You're blaming a seven-year-old, Summers? That's a little immature," he tells me.

"You're more immature than me!" I exclaim. "You should have heard what she told me! She said she wanted a pretty sister and that she was my dad's princess and he loved her more."

He sighs. "And what did you tell her?"

"I told her she was probably right."

"Riley…"

I sit up and lean back on the pillows on the bed. "Well, it's the truth."

"First of all, she's seven. She doesn't know what she's saying. And second, you are pretty."

My heart beats a little faster. Then I realize that he can be messing with me again. "You don't have to lie, Aiden. Just stop," I tell him.

"Stop what?" he asks. "You know, you don't take compliments very well."

"Not from you," I say. "I don't trust you as much as I used to."

I hear him sigh in frustration. "What would you say if I told you that you really are beautiful?"

I end the call right there.

Chapter 24

The next morning, I wake up feeling refreshed. The bed in my room is extremely comfortable, and I actually don't want to leave. But a knock on my door interrupts my thoughts on stealing this mattress when I leave.

My door opens slowly and Alyssa walks in. She offers me a smile. "Morning," she says slowly.

I sit up in my bed. "Morning," I say, looking down. I feel guilty for the way I acted yesterday. It was childish, and I regret some of the things I had said.

"We're going out for breakfast in an hour and a half. I thought I'd let you know ahead of time so you can get ready," she tells me.

"Okay. Thanks, Alyssa," I say as I pull the covers off. I slide my legs over the bed and my feet meet the carpeted floor.

Alyssa stands at the door for a moment. "Riley, can I talk to you about something?" she asks cautiously.

"Um, sure," I say awkwardly. She walks towards me and sits next to me on the bed. I smooth out my hair since it probably looks like a disaster right now.

She sighs before she starts talking. "Riley, I know it must be a little difficult seeing your dad right now. I'm not trying to become your best friend or anything, but I want you to know that I'm here if you want to talk."

I nod, understanding. "Thanks." I offer her a small smile then take a deep breath. "I'm going to be honest with you, Alyssa. It hard seeing my dad, especially with you and Amanda."

She purses her lips. "I know, Riley. I talked to him about all of this last night and he told me he doesn't expect you to forgive him for leaving you and your mom when you were younger. But I can tell you that he really wants you to know that he does love you."

I look down at my hands. "I'm sorry for snapping yesterday. It was uncalled for and childish of me. I guess I just got jealous that he's here for Amanda and he wasn't there for me when I was growing up."

"I'm going to tell you right now that I had no idea he left you and your mom when I was first with your dad," she tells me. "I found out about you a few weeks after Amanda was born." I lift my eyebrows. "He told me that he already had a daughter and wife before me. I'm going to be honest also and say that I was not happy. I thought he was going to leave Amanda and me and go back to you and your mom."

"But he didn't," I comment.

She shakes her head. "I wasn't sure what to think when he told me that he wanted to see you after all these years."

"I wasn't sure what to think either." I shrug. "But with the help of a friend, I decided that it wouldn't kill me to visit."

She smiles. "I know it's none of my business and I shouldn't have been eavesdropping, but it sounded like you were on the phone with a boy yesterday."

My cheeks flush. Oh God, she heard my conversation with Aiden yesterday. I sigh. "I was," I admit. "A very frustrating, annoying boy." I shake my head.

She chuckles. "All boys are frustrating and annoying."

"I know that *now*," I tell her.

She smiles and stands up from the bed. "Well, if you ever want to talk some more, just know I'm here."

"Thank you," I say to her. She walks out of my room and shuts my door behind her.

Soon enough, I start to get ready. I start off by taking a shower. My room has its own bathroom, which I'm thankful for. I strip out of my pajamas and take a nice shower. After that, I let my hair dry naturally as I usually do and pick out some clothes. I decide to wear some jeans with my AC/DC band t-shirt and my Converse. Once I'm somewhat happy with my appearance, I walk out of my room and make my way to the kitchen.

As soon as I walk in, I notice Alyssa and my dad drinking coffee at the island while Amanda sits and plays with what looks like a Nintendo DS.

My dad looks up and sees me at the doorway. "Good morning, Riley," he says, offering me a smile.

"Morning," I speak softly. I take a few steps further into the kitchen.

Alyssa nudges Amanda and Amanda looks up at her mom. "Amanda honey, I want you to apologize to Riley."

Amanda sighs and looks at me. "I'm sorry, Riley," she says with no emotion.

"It's fine," I mumble.

"So, who's hungry? I know I am," my dad says.

Amanda hops off her seat and raises her hand. "I'm hungry!"

I feel my pocket to make sure I have my phone before we leave. We all walk out of the house and get into one of their vehicles. I sit in the back with Amanda. My dad pulls out of the driveway, and we're on our way.

My phone buzzes in my hand and I look down. It's a message from Aiden.

Good morning Led Zeppelin Girl ;)

I stare at the screen, debating whether or not I should respond to him. I give in and type a message back.

Hi

Plain, I know. But he isn't completely forgiven.

—All I get is a hi?

—Yes. Be lucky you even got a response from me.

—I know you love me Summers ;)

I smirk. I don't love him. Sure, I have a slight crush on him, but I don't think I can ever love Aiden Callaway.

—You just keep telling yourself that

—Oh I will. Can I ask you something?

I brace myself.

Sure

I wait for him to respond. Though it only takes a couple of seconds for him to respond, it feels like an hour.

Wanna hang out when you get back?

Part of me feels like that isn't what he wants to ask me. But I brush that aside and think about it.

"Who's Aiden?" Amanda suddenly asks.

I look at her and frown. "What?"

"The Aiden you've been talking to," Amanda says to me. "Who is he?"

Has she been reading my text messages? "Um, he's a friend," I answer plainly.

"Is he your boyfriend?" Amanda asks in a teasing tone.

I feel my face heat up as soon as she says *boyfriend.* Alyssa looks back at us and shakes her head. "Amanda, I don't think that's any of your business," Alyssa tells her.

"He's not my boyfriend," I tell Amanda anyway.

I text Aiden back, but I make sure Amanda can't see.

—Sure, why not

"We have arrived," my dad says. I look out the window and notice we're at Village Inn. My stomach instantly growls.

Aiden

The doorbell rings, and Alex and I look at each other. It's Saturday morning and we're just lounging around. We usually don't do anything until the afternoon.

"Did you invite someone over?" Alex asks me.

I shake my head. "Did you?"

"If I did, I would have told you," he says as he stares at the TV. Seeing how he isn't the one who will answer the fucking door, I stand up and start walking in that direction.

I unlock the front door and open it. I'm surprised to see Ryan Dixon standing in front of me with his hands in the pocket of his Nike hoodie. "Well, if it isn't my loving stepbrother," I remark.

He rolls his eyes. "It's good to see you too, Aiden."

"How can I help you this fine morning?" I ask in a bored tone. I lean against the doorway as my phone buzzes in my hand. It's probably Riley texting me back.

"Your dad wants to have a big family dinner tonight, and he wants you to know that you're invited," he informs me.

I smirk. I'm actually invited to a *family dinner*? "Why did he send you?" I ask curiously.

"He didn't send me. I volunteered to come over here," he says.

I narrow my eyes at him. "I'm getting the feeling that you didn't just come to tell me that."

He smirks. "And you're right."

I sigh and glance behind me. "Come in." I hold the door open for him. He walks inside and looks around. "Let's go in the kitchen," I say, walking past him. He follows me to the kitchen, and I go straight to the fridge. "You want anything to drink? Water? Vodka? Jack Daniels?"

He takes a seat at the bar in front of the sink. "Thanks, but I don't want anything."

I grab a water bottle for myself since I'm feeling a bit thirsty. "So what else did you want to tell me?"

"Have you talked to Riley?" he asks curiously.

That question takes me slightly off guard. Why is he asking that? "Why do you want to know?" I ask him.

"I'm just curious," he says, looking down at the counter in front of him.

I'm pretty sure he's not *just curious*. I squint at him. "You like Riley, don't you?" I find myself asking him.

He looks back up at me and shakes his head. "I don't know. I mean, I really thought I just liked her as a friend when I got to know her, but now…"

The thought of Ryan liking Riley makes me feel weird. If he ends up asking her out, she'll spend more time with him than with me. I honestly like spending time with Riley. She's like no one else I know.

"Now you like her more than a friend." I finish for him.

He shrugs. "With Nicole off my back, I actually want to hang out with Riley more. But I wanted to ask you…"

"You wanted to ask me…what?" I ask.

"Do *you* like Riley?"

He catches me off guard with that question too. I frown when he asks. Do I like Riley? No. I can't. And even if I do, she probably won't like me like that anyway. I pissed her off, and I'm still not forgiven.

"Why does it matter?" I ask, turning around and taking a drink from my water bottle.

"We all know you like Riley, Aiden," he tells me.

What the fuck does he know? I turn back around and look at him. "Oh really? Well, you're wrong. I don't like Riley like that." I snap at him.

My answer seems to amuse him. He smirks. "So, you're okay with me asking her out then?"

I clench my jaw. No, I'm not okay with you fucking asking her out. Dammit. "Do whatever the fuck you want, Ryan."

He smiles. "Great. Well, I'm out of here." He stands up and walks out of the kitchen. I don't move from my spot. My mind is still trying to process what the hell just happened.

Alex walks in with a puzzled look on his face. "Who was that?"

"My stepbrother," I say, taking a drink from my bottle of water.

"Oh," he says plainly. "That's interesting."

I tap my fingers on the counter in front of me. I find myself thinking about everything that has been going on. I look at Alex who's still in the kitchen.

"How do you know when you like a girl?" I find myself asking him.

He raises his eyebrows. "Um, I don't know." He frowns. "I guess when you like being around her more than anyone else. Why?" He looks at me skeptically.

Hmm. "No reason." I shake my head. I start towards the hallway.

"Get your ass back in here," Alex says behind me. "You can't just ask a question like that and get away with it."

I roll my eyes. Leave it to Alex to be a drama queen about this.

"Do you like someone?" He grins as he asks me.

"No," I answer flatly.

He smirks at me. "You're a damn liar. Fess up, Callaway. I know you like someone."

"You don't know what the fuck you're talking about, Alex." I deny.

"I already know who you like actually. I just want to hear you admit it," he says, continuing to smirk.

I don't like anyone. Alex and Ryan have both gone off the fucking deep end. "Who do I like then, Alex? Please enlighten me," I say to him, crossing my arms.

"You like that Riley girl." He has a smug smile.

Why does everyone assume I like her? "We're *friends*, Alex. Besides," I say, "Ryan likes her. And since he's *Ryan fucking Dixon*, he always gets what he wants."

"What do you mean?" he asks, raising his eyebrow.

"I mean, he's going to ask her out and she's going to say yes, then they'll be the happiest damn couple around," I ramble.

Alex shakes his head when I finish talking. "Why are you shaking your head?" I demand from him.

"You don't realize how *jealous* you sound." He laughs. "Seriously, Aiden, just admit you like the girl, tell her, then both of you can live happily ever after."

I turn around and walk into my room, slamming the door in his face.

Chapter 25

Riley

When I get back home, it's about six in the afternoon. I sigh when we pull up to the house.

"The trip wasn't too bad, was it?" my mom asks me.

I shrug. "No, not really."

"I'm glad everything is fine now," she tells me.

Me too, I think. I grab my bag and my phone and get out of the car. Mom and I walk up to the front door and she unlocks it. When she walks in, she turns and smiles at me. I frown in return. "Why are you smiling at me?"

She continues to grin. "I know you're eighteen already, but it's starting to settle in that you're going to be off doing great things in the near future. Soon enough I'll have a son-in-law and a grandchild—"

I stop her right there. "Mom, please." I don't know what brought on this sudden speech and it's kind of weird. "It'll be a while before you get grandkids, much less a *son-in-law*." I scoff.

She smirks. "Well, don't be in a hurry to have kids just yet. I wouldn't mind a son-in-law though." She winks. I roll my eyes and she chuckles at me. "Just put your stuff up and come back down for dinner."

I nod and make my way up the stairs to my room. When I walk in, everything seems to be in place. I throw my bag on my bed and turn around. My attention is immediately directed towards the flowers on my dresser.

I slowly approach the lilies and smell it . They're all white and are placed in a glass vase that's sitting on my dresser. I look around the flowers for some sort of hint of who they're from. But I can't find anything.

"Mom!" I yell as I run down the stairs. I find her in the kitchen, and she looks up at me. "Where did those flowers come from?"

She smirks. "I'm not supposed to say."

What? My own mom is turning against me! "Mom, that is not fair," I say, crossing my arms. "Who are they from?"

"He told me not to tell you." She smiles. "It was quite sweet of him, don't you think? The flowers are absolutely beautiful."

"That is cruel, Mom. Why can't you just tell me?"

She grins. "I told you I can't say! He said he'll tell you eventually though."

I huff and goes back up to my room. As soon as I walk in, my phone starts buzzing on my bed. I sit down and look down at the screen. I roll my eyes but answer anyway.

"Yes?" I ask.

"A simple hello would have been nicer," Aiden responds.

"Why did you call?" I ask as I lay back on my bed.

He sighs. "Isn't this what friends do? Call each other for no reason?"

"How would I know?" I ask him. "I never had any friends before I met you, Kelly, and Ryan."

"Well, now you do," he comments. "And I'm glad you can refer to me as a friend again."

I smirk. "Yeah, I guess I'm not *that* mad at you anymore."

"I want to say something though, and I don't want you to get pissed off about it, okay?"

What's he going to say? "That depends on what you're going to say."

"Just let me clarify a few things," he says. "First, Nicole and I are not together. I know that stupid rumor was going around about us, but it's not true."

For some reason, I feel some kind of relief in me after he says that.

"Second, that time I went to her house was a one-time thing. It won't happen. Never." He continues. "And last, those messages that Nicole showed you were real. It was a mistake going to her house though."

I close my eyes and sigh. I feel like hanging up, but I want to hear what else he has to say.

"And now I want to ask you a serious question that only requires a yes or no," he says finally. My heart starts to beat rapidly in my chest. "Riley, did I steal your first kiss?"

Part of me wants to lie and say no. "Yes," I answer.

"Seriously?" he asks. I can already see him smirking.

I frown. "Go ahead. Make fun." I groan.

"No, I'm not making fun of you," he says. "I've just never been someone's first kiss."

My cheeks heat up. "How many girls have you kissed?" I blurt out.

He laughs. "Not as many as you think."

My eyes flicker to the flowers and I sit up on my bed. "It's my turn to ask you a question that only calls for a yes or no."

"Okay, what is it?"

"Did you bring flowers to my house?" I ask him.

"No?" His answer comes out as a question. There's a slight pang of disappointment in me. "Wait, someone sent you flowers?"

I play with one of the petals on the lily. "They were here in my room when I got home a while ago."

He doesn't respond for a minute. "Shit. That son of a bitch!"

I raise my eyebrow from his sudden outburst. "What?"

"I'll see you tomorrow at school, Riley," he says then hangs up.

***

Turns out I won't be seeing anyone for school. I woke up last night not feeling well and I ended up puking up everything that was in my stomach. Not pleasant *at all*. I'm now stuck in bed for the rest of the day. I honestly feel miserable. I don't even remember the last time I got sick like this. Maybe those mystery flowers are cursed or something.

"Call me if you need anything, Riley. I'll be right over," my mom says.

Since I have a headache too, it sounds like she's yelling at me through a megaphone. I roll over on my bed and groan. "Okay, Mom. I'll be all right," I say, closing my eyes. I didn't get much sleep, so I intend to sleep all day if I have to.

My mom eventually walks out of my room and I hear her leave the house. I sigh and try to fall asleep. That doesn't work out. About fifteen minutes after my mom left, I run to my bathroom and throw up again. I eventually fall asleep around ten o'clock.

"I'm just checking on her. Why does that even matter, Alex? Listen, I'll call you back. I think she's waking up."

I groan and roll over on my bed. The headache is still there and so is the nausea. My eyes slowly open and I look around my room. I raise my eyebrow when I see Aiden sitting at the end of my bed, putting his phone in his pocket. "What are you doing here?" As soon as I ask that, I feel something in my stomach. Before he can respond to my question, I get up from my bed. At the same time, Aiden stands up, and I push him out of the way to get to the bathroom where I shut the door behind me.

When I finish throwing up, I emerge from the bathroom and walk back to my bed.

"Well, don't you look lovely today?" I hear Aiden say.

I roll myself in the blankets. "Shut up," I mumble.

"Friends are supposed to be honest with each other, so I'm going to be totally honest with you," he says, sitting back down on my bed. "You look like death, Riley."

"Gee, thanks." I roll my eyes. I'm not in the mood for this.

"No problem." He grins. "And you're pretty strong, you know that?" I frown at him. "You nearly knocked me down when you ran for the bathroom."

I pull the blankets tighter against my body, suddenly feeling cold. "You were in my way. Be lucky you didn't get thrown up on."

He smiles. "I see being sick hasn't affected your charming personality."

I look at the clock on the small table next to my bed. It's around one in the afternoon. "Shouldn't you be at school?" I ask him. Lunch was over at twelve thirty.

He shrugs. "I thought I'd check on you since I didn't see you this morning."

"Thanks," I mumble. I start to think about how much work I have to make up since I missed Friday and today. I wince and stop thinking about that for now.

"Are these the flowers you got?" Aiden says, gesturing to the lilies.

"No, they aren't. How did those get here?" I ask sarcastically.

Aiden chuckles and shakes his head. "Do you even like lilies?"

I shrug. It isn't my favorite flower, but they are beautiful. My favorite flowers are white roses. I don't know why, but there's just something about them. The average person would like the romantic red rose, but I'm not average.

Aiden smirks. "Someone is trying too hard."

"Wait, you know who sent them?" I ask, slightly sitting up.

He hesitates but shakes his head. "Nope."

I know he's lying, but I don't push the subject.

"Have you had any water today?" he asks me. I shake my head. "I'll be right back." He stands up and exits my room. I sigh and sink into my bed. I move around until I'm comfortable. But when Aiden walks back in, he tells me to sit up so I can drink some water.

"You know, I've seen you at your best, and now I'm seeing you at your worst," he says to me as I take a sip of the water.

I raise my eyebrow. "You've seen me at my best?"

"Yeah." He shrugs. He takes the water and sets it on the small table next to us. "At the rehearsal dinner when you were all dressed up. I never would have guessed that you're a nerd."

I roll my eyes. "Thanks."

"That was a compliment, Summers." He smiles. "You looked good that night."

I feel the blood rush to my cheeks while he chuckles. "Well, that was probably the last time you will ever see me in a dress," I tell him.

He reaches in his pocket suddenly and pulls out his phone. He looks down at it and frowns. Then he shakes his head and puts it back in his pocket.

"Not going to respond to your girlfriend?" I find myself asking him.

Aiden smirks. "If you would call Alex my girlfriend, then no, I'm not going to respond. He's being stupid."

"How?" I ask curiously.

He purses his lips. "That's confidential information." A slight smile forms on his face.

"Ah, I see." I nod.

"So, you seem fine to me. How about I take you to school?" he asks, smirking. I roll my eyes at him.

"I am *not* fine. And it's already the afternoon," I say, pulling the covers tighter around me. I'm surprised I'm not freaking out over Aiden being here while I'm still in my pajamas. Whatever, I'm sick. And if he has a problem with that, then he can leave.

We fall into a somewhat comfortable silence and I notice Aiden looking around my room. I'm starting to feel nauseous again, but I take deep breaths hoping the feeling will go away. I feel Aiden's gaze on me again.

"So, how did everything go with your dad?" I hear him ask.

I don't have time to answer. I scramble out of my bed and run into the bathroom, making sure to shut the door. When I finish, I slump over the toilet, ignoring the fact that doing so is disgusting.

"Are you okay in there?" Aiden asks from the other side of the door. When I don't answer, he asks, "Riley?"

I take a deep breath. "I'm fine." I stand up shakily and clean up before walking back out. I crawl into bed and make myself comfortable.

"You wanna tell me what went down up there?" he asks as he sits down next to me on my bed.

I sigh and nod. I inhale before telling him what happened with my dad over the weekend.

Chapter 26

After we had got back from *Village Inn*, Alyssa suggested that she and Amanda should some time by themselves for part of the day. Amanda, of course, complained that I'd get to spend time with her daddy, but Alyssa promised to buy her some candy at the mall, and if she'd stop her pouting.

Alyssa told me that it would be a good time to start bonding with my dad. I'm about to protest, but then I remembered that the whole purpose in going there was to get to know him and "bond." So Alyssa left with Amanda, and I joined my dad in the living room where he's watching TV.

"Food from *Village Inn* really hits the spot, don't you think?" my dad asked me.

I nodded. I loved *Village Inn*. I loved it so much that I overate that's why, for the rest of the day, I felt like an inflated balloon. "Yeah. *Village Inn* is great."

He stayed quiet for a few minutes. He grabbed the remote and changed the channel to ESPN. Then he spoke again. "So, everything is good at home?"

Once again, I nodded. "Yep. Mom keeps up with the house chores and I look after our dog." At the mention of Sassy, I instantly missed that fur ball.

"Let me guess, it's a Pomeranian isn't it?" he asked, sounding amused.

"How did you know?" I asked back, raising my eyebrow.

He shook his head and chuckles. "Your mom always wanted a Pomeranian."

"We got her when I was about twelve," I said to him.

Another silence followed. My dad eventually sighed and turned the volume down on the TV. "Riley, I know you want to know why I left you and your mother…"

I took a deep breath. I knew the conversation would come up at some point. "I do," I said.

"There are some things you have to understand, Riley. Your mother and I were only twenty years old when she had you. It's not too young, but it's not that old either. We were both still growing up ourselves, and raising a child was difficult for both of us. As much as I loved your mom, things were only getting harder instead of better," he said then sighed. "I started to think that I wasn't fit to be a dad, and if I stayed, I would only screw things up."

"Doesn't that cross every parent's mind though?" I found myself asking him.

He nodded. "I didn't realize that at the time. Let me tell you, it wasn't easy leaving you and your mom. You were *such a cute kid and I loved spending time with you and her. I was going through a rough time with my family and everything seemed like it was crumbling down around me. So I did end up leaving."*

"*You gave up," I said. He was beating around the bush and I hated it when people do that.*

"*I did." He admitted, slumping his shoulders. "A few years later, I met Alyssa. I didn't expect to find someone else, but I did. And I ended up lying to her. I had told her that I was never married or anything, which was a huge mistake."*

In all honesty, I didn't want to talk about Alyssa at that point. "So, instead of trying to reach out to your own daughter, you went out and found a new wife?" I asked, trying so hard to keep my voice steady.

"*When you put it like that—"*

"*You know, I never really cared that you left us." I cut him off. "Because I honestly thought I would never speak to you, ever. I thought I could go on in life and not make a big deal about this. Then I see that you're married again and had another daughter. Do you have any idea how that makes me feel?" I asked, pointing to myself.*

"*Riley—"*

"*It makes me feel like I'm not wanted. As much as I hate to admit it, I am jealous of Amanda because you're here for her and you weren't even there for me. She gets to have the childhood I never had." I ranted. I was already on a roll and I didn't want to stop.*

My dad wore a sad expression. "I was afraid your mom wouldn't let me see you after what I did."

"You could have tried still," I told him. "The thing is, though, I wouldn't change my childhood. I think Mom did a pretty good job raising me on her own."

"She did." He nodded. "She raised a beautiful young lady who is going to do great things later in life. Even though I wasn't there to see you progress to where you are now, I'm still proud of you. And I don't want you ever to think that I love Amanda more than you."

I took a deep breath and calmed myself down. I knew this would happen, and I wanted to handle it well.

"What I want from you, Riley, is your forgiveness. I haven't been the perfect dad, hell, I haven't even been a dad to you, but I want you to forgive me more than anything. I promise I will try to be there for you whenever I can."

We both stood up and I wrapped my arms around him in a tight hug. I didn't have to say it, but we both understood that he was forgiven.

***

After I finish telling Aiden about my conversation with my dad, he whistles. "Pretty emotional stuff," he says to me.

I nod in agreement. "Everything was fine after that. Alyssa was nothing but nice to me for the remaining time I was there and Amanda even complimented me on my eyes," I tell him. I almost choked on the water I was drinking when the girl said that to me.

Aiden grins. "At least things didn't take a turn for the worst."

"I'm glad for that," I say, leaning back into my pillow. I'm feeling a little better at this point.

Sassy walks into my room at that moment and jumps onto my bed. She goes straight for Aiden and starts licking his arm.

"Awe man!" Aiden yells. I chuckle at the sight before me.

Aiden points to Sassy. "You are an evil dog. You lost my respect." Sassy just tilts her head then comes and sits beside me.

I pat her back. "Good dog."

Aiden shoots me a glare. "You're real funny. I now have dog saliva on my arm."

"You can easily clean it off." I shrug. "You're being a drama queen."

He smirks then. "You wanna lick my other arm, so it'll be even?"

"No, I don't want to *lick your arm*. I don't want to get even sicker than I already am. I don't even know where your arm has been," I say to him, crossing my arms.

He chuckles. "I promise my arm is clean."

"Aiden, I am *not* going to lick your arm. That's disgusting and weird." *Seriously, who licks someone's arm?*

I hear a buzzing noise and I turn my head. My phone on my dresser goes off. I look at Aiden. "Can you grab my phone for me?" I ask as nicely as I can.

"What do I look like, your goddamn servant?" He crosses his arms.

"Yes, you do. Now, get my phone." I point to it.

He sits there and sticks his nose up in the air.

"Please?" I plead. "It could be my mom."

He sighs and stands up. "Dammit. This is the only time I'm doing this," he says as he grabs my phone.

"Whatever." I roll my eyes. I see him glance down at the screen and he smirks. He then hands it to me and I see that I have a text from Lucas.

"You still talk to that guy?" Aiden asks me.

"Not in a while." I shake my head as I open the text.

Hey Riley (: did you like the flowers?

A smile creeps onto my lips. So Lucas was the one who sent me the flowers.

I did. That was nice of you

Aiden stands up from my bed and I look up at him. He paces for a minute before looking at me. "Why are you staring at me, Summers?" he asks, sounding amused.

"Why are you pacing?" I ask him.

"I'm thinking." His eyebrows knit together.

I purse my lips. "Lucas was the one who gave me the flowers," I inform him.

Aiden looks at me and frowns. "It was *him*?" I nod. "I better get going," he says suddenly.

"Okay…"

"Don't miss me too much." He smiles as he exits my room.

I don't bother responding.

***

"Riley, wake up." I feel someone shaking my shoulder. I groan and rub my eyes before slowly opening them. I find my mom hovering over me.

"Yes?" I ask, feeling a bit irritated. I'm sleeping so well and she has to come and wake me up.

"Riley, sit up. I have to talk to you," she says, sounding serious.

I eye her suspiciously and sluggishly sit up and lean against my pillows. "About?" I question.

"The neighbor said they saw an unfamiliar car sitting in our driveway for a while," she says, putting her hands on her hips. "They also said they saw a boy leaving. Care to explain?"

I frown. "Why do the neighbors have to be so nosy?"

"Just answer me, Riley. Was there a boy here or not?" she demands.

"There was," I say hesitantly. "It was only Aiden though. He just came over to check on me."

She sighs. "Riley, I don't really trust that boy. From what I've heard from Anna, he isn't the best company to have around."

"It's not like we did anything." I glare at her. "I was *sick* today in case you forgot. And I'm not even like that."

"I don't care, Riley." She crosses her arms. "I don't want you around that boy. What about the one who brought you flowers?" she asks

I groan. "Mom, I don't even like Lucas like that. We're friends. And so are Aiden and I."

"If I see you hanging around that Aiden boy, I will ground you and take your phone away." She threatens me.

"I'm eighteen, Mom. You can't do that." I complain. Why is she so mean all of a sudden?

"I'm your mother and you will listen to me. I don't care how old you are."

I flip over onto my stomach and sigh loudly. "This is so unfair," I say into the pillow.

"If I find out you've been hanging around him again, I will not let you move out after you graduate," I hear her say.

I instantly look at her. "You can't do that."

"I can and I will."

I lay back down and don't bother replying to her. I hear her walk out of my room and shut the door behind her. As much as I hate to admit it, spending time with Aiden isn't awful.

My mom was the one who told me to make new friends. So here I am making new friends and what does she do? Flips out.

I'm sure every normal teenager says this, so I'm going to say it too.

Life is so unfair.

Aiden

"Alex, where are the goddamn keys?" I call out. I've been looking everywhere for those stupid keys and I still can't find them. If I don't want to be late to school, I have to leave *now*. I already missed yesterday, since I went to see Riley.

"Did you look in the refrigerator?" I hear him ask.

What. The. Fuck. "Why would they be in the damn fridge?" I demand. But I walk up to the fridge anyway and open it.

And sure enough, there are the keys, sitting on one of the shelves.

I don't bother asking Alex why they're in the refrigerator. I grab the keys and slam the fridge shut. I then grab my leather jacket, my pack of cigarettes, and my backpack. I run out the door and unlock the car.

By the time I park the car in the student parking lot, the class has already started. I walk swiftly through the halls and approach my first class of the day. I open the door and immediately everyone's eyes are on me.

My teacher, Mr. Richards, looks at me and sighs. "It's nice of you to join us on this fine morning, Mr. Callaway."

I ignore him and walk over to my seat. I quickly sit down and lean back. Mr. Richards just continues talking after I sit down. He hands out a worksheet for us not too long after and then sits at his desk and starts going through papers. The classroom instantly becomes noisy from everyone talking with their friends.

"Hey, Aiden." The voice comes from the girl in the seat next to mine. I think her name is Leah. I'm not quite sure.

"Hey." I nod at her. I give her a once-over, and I become slightly interested in her. Her blonde hair is pulled up in a ponytail, and she has on a short skirt with a V-neck shirt.

"I didn't see you at lunch yesterday," she says, batting her eyelashes. I become less interested when I notice her voice is a little too high-pitched for my liking.

"I left." I shrug. I tap my pencil on my desk instead of working on the paper in front of me.

She leans forward a little in her seat. "Nicole was looking for you also." She smirks.

I cringe. Nicole won't leave me the fuck alone now. I don't understand how Ryan put up with her. "Oh joy," I say sarcastically.

"She doesn't seem like your type, you know," she comments.

"I don't even have a type," I say to her. I'm getting somewhat annoyed with her at this point.

She smirks. "Do you wanna go out Friday night? I'm pretty sure I can prove that *I'm* your type."

"Not interested," I say as I start working on the worksheet.

This girl obviously doesn't get the hint though. "C'mon, Aiden. It'll be fun."

"I already said no, so drop it." I snap at her. She shuts up after that. I don't understand why all these girls won't just leave me alone. I thought sleeping with Nicole would get her off my back, but that only made things worse. It's better to just ignore them.

For the rest of the time, I focus on the paper in front of me.

***

Lunch comes around soon enough. After I stop by my locker, I head in the direction of the library. I know Riley would be in there.

When I walk into the library, I instantly notice Ryan sitting with Riley at a table off to the side of the library. I see her laugh at something and he just smiles at her. I clench my jaw but immediately calm myself down. I don't know why it bothers me when I see them hanging out. I shouldn't even care.

As I approach the table, Ryan notices me and he raises his eyebrows. "Aiden." He acknowledges me when I'm close enough.

"Ryan," I say to him. I sit down next to Riley and smile at her. "Hey, Riley."

"Uh, hey," she says, not looking at me. She instantly starts to gather her things. "I should go."

"Are you sure?" Ryan asks her.

She nods. "Yeah. Um, I'll see you later, Ryan." She starts towards the library doors and I frown.

"What was that all about?" I ask Ryan.

He shrugs. "Maybe you should just leave her alone for now. I've already won her over anyway."

"What do you mean?" I narrow my eyes at him.

"I asked her if she wanted to hang out later and she said yes." He grins. "Just give up, Aiden. You had your chance, but now it's mine."

"What the fuck are you talking about, Ryan. What chance are you talking about?" I demand from him.

He stands up and pushes his chair in. "The chance to ask her out." And with that, he leaves the library.

I'm not even going to ask her out. Ryan is just making up all this shit.

I leave the library and walk in the direction of Riley's locker. Something is obviously bothering her and I intend to find out what it is.

And there she is, standing at her locker. I quickly approach her and lean against the locker next to hers. "Is something wrong?" I ask her.

"Yes," she says, avoiding my gaze. "I need you to leave me alone for a while."

What?

"What? Why?" I question. Everything had been fine with us yesterday when I went to see her.

She sighs. "Just leave me alone, Aiden."

I'm about to respond when I feel someone besides me. I look to my right and see Nicole smiling at me. "Hey, you," she says to me.

Riley slams her locker shut, making Nicole look at her. "Oh look, the nerdy whore is back. We all thought you killed yourself or something."

Riley just rolls her eyes and walks away. Nicole snarls. "*Bitch*."

I push Nicole away from me. "Nicole, leave me the fuck alone."

"But, Aiden—" she says, laughing slightly.

"No." I shake my head. "You think talking to Riley like that is funny? Well, it's not. You're the bitch." I snap at her.

"That's not what you were saying when you were screwing me," she retorts.

I wince when she says that, but I hold my ground. "Doing you was the biggest mistake I've ever made. I want nothing to do with you now," I tell her.

She glares at me then makes her way down the hallway. A few people around me start whispering about our argument. But I don't care about that.

I need to find out why Riley wants me to leave her alone.

***

I arrive back at the house and park the car in the driveway. I walk up to the door and open it. I throw my backpack on the couch and go straight for the kitchen.

Alex is talking to someone on the phone when I walk in. I walk past him and go straight to the cabinets. I decide that a nice bowl of cereal sounds good. Alex ends his call and looks at me. "How was school?" he asks me.

I stare at him. "You sound like a parent."

"I'm just asking." He holds his hands up.

"It sucked," I say as I grab the milk from the fridge. I pour the cereal into the bowl then the milk. I put the stuff away and start eating the cereal.

Alex chuckles. "That's high school for you."

I pull my phone out of my pocket and text Riley again. I know she's ignoring me, but that isn't going to stop me from texting her.

"You seem very tense," he comments. "I'm going to take a wild guess and say that something happened to you today."

I don't answer him. I just continue eating my cereal.

"Fine. Don't tell me," Alex says then. "It's not like we haven't been friends for four years or anything."

Alex can be a drama queen about everything. He'll keep pushing you until you tell him what's wrong, and then he tries to go all Oprah on you.

I sigh. "Riley told me to leave her alone, and I have no idea why," I say to him.

He grinned. "Why don't you just admit to yourself that you like this girl? It's pretty damn obvious but you're so oblivious."

"We're *friends*, Alex." I snap. "Even if I did like her, I wouldn't have a chance with her. She's got two other guys after her and she's not even talking to me right now." I rant.

Alex has a smug look on his face.

"What?" I demand.

He just walks into the living room. I slam my fist on the counter and sigh in frustration. I don't know why I'm getting so worked up about all of this. I shouldn't even care. But I do.

I have to find out why Riley doesn't want to talk to me. And I think I know how I'm going to do it.

Chapter 27

Riley

Ryan pulls into my driveway and I smile. I had spent the afternoon with him and it was actually quite fun.

"So, I'll see you tomorrow at school?" he asks, turning to look at me.

I nod. "Yup." I then grab my bag and get out of the car. I wave to Ryan before he drives off.

When I walk inside the house, I notice my mom by the kitchen window and I automatically know she's trying to see who I'm with.

"That was Ryan, for your information," I tell her then run up the stairs.

Once I finish my homework, it's around five o'clock. I'm in my room listening to music on my iPod when my mom comes. I pull my earphones out of my ear and look at her.

"Riley, I've been calling you from downstairs for the past five minutes," she tells me. "You have a visitor."

She makes it sound like I'm in a jail or something. I get up and walk out of my room to see who came to see me. I know it isn't Aiden because my mom probably wouldn't have told me if it's him.

I raise my eyebrows in surprise when I see who's at the door. "Kelly."

She smiles at me. "Hey, Riley."

"What are you doing here?" I ask her slowly. I haven't really talked to her much lately.

"I was wondering if you wanted to take a trip to the park. You know, just catch up and stuff," she says, continuing to smile.

"Uh, okay," I tell her. "Mind if Sassy tags along?"

When Kelly says she doesn't mind, I tell my mom where I'm going and grab the dog leash. I call Sassy to the door and the three of us then head down the sidewalk.

"So, how's everything with Robert?" I ask her.

"Everything is fine. He makes my mom happy and I don't have anything bad to say about him." She shrugs. "What about you? What's new? Still watching *Star Wars* at home?" She teases.

"I haven't watched it in a while actually," I tell her. "I don't know if Ryan told you, but I went to visit my dad over the weekend."

She raises her eyebrows. "You did? Didn't you say he left, like, when you were little or something?"

I nod. "Yeah. It was a little awkward at first when I found out he had another wife and daughter. But everything worked out."

"Damn." She shakes her head. "I don't know how you managed to work things out. I found out that the woman my dad cheated on my mom with is pregnant with his kid."

We're both basically in the same situation. Only I worked my way through it and she hasn't. "How are you dealing with it?"

Kelly sighs. "It sucks. I know my mom has moved on and everything, but knowing that my dad is going to have another kid with that woman…"

"Have you talked to your dad?" I ask curiously.

She shakes her head. "No. The day I found out about him cheating on my mom is the day I stopped talking to him. Ryan talks to him every now and then, but I can tell he is still trying to handle all of it."

I remember telling Aiden that Ryan could be feeling the same way about his dad also. Maybe they should just sit down and try to understand each other instead of disliking one another.

We pass by Aiden's old house and I glance at it for a few seconds before looking down at Sassy.

"Let's talk about something else," Kelly suggests. "I don't feel like going home depressed."

I chuckle. "Okay, what do you want to talk about?"

"Boys." Her eyes sparkle as she says it.

"Okay…"

"So, I met this guy…Not recently though. I've known him for like almost a year now. Anyways, we've been texting non-stop for like, three days now." I smile. "But he told me yesterday that he's been dating this girl for about a month." Her smile falters.

I frown. "He's been dating this girl for a month, but he barely mentioned it now?" I ask her. That seems a bit odd. But then again, I'm actually having a girly conversation. *This is odd.*

She nods. "Yeah. It sucks because I did develop a small crush on the guy and he has a girlfriend already. And it sucks even more because he said he's only known her for three months. I've known him longer."

I feel like I need to give her some encouraging words, but I don't know exactly what to say.

She sighs. "Well, enough about me. What about you?"

"Me?" I ask.

"Yeah, I know you and Ryan hung out today. But what about Aiden or Lucas?" she asks me.

It's my turn to sigh. "Lucas is just a friend and so is Ryan. And I...uh...I'm not exactly allowed to see Aiden anymore," I tell her.

She frowns. "You're not *allowed to*? What the hell does that mean?"

"My mom doesn't like me hanging around him and she threatened that she'd keep me at home after graduation instead of helping me move out on my own," I inform her.

"I'm sorry, Riley, but that is just stupid. You're eighteen, right? You can move out even if your mom says you can't," she says to me.

I know that. But I'm afraid that if I start all this crap right now, my relationship with my mom will never be the same. "I know," I tell her.

"It's okay to rebel against your parents every now and then Riley." She laughs slightly. "I think it would be quite healthy for you to go against your mom."

I think about it and she's right. I've never done anything bad in my life. Well, besides spray painting on the back wall of the library. I won't go so far to when it will affect my grades at school or anything, of course. "You're right." I nod.

"So, what are you going to do?" she asks, raising her eyebrow.

"To start things off, I'm going to continue talking to Aiden," I tell her. I feel kind of nervous for this. I mean, I've never gone against my mom's rules.

This is going to be interesting.

Aiden

"See? It was nothing you did so calm down, bro," Kelly says through the phone.

"*Step*-bro." I correct her. She replies with a quick whatever. "Is that all you guys talked about?" I ask curiously. I don't want Kelly to make it obvious that I'm the one behind all of this.

"Well, no." I can practically see her rolling her eyes as she answers. "We talked about our dads too."

I don't know a whole lot about Kelly, Ryan, and Jenna's dad. I just know that he had cheated on Anna before they got divorced. "Oh" is my reply.

"I gotta go. Is that all the information you need?" she asks.

"Yup," I tell her then hang up.

I pace around in my room and think about what Kelly told me. Of course, Riley, being Riley, decided not to go against her mom and talks to me anyway.

My bedroom door suddenly opens and Alex enters. "Hey, I invited Jake and Isaiah over tonight. Just thought I'd let you know if you wanna go out with us tonight."

I think about it then shake my head. "Nah, I'm good man. I'm gonna stay here."

"Really?" he asks, shock evident on his face.

I nod slowly. "I'm sure."

He walks up to me and puts his hand on my forehead. I frown. "What are you doing?" I ask him.

"Seeing if you have a fever. You never turn down an offer like this," he says, dropping his hand.

"Get outta here, man." I push him away.

"Whatever. You're going to miss a great night!"

I shove him out of my room and shut the door behind him. I need time to think, so going out isn't a great idea.

I end up going to bed pretty early that night.

***

Alex isn't awake when I get up in the morning. I figure he won't wake up until about eleven or so. I continue getting ready for another wonderful day at school. Note the sarcasm.

My phone buzzes on the counter while I eat breakfast. I glance at the screen and see that Riley had texted me. I smirk when I see her name and read the message.

Meet me at my locker when you get to school?

I decide to mess with her.

I don't know. You didn't say please.

You frustrate me, you know that?

I chuckle before replying, *It's okay Led Zeppelin Girl. I know you secretly love me*

Just meet me when you get to school.

And so I do. When I get to school, I stop by my locker first then head for Riley's. I slowly creep up behind her and grab at her sides, yelling, "Boo!"

She jumps and whirls around. She instantly smacks my arm and glares at me. "You scared me half to death!"

I chuckle when she yells at me. She looks cute when she's angry. Wait, what? I clear my throat. "So, why did you want me to meet you here?"

She sighs. "I want to apologize."

"For?"

"For how I acted yesterday," she says slowly. "My mom told me to stay away from you since she found out you were over when I was sick. She said she wouldn't let me leave the house after graduation if I had continued hanging out with you and I was just so mad at her and I actually went through with not talking to you—"

I put my hand over her mouth. "Riley, shut up."

She frowns and crosses her arms.

I uncover her mouth and smile at her. "I forgive you."

"Really?" she asks.

I shrug. "Sure."

She looks at me suspiciously. "That was a little too easy."

"I'm a forgiving person," I tell her. She shuts her locker and looks at me. I put my arm around her and we start walking down the hallway. "Anyways, I think we should hang out this weekend."

She looks at me and smiles. "Okay."

I raise my eyebrow. I wasn't expecting a quick answer like that. "Okay." I smile at her. "Do you want to hang out at lunch?"

She nods. "Sure." She takes my arm off her shoulder. "I need to get to class now." With that being said, she turns around and walks away from me.

Riley

It's now Saturday and I'm getting ready to go see Aiden. Of course, I told my mom that I was going to hang out with Ryan and she seemed pretty happy at the thought of me being with him. In all honesty, I don't like Ryan in that way. I think of him as a great friend and nothing more. I also think of Lucas as a friend.

Aiden had told me to meet him at the park so my mom wouldn't see him. I quickly throw on my Led Zeppelin t-shirt, which I found on the floor in my closet last night and washed it as soon as I found it. I then put on some jeans and my Converse and brush out my hair. I had showered earlier, so I let it dry naturally.

When I go downstairs, I let my mom know I'm leaving. She's in the living room watching TV.

"Isn't Ryan going to pick you up here?" she asks me.

"No. I told him I'd meet him at the park," I tell her. It isn't a complete lie.

She nods. "Okay. Call me if you need anything."

I tell her I will and head out the door. The air is nice and it seems like a good day to spend your time outside. But I have somewhere to be, so I continue walking along the sidewalk.

Once I get to the park, I notice Aiden sitting on a bench with his phone in his hands. When he hears me approaching, he looks up and a smirk forms on his face. "It's about time," he says, standing up.

"Shut up." I glance down at my phone. "I'm here on time."

"Okay, let's move on," he says as he starts walking. I catch up with him and walk next to him.

"So, where are we going?" I ask curiously. He just mentioned that he wanted to hang out, but he didn't specify where.

He glances at me and smiles. "It's a surprise."

"Of course, it is," I mumble. We continue walking until we exit the park and start walking near some small shops. After a few minutes of silence, Aiden decides to speak up.

"Why are you quiet?" he asks.

I shrug. "I don't know."

He raises his eyebrow. "You're acting kind of strange, you know that?"

I keep thinking about how I lied to my mom about meeting Ryan to spend time with Aiden. It really sinks in how I'm disobeying her and I find myself smiling. My mom didn't even suspect a thing!

"Now you're really starting to scare me with that smile," Aiden says.

I chuckle. "Sorry. I'm just suddenly in a good mood," I tell him. At that moment, Aiden grabs my hand and I gasp in surprise. I look up at him immediately. "What are you doing?"

He looks at me. "I'm holding your hand. What does it look like I'm doing?"

I look down at our intertwined fingers and glance back up at him. My heart starts racing in my chest. "Why?"

"Well, why can't I? It's a free country, isn't it?" he asks, smirking. I notice that he hardly ever gives me a straight answer.

Aiden ends up taking me to a diner not too far away from the park. We're still holding hands when we walk into the place. We find a booth off to the side and quickly sit down.

"Have you ever been here?" Aiden asks me.

I shake my head and take a glance around the place. It isn't one of those cliché '50s diners. It just has a vintage feel to it. "Have you?" I ask.

He nods. "A few times."

A waitress eventually comes up to us and hands us menus and asks us what we want to drink. She leaves once we tell her what we want.

"So..." Aiden says.

Things are suddenly getting awkward. "So..." I copy him.

"Alex wants you to come by again," he tells me as he leans back in his seat.

"Come by?" I question.

"Yeah, come back to the house," he says.

The waitress gives us our drinks and asks us what we would like to eat.

After ordering, I think about what Aiden said. It won't be so bad if I go back. I didn't really get to know Alex the last time I was there.

"So, what do you say?" Aiden asks me.

I nod. "Okay." I smile at him.

Chapter 28

"This is all your fault." I point to Aiden. "You're the reason I'm *here*." I gesture to the holding cell we were in. I pace around and run my fingers through my hair nervously. This can't be happening.

Aiden has been rubbing his face and staying quiet the whole time. "No," he says, shaking his head. "Would you stop blaming me? You took part in it."

My mom is going to kill—no, *brutally murder* me when she gets here. She's going to know that I lied to her to see Aiden and I'm going to be in even more trouble with her.

And now Aiden is blaming me. "I wasn't the one who drove us—" I stop when Aiden stands up and walks towards me menacingly. I back up and my back hits the wall behind me. Aiden stands dangerously close to me and he looks really scary at the moment.

As much as I'm trying to forget it at this moment, I remember what we had done earlier. My heartbeat accelerates and I find myself blushing. "Get away from me," I say, trying to sound confident.

He frowns and walks up to me. "Or you'll do what?" He challenges me. His face is only inches away from mine and my breath hitches in my throat.

"Riley?" I hear my mother's voice.

***

Five Hours Earlier

We made it to Aiden and Alex's place eventually around noon and walked inside. I remembered my way around as soon as I walked in.

"Aiden is that you?" I heard Alex call out.

"No, it's the Easter Bunny." Aiden rolled his eyes and I chuckled. We walked into the kitchen and found Alex eating a slice of pizza.

Alex smiled when he saw me. "Hey, it's you again."

"Hi," I said awkwardly.

"So now I know what Aiden has been doing all day." He grinned at Aiden. Aiden responded by punching him in the shoulder before heading towards the fridge.

Alex gestured to his pizza. "You wanna slice?"

I shook my head. "No thanks. I ate a while ago." The food at the diner was amazing and I might have overeaten.

I looked at Aiden who's warming up a slice of pizza in the microwave. "You're still hungry?" I asked him, raising my eyebrows. He ate more than me and he's still eating?

He shrugged. "What? You might have a small stomach, but I don't."

I took a seat at the island in the kitchen and rested my hands in front of me. Alex took a seat next to me and looked at me.

"*Tell me about yourself, Riley. Aiden doesn't know how to give details,*" *he said, smiling at me. Is he implying that Aiden talked about me sometimes?*

"*What do you want to know?*" *I asked, smiling back.*

"*Tell him about your obsession with* Star Wars," *Aiden said.*

I shot him a glare. "*It is* not *an* obsession. *I just really like* Star Wars."

"*Nice shirt by the way,*" *Alex said, glancing down at it.* "*Led Zeppelin is the shit.*"

Aiden sat down in front of me and starts to eat the pizza. "*That's where she got the nickname Led Zeppelin Girl. She was wearing it when I first met her.*" *Aiden grinned.*

Hearing him say that makes me all giddy inside. It's nice to know that he remembers the first time we talked.

"*Ah, I see,*" *Alex said sounding amused.* "*That's cute.*"

"*What about you?*" *I asked Alex.* "*Tell me about yourself.*"

Alex put his hand over his heart. "*Oh, I'm not that interesting. My life is quite boring,*" *he said dramatically. I glanced at Aiden and he just shook his head.* "*But since you asked, my name is Alexander Harris, Alex Harris for short. I've lived in this house all my life. My parents moved to Spain and left it to me about two years ago, but they still help with payments and stuff. I'm twenty-one and still single. And*

I also have a part-time job. I don't want you to think I just live off my parents or anything," he explained.

"How did you and Aiden become friends?" I asked curiously.

Aiden groaned. "Don't ask him."

"This story never gets old." Alex laughed.

"Yes, it does," Aiden said.

"Shut the fuck up, Aiden." Alex rolled his eyes. "Anyways, I was taking a walk through the park one day when I noticed two kids fighting on the playground. No one else was around so I decided I should at least try to stop the damn fight. I pulled them apart and yelled at them to go home, like the responsible person I am. The other kid ran off, but Aiden stood directly in front of me and told me to fuck off." Alex started to laugh. "So I started arguing with him. I was seventeen then and there was no way I was going to get told off by a little fourteen-year-old."

Aiden shook his head and chuckles. "I don't know why I stayed friends with this douche bag."

"You should be lucky otherwise you'd have nowhere else to stay," Alex told him.

"I could have just stayed with Riley," Aiden smirked at me.

I scoffed. "And if my mom found out you were staying at my house, she would've skinned you alive."

They both laughed and I smiled. I'm comfortable hanging out with these two. Alex grabbed his and Aiden's plates and walked over to the sink.

"She wouldn't have found out," Aiden said to me, standing up in the process. He walked over to me and leaned

down. He whispered in my ear, "Maybe she would have suspected something if she heard you screaming and moaning my name in the middle of the night."

I gasped quickly and smacked his arm while he laughed and walked away from me. I felt my cheeks heat up instantly at his innuendo.

Aiden rubbed his arm as he sat back down in front of me. "You didn't have to hit so hard."

"Yes, I did." I crossed my arms.

"Well, children, I have to get to work," Alex said to us. "Behave yourselves and don't get into too much trouble."

Aiden smirked. "No promises."

And with that said, Alex left Aiden and me alone in the house. We decided to watch a movie in the living room. Aiden put me in charge of finding a movie while he made us some popcorn.

"No chick flicks and definitely no Star Wars*," Aiden told me.*

I roll my eyes. "Whatever." I search through the DVDs they had and tried to find something good to watch. My eyes landed on a movie and I grin. "What about Harry Po—"

"No," Aiden said as he walked in with a bowl of popcorn.

I pulled out another one. "How about The Dark Knight Rises*?"*

Aiden shrugged. "Sure."

I handed it to him since he knew how to work the DVD player. I sat on the couch and grabbed the bowl of popcorn. Once Aiden got everything set up, he sat down beside me and grabbed a handful of popcorn.

"You're going to eat it all before the movie even starts," I told him.

He didn't answer. The movie started and gained both our attention.

Sometime during the movie, I found myself getting tired. My eyelids started drooping and I struggled to keep them open. I decided I couldn't fight it anymore and I doze off.

"Uh, Riley?" Someone shook me.

I groaned and buried my face deeper into the pillow. Wait. Pillows couldn't breathe. My eyes shot open and I glanced around. I sat up and saw that I had been laying on Aiden. I rubbed my eyes and my gaze landed on him. "How long was I asleep?"

"Well, the movie just ended. I would say about forty or so minutes," he said, shifting on the couch.

"Sorry I fell asleep on you." I laughed slightly. "I didn't feel tired until we started watching the movie."

Aiden smiled. "I guess I can be a good pillow then."

There's a buzzing noise then and I looked at the small table in front of the couch. Aiden's phone was ringing. He picked it up and glanced at it but then threw it to the side of him, ignoring whoever was calling him.

"Who was that?" I asked curiously.

"My dad." He sighed. "He's been calling me lately but I've been ignoring him."

"Aiden, why don't you just talk to him?" I asked him. "Just let him know that you're okay."

He leaned back into the couch. "I just don't want to talk to him right now."

I remembered what Kelly had told me when we hung out that afternoon about her dad. "Maybe you should talk to Ryan," I suggested.

He looked at me like I'm crazy. "Why would I talk to him?"

"Because he's in the same position as you are," I said as I scooted closer to him.

"Yeah right," he mumbled.

I sighed. "You should stop being so stubborn and listen to me. He's having issues with his dad too and I bet talking to him would make things a little easier."

He glanced at me but didn't say anything. His eyes searched my face, making the butterflies in my stomach go crazy. "Maybe I should start calling you Dr. Phil or some shit like that," he said, scooting closer to me.

I chuckled. "I'm no Dr. Phil. I'm just telling you what I think you should do about all of this."

I noticed him leaning closer towards me. "And what do you think I should do right now?" he asked slowly. My breathing slowed down and my heart beats rapidly in my chest.

"I-I don't know." I stuttered.

"I think you do know," he said to me. His eyes flickered to my lips and I felt like my heart was about to leap out of my chest. "Just ask and I'll do it."

I didn't have to ask him what he meant by that. "Kiss me," I find myself saying.

Aiden wastes no time leaning in and connecting our lips. This one is way different than our first one. The first one was short and kind of awkward for me. But this one is longer and definitely more enjoyable.

One of Aiden's hands was on the back of my neck, pulling me closer to him, while the other found its way to my waist. I, however, am not as experienced as he was, but I got the general idea and just go with it.

Aiden ended up pulling me onto his lap and I straddle him. If I'm not so caught up in the kiss, I would have gotten flustered right away. I was slightly out of breath when we pulled away eventually. Our foreheads rest against each other.

My gaze met Aiden's and there's something in his eyes that I couldn't explain. I thought both of us were surprised that we just did that. I was still trying to process everything in my head.

"Riley...I—"

"I'm back!" Alex cut Aiden off, walking into the living room. I quickly moved from Aiden's lap and I blushed furiously. This was the second time Alex had caught us in a suggestive position. He raised his eyebrows and I'm pretty sure he knew we just made out on the couch.

"What are you doing back early?" Aiden asked him right away.

"Things were slow, so the boss man let a few of us go," Alex told us. "Perfect timing though. Jake and Isaiah are coming over later on, just so you know."

I felt so embarrassed at the moment; I couln't even look at either of them. And I couldn't even left since I came here with Aiden.

"I'll just be in my room if you guys need me," Alex said when we didn't answer him. He walked out of the living room.

Once Alex was gone, Aiden turned towards me. "You look like you're going to pass out. Are you okay?"

I nodded. "I'm fine. I'm just..."

"Hot and bothered?" Aiden smirked. I glared at him and smacked his arm for the second time today. "Ow, I was just kidding."

I didn't respond. All I could do was think about the kiss that just happened.

"Okay, I'm just going to be straight up with you," Aiden said suddenly. I finally looked at him and he continued talking. "That was the best kiss I've ever had with someone."

Once again, my face turned red and I looked down at my hands.

"Riley, why are you so embarrassed?" Aiden asked me. "We've kissed before."

"Not like that," I argued back. My heartbeat started to slow down back to its normal pace.

He smirked. "I'm pretty sure Alex knows we kissed."

I nodded but don't say anything.

I heard him sigh. "Listen, Riley," he started. "I'm going to tell you something." And now my heartbeat was going crazy again. "I care about you, Riley. I care more than I should and it kind of scares me."

Yup. I'm pretty sure my heart was going to leap out of my chest.

He looked like he wanted to say more but the doorbell rang through the house and interrupted him. He groaned and immediately stood up. While he's away, I tried to compose myself. No matter how hard I tried, I couldn't stop thinking about that kiss. It just keeps replaying in my head.

I heard Aiden talking to someone, then I heard a third voice. I shifted slightly on the couch when I saw Aiden walked back into the living room with two other guys. One was a tall blonde guy and the other one was about Aiden's height and he had short light brown hair.

"Jake, Isaiah, this is Riley," Aiden told them as I stood up. "And, Riley, this is—"

The blonde one held out his hand. "I'm Jake."

I hesitantly shook his hand. "Hi."

"And I'm Isaiah," the brown-haired one said.

Alex walked into the room and smiled. "I thought I heard you guys."

"We're here to fuck shit up!" Jake exclaimed.

"Dude, watch your language," Isaiah told him then glanced at me. "Sorry for his nonexistent manners."

I shrugged. "I don't mind."

Jake looked at Isaiah. "See? She doesn't mind."

Aiden made his way around them and stood next to me. "So, what were you guys planning on doing?" he asked them.

"What we do every Saturday night." Isaiah grinned.

"Get wasted and pass out wherever." Jake finished for him.

I couldn't imagine getting drunk every Saturday night. I've never even been drunk before. The only alcohol I've tasted was the wine that my mom let me have at a Christmas party last year.

Jake looked at Aiden. "Were you guys going to hang with us?"

Aiden and I looked at each other and he smirked before turning back to them. "I might take this one home. She hasn't had much experience with this kind of stuff."

I frowned when he said that.

"Awe, well, it was nice meeting you, Riley," Isaiah said to me.

"You too." I nodded.

Aiden grabbed my hand and started pulling me away from them.

"See you soon, Riley!" I heard Alex call out before we walked out of the door.

I looked at Aiden as we approached the car. "It seems like you don't want me around now."

We both got into the car and Aiden started it. He sighed as he backed out of the driveway. "It's not like that, Riley," he told me. "When Jake starts drinking, he can turn into a real asshole and I don't want him messing with you."

He sounded very protective.

"Are you really taking me home?" I asked him.

He smirked. "No. I'm not quite ready to give you up yet."

I didn't know why but there was a feeling of butterflies in my stomach when he said that. "So where are we going?"

"I thought we could go see if our names are still on the wall at the library," he told me.

And they still were. Aiden's name was still in the bright pink and my name was in the bright blue. But someone had sprayed painted over the word Outcasts *under our names. And they also put a plus sign in between our names and added* Love *next to my name.*

Aiden + Riley=Love

"Who did that?" I asked incredulously.

"How should I know?" Aiden responded. I noticed he had the black backpack with him. He set it on the ground and opened it up. He pulled out a spray can and walked up to the wall. He looked at me. "Write down something I've said before and I'll do the same." He smiled.

I thought about what he's said that I could put on the wall. I reached into the black bag and pulled out a spray can. Aiden and I wrote at the same time. When we finished, we both took a step back and looked at what each other wrote.

He had written: you're just misguided.

I, on the other hand, had written: don't think.

"When did I say that to you?" I asked, not remembering that at all.

"It was the morning after the wedding when we met at the park and I called myself a screw-up. But you told me I was just misguided." He explains.

I automatically remembered. "I remember now." I nodded.

Aiden smirked when he saw what I had written. "I definitely remember when I said that."

Of course, he does. "So do I." *I nodded as I look at the wall.*

We stayed quiet for a minute or two. Then Aiden spoke up. "Riley, there's something I want to tell you—"

"Hey! What are you two doing?" someone yelled behind us. We both turned immediately and saw an officer walking towards us.

"Riley?" Aiden whispered.

"Yeah?" I squeaked.

"Run!"

***

And that's how we ended up in this stupid holding cell.

I shouldn't have listened to Aiden when he told me to run. Doing that only made us look even more guilty.

The cop had eventually caught Aiden and me and we ended up in the back of the cop car. I was on the verge of hyperventilating since that was my first time basically being arrested.

"Mom." My eyes widen when I see her on the other side of the bars.

Her eyes flicker to Aiden and I can see the rage in them. But she keeps her composure and looks at me. An officer appears at her side and unlocks the cell door.

"You can go now," he tells me.

I hesitantly step out of the cell and the officer shuts it behind me, leaving Aiden alone. I glance at him and he just stares at me.

"Let's go, Riley," my mom says sternly.

I finally look away from Aiden, and my mom and I walk out of the police station. On the way out, we run into Robert and Anna.

"Carol!" Anna says, sounding surprised. "Riley? What are you two doing here?"

My mom stiffens. "It seems Riley and Aiden were caught spray painting on the back wall of the public library together."

I look down, feeling embarrassed.

"Oh, Riley." Anna shakes her head. "When the officer told me he was with another person, I had no idea it would be you."

Her comment makes me angry all of a sudden. "Because I'm supposed to be this perfect straight-A girl, right?" I ask angrily.

Her and Robert both raise their eyebrows at my outburst.

My mom glares at me. "Riley, that is no way to talk to someone."

"I'm going to wait in the car," I say, pushing past her. I walk up to the car and open the passenger door. I slam it as I get in.

I feel my phone vibrate in my pocket and I swiftly pull it out. I have a text from Aiden.

Tell me you don't hate me

I sigh and quickly reply. *I don't hate you*

I see my mom walking towards the car and I immediately shut off my phone. I know she will ask for it as soon as she gets in.

She opens the driver's door and gets in. She holds out her hand. "Phone. Now."

I set it on her palm and wait for the lecture. But she surprises me when she doesn't say anything. She simply turns the key in the ignition and drives us home.

Chapter 29

The suspense is driving me insane.

I don't know why my mom is doing this to me, but I don't find it amusing. Here I am, sitting at the dining table while my mom is just finding things to do or clean the kitchen. Can't she just punish me and get it out of the way? I tried going to my room, but she said she wanted to talk to me.

And there's no talking going on.

"Mom, please just say something already," I say, running my fingers through my hair. "I don't like just sitting here."

She glances at me and then looks down. "Riley, you have no idea how disappointed I am in you," she finally says.

I just want to get this conversation out of the way. "I know, Mom." I lean back in my chair and cross my arms.

"No, you don't know, Riley," she says sternly. "Do you know how nerve-racking it is going to the *police station* to pick up your daughter?"

I stay quiet.

"And you completely disobeyed my orders by going with that Aiden boy." She shakes her head.

I remember what Kelly said that day we walked to the park. "Mom, I'm eighteen. I'm practically an adult now so I can make my own decisions without talking to you about it."

It's her turn to stay quiet now.

"I know you're mad at me for not listening to you, but name another time I didn't listen to you," I tell her. "I'm not an average teenager, Mom. I never went out partying or hanging out with my best friends or anything like that. I don't even have a best friend. But now, I can do that. I have friends and I like hanging out with them."

"You like getting arrested?" She snaps.

I groan. "No, Mom. But it's not like I'm going to go and get myself arrested every weekend. Sure, I made a mistake, but that's the thing. I'm supposed to learn from my mistakes, right?"

She walks out of the kitchen and sits across from me at the dining table. She doesn't say anything, and neither do I. I want to know what she's thinking though.

"You're right," she says, not looking at me. "As much as I hate to admit it, you are right, Riley. I knew you would break out of this shell of yours at some point." She shakes her head. "You don't know how hard it is to realize that your child is growing up and you can't stop it." She looks like she's going to cry.

I sigh. "I'm sorry I acted out. But I have to learn from my mistakes and to do that I have to *make* mistakes."

"I'm not going to punish you," she tells me. "You're eighteen, and you've been old enough to know the difference between right and wrong."

Relief washes through me when she says that. I wasn't sure how she would take my rant.

"So," she says, smiling a bit, "tell me a little bit more about this Aiden."

Oh, God. I wasn't sure if she was going to mention him again and she did. "Why?" I ask hesitantly.

She shrugs. "I've noticed that you've been spending a little bit more time with him more than anyone else and I'm just curious about him. You know I've only heard bad things about him."

I look down at my hands. "He's not as bad as everyone says he is," I tell her. "No one bothers to listen to what he has to say, so they don't understand him."

"Riley," she says, "as long as you trust him, then I'm okay with you being with him. Just promise me I won't have to go and get you from the police station again."

I smile. "I promise."

She reaches into her pocket and pulls out my phone. She then slides it across the table and puts it in front of me. "Here."

"Thanks," I say.

I make my escape to my room and shut the door behind me. I text Aiden and ask him how much trouble he got into. But instead of him texting me back, he ends up calling me.

"Hello?" I answer.

"I think that is the first time you've given me a decent greeting over the phone," he says. "And I didn't get in too much trouble, to answer your question. What about you?"

I sigh. "I got let off the hook."

"Are you serious?" he asks. "So you aren't grounded or anything?"

I lay on my bed and stare at the ceiling. "Nope. I'm eighteen, so my mom technically can't ground me."

"Then we should hang out again tomorrow," he suggests.

I smile. "Did you ever think that we would become friends?" I ask randomly. I never would have thought that I would start hanging out with Aiden Callaway.

"Honestly, I didn't know who you were until that day I dragged you along with me," he admits. "But I'm kind of glad I ran into you."

My smile grows wider. "I guess I'm glad you ran into me too."

"Seriously, Riley," he says, "what would you do without me?"

I laugh. "I bet I could live without you."

"I highly doubt that. You wouldn't have had your first kiss if it weren't for me."

He did *not* just say that. "How do you know?" I challenge.

"I just know."

"You never know. Maybe I would have had my first kiss with Ryan," I tell him. Even though I don't think I can ever see myself kissing Ryan.

"Ryan?" he asks. "Oh please. A kiss from Dixon can't possibly top a kiss from me."

I'm not good at this kind of thing, but that sounded like a challenge. "I guess that would be up to me."

He stays quiet. "I don't want you kissing *Ryan Dixon*."

"You don't want me kissing him?" I ask. Why doesn't he want me to kiss Ryan?

"Hell no," he answers. "Listen, Riley, I don't usually say this but—"

My door suddenly opens and my mom walks in. "Hold on," I tell him quickly.

My mom looks at me. "I'm going to bed, Riley. Don't stay up too late," she says.

I nod. "Okay."

"I'll see you in the morning," she says.

"Good night," I tell her. She then walks out of my room. "Sorry, that was my mom. What were you saying?" I ask.

I hear him sigh. "It's nothing important. Can I see you again tomorrow?"

"Yes, you can."

"Good night, Riley." And he hangs up.

Aiden

You're going to fuck things up, Aiden.

No, I'm not. I'll be fine.

No, you're not. You're never fine.

Am I having a conversation with myself?

"Aiden?"

I shake my head and blink. Alex stands in front of me, looking confused. "Are you okay?" he asks.

I nod. "Yup. Totally fine." *Not.* "Why?"

He frowns at me. "You just seem jittery and it's kind of worrying me."

"I'm fine," I say to him.

"Are you doing anything today?" he asks, changing the subject. "If you want to, we can go to Pancake Alley and pig out."

Pancake Alley is the best diner out there. Their food is just amazing. "As good as that sounds, I can't. I'm going to hang out with Riley today." Even when I say her name, I get goosebumps.

Alex smiles. "Riley?" he asks. "So that's why you're all fidgety."

I don't deny it. But I'm finally going to admit it. "I guess so." I make my way around him and decide to eat some cereal.

"Say it, Aiden." Alex teases. "Just say it out loud."

I pull out the milk and grab a box of cereal. "Say what?"

"Just say that you like the damn girl already! Or tell me you'll ask her to be your goddamn girlfriend or something!" he exclaims.

I chuckle. "Okay." I nod. I take a deep breath and look at him. "I like Riley and I want to ask her to be my girlfriend."

Chapter 30

Riley

After eating breakfast and getting dressed, I sit in the living room watching a show on the *Investigative Discovery* channel. I'm really getting into the show that's on. But, of course, my phone has to go off.

"Hello?" I answer.

"Riley, can you come over right now?"

I glance at my phone. "Ryan?" I ask. "Go over to your house, you mean?"

"Yeah. It's kind of an emergency."

I think about it. Aiden asked me to go over in a while. "Well, I was kind of planning on going over to see Aiden in a bit," I tell him truthfully. "Can I go over later?"

"It'd be great if you could come over right now. But if seeing Aiden is really that important, then it's fine I guess."

I rub my forehead. He's trying to make me feel guilty now, and it's working. "Fine, I'll go over."

"Thanks, Riley."

After I hang up with Ryan, I text Aiden and tell him that I can't go over right away. And exactly one minute after I send the text, I get a call from him.

"Hello?" I answer.

"What do you mean you can't come over right now?" he immediately asks.

I sigh. "Ryan needs me to go over to his house."

"Why?" he asks, sounding irritated.

"He just said it was an emergency," I tell him. "It shouldn't take too long, I don't think." I hear him sigh in frustration and I frown. "Does it really bug you that I'm going over there? I'm just going for a while," I say as I make my way upstairs to put some shoes on.

"Just—" he stops for a moment "—just get over here as soon as you can. I need to talk to you about something."

I locate my Converse in my room as soon as I enter. "Will do."

***

"So what exactly was the emergency?" I ask Ryan as I sit down on the familiar couch in his house. I'm really curious about this "emergency."

Ryan is wearing a dark blue t-shirt and some jeans. It doesn't look like he's going to do anything exciting today. "I know who spray painted the wall with the whole *Aiden + Riley* thing," he tells me.

I raise my eyebrows. I too have been wondering who did that. "How did you know it was there in the first place?" I ask, thinking about it.

"I, uh, heard my mom and Robert talking about it after they picked up Aiden at the police station," he quickly says.

"So, who did it?" I ask him.

"I need you to tell me something before I tell you," he says. "Is that fine?"

I'm sure where he's going with this. "Yeah..." I say.

"I need to know how you feel about Aiden."

Puzzled.

That's the word that describes how I'm feeling right now.

But then I feel the anxiety kick in. I can't tell Ryan that I have a slight crush on Aiden. He might run off and tell Aiden, then my friendship with Aiden can become nonexistent. "He's a good friend," I say.

Ryan rolls his eyes. "Obviously, otherwise you wouldn't hang out with him."

He has a point.

"Do you like him more than a friend?" he questions.

My hands start to get sweaty and I feel a slight blush creep onto my cheeks. "No." My voice is almost inaudible.

Ryan cracks a smile. "Yes, you do."

"Why are you even asking this?" I probe.

"Because," he says, "I want you to know that I'm the one who spray painted the wall."

I stare at him for a moment as I process what he just told me, then I say, "But why?"

Ryan continues to smile. "So Aiden would realize that he likes you more than a friend also."

"What are you cupid or something?" I ask without thinking. "Aiden doesn't like me like that and I don't either." The last part is a lie, of course.

"Please, Riley." He scoffs. "You are such a liar."

I narrow my eyes at him. "Why do you want me and Aiden to admit to liking each other anyway?"

Ryan sighs. "Riley, I don't know what your first impression of me was, but I want you to know that I'm not just some conceited popular guy, okay?" he asks. "I do care about certain things. The reason I'm doing this is because Aiden needs to realize that he can't act like a delinquent forever. He needs to grow up at some point and I think you're just the thing to make him realize that."

Basically, Ryan is convinced that I can change Aiden for the better

"I've talked to Robert," Ryan says, interrupting my thoughts. "He thinks that if Aiden doesn't change a few things about how he lives, then he'll end up losing him more than he already has."

"Are you always the good guy?" I ask Ryan.

"Most of the time." He shrugs. "I have to tell you something though."

"Okay..."

"I told Lucas to hang out with you and send you flowers so Aiden would get jealous."

Seriously? "So Lucas doesn't really like me then?" I ask, feeling hurt and slightly relieved at the same time. I mean, I never liked Lucas like that anyway, but it still hurt that he only hung out with me because Ryan told him too.

Ryan shrugs. "I don't know honestly. But that doesn't matter. What is important is you and Aiden."

I'm about to protest, but he stops me. "Don't deny it, Riley. I already know." He grins.

I sigh. "Fine. I might like him a *little bit*."

"There's one more thing I need to tell you…"

What more can there possibly be?

"I may have told Aiden that I like you more than a friend also. But I need you to remember that I don't really see you that way. I mean, being your friend is good enough for me," he tells me.

"Okay, good. I don't like you like that either," I say to him.

He laughs. "Thanks. Now, there are some things I want to go over with you."

"And those things are?" I ask hesitantly. This is already a lot to take in.

"First thing—" he smiles "—keep Aiden out of trouble as much as possible. Don't tell him you like him or anything, just keep being yourself."

That shouldn't be too hard.

Ryan is still smiling. "I really do think you'll help Aiden in the long run, Riley. You're the perfect thing he needs in his life."

It's weird hearing that from Ryan. I've never been someone who another person needs in their life. Heck, I've never even had a boyfriend before. This is definitely going to be an adventure for me.

Aiden

I tap my fingers on the counter impatiently. Riley had texted me over an hour and a half ago that she would be at Ryan's for a little bit. But it's been more than a little bit and I'm started to get pissed off.

Is she blowing me off for Ryan?

I shake my head.

C'mon, Aiden, this is Riley we're talking about. I bet she can't hurt a fly.

Instead of talking to myself in my head, I decide to take a trip to the store. We need some more groceries in the house anyway, so might as well use this time to do that.

"Alex, I'm going to the store!" I call out as I grab the keys. I feel on edge, so I'm taking sharp turns around the house and end up hitting my leg on the corner of the small table near the couch.

"God dammit." I bend down and rub my leg.

Stupid table. Stupid corner. Stupid me for hitting the damn thing.

I yank open the door and turn to shut it. As soon as I turn around, I collide with something else and lose my footing. I end up falling and taking down whatever I hit.

Whatever it is lands on me and I hear a small squeal.

"Riley?" I ask when I see her lying on me.

Her cheeks tint pink as her eyes meet mine. "Sorry!" she exclaims. "Y-you came out kind of in a r-rush, and I guess I was standing in the way."

I chuckle when I hear her stumble over her words. "It's fine," I say when I notice that she's lying on me. "I don't mind."

She buries her face in her hands which lay on my chest. Amused at her reaction, I just stare at her. I'm kind of hoping that she won't notice my heart beating at an unhealthy rate.

"I'm going to get up now," she mumbles. Before she can sit up, I wrap an arm around her and pull her close.

"Why don't we just stay like this for a minute?" I ask her.

She gives me a small smile. "Because there're ants like two inches away from us and I don't want to get covered in them."

Shit. "Good point." I nod. We both stand up and dust ourselves off. "I have to admit, Summers, I was starting to think that you were blowing me off for Dixon."

"I wouldn't blow you off." She waves her hand. "But where are you going—and in a rush too? It seems like you're the one thinking of blowing me off." She crosses her arms.

Now that we're standing, I have to look down slightly at her since I'm taller. I end up laughing. "You look like a small child."

"Don't change the subject," she says to me. "You were just leaving."

I sigh. "Well, thinking that you weren't going to show up, I decided that I was going to head to the store to get some groceries," I explain.

"Oh." Her arms drop to her sides. "I'll go then. I don't want to be a bother—"

I cover her mouth with my hand and push her towards the car. "Just get in the car, Riley. You're coming with me."

Riley

"So what do you need to buy?" I ask Aiden curiously as we enter the supermarket. I glance around at the familiar store then look at Aiden.

"First things first, we need milk. We can't have cereal without milk," he says as he grabs a basket and starts walking with it.

I walk alongside him as we make our way to the dairy section. "We, as in you and Alex?" I question.

He grins. "We as in me, Alex, and you. You're staying over at my place tonight."

I feel butterflies in my stomach as soon as those words leave his mouth. Stay over at his house? I've never actually spent the night at a non-family members' house before. "Um, when was this decided?" I ask hesitantly.

We approach the milk gallons and Aiden grabs one from one of the shelves. "Just now. We're close friends, right? And close friends stay at each other's houses"—he steps in front of me—"right?"

I gulp as his gaze meets mine. "I don't know how my mom would feel about—"

"You're eighteen, aren't you?" he asks as we start down another aisle. "C'mon, Riley. You gotta live a little."

I guess he has a point. I am eighteen and I already had this talk with Kelly. "Yeah, but I mean, it's *your* house," I mutter.

We're passing the cereal section when Aiden stops and grabs a box of Cinnamon Toast Crunch. "What, are you afraid you might not be able to control yourself around me?" he asks, sounding amused.

I hit his arm. "You are so full of yourself." I shake my head. "It's unhealthy."

He chuckles. "I've just learned to love myself." He smiles. "And you should do the same."

I think about it. I guess I'm happy with myself. I can be a little more confident, but I won't say I'm really insecure or anything. "Anyways, what else do you need?" I change the subject.

"All the unhealthy junk food," he says seriously.

"Ah, of course." I nod.

"Alex can't live without those Little Debbie Cosmic Brownies," he explains. "He goes mad when we run out."

I laugh at that. I admit those brownies are amazing. But I can live without them if I have to. "What about you? Is there something sweet you can't live without?" I ask as I glance at all the small cakes and cupcakes around us.

"Do *you* count as something sweet I can't live without?"

I whirl around and face him. But he's too busy grabbing a box of Hostess cupcakes to notice me looking at him. "What?" I stupidly ask.

He grins. "Never mind."

Aiden gets a few more things and tosses them into the basket. We get in line at one of the registers and Aiden pays.

As soon as the bags are put in the car, we both get in and drive back to the house.

"So, do you want me to drop you off at home to get a change of clothes?" Aiden asks as he drives.

"For what?" I ask.

"You're staying over, remember?" He raises his eyebrow.

Once again, the butterflies fill my stomach. "Um…"

He covers my mouth with his hand and smirks. "I'll take that as a yes."

Chapter 31

I return home after the interesting shopping trip with Aiden. Deciding that I want to have a fun night, I end up lying to my mom and tell her I will be with Kelly. To be safe, I inform Ryan about the little white lie and he assures me he will back me up if anything happens. To say I'm nervous for tonight is an understatement. I'm completely and utterly terrified. It feels as if I have pterodactyls in my stomach instead of butterflies.

I arrive at Aiden's house once again. As I approach the door, Aiden swings it open before I can even reach out to knock.

"Are we excited for tonight?" Aiden asks as I enter the house.

I laugh. "It seems you are. How did you know I was at the door?"

"We have cameras everywhere. There's no hiding anything around here." He smirks. "I might have peeked out the window at the right time."

"Sure." I nod. My overnight bag is instantly taken from me by Aiden and is put on the couch. Without saying a word, Aiden makes a beeline for the kitchen. I follow, wondering if he's joining Alex.

Walking into the kitchen, Alex's grin is the first thing I see. "Riley!" he exclaims. His arms open wide for a hug. Once I'm close enough, he engulfs me in his embrace. "How are you today?" he asks.

I notice the comparison between Alex and a typical mom. "I'm fine," I say, pulling away from him while feeling a bit awkward.

Alex continues to smile as he glances at Aiden. They stay silent for a moment as if they're having a silent conversation. Aiden tears his gaze away first and walks towards the fridge.

"When Aiden told me you were going to stay with us, I decided to make dinner." Alex beams.

"I didn't know you cook." The words spill from my mouth before I can stop them.

Alex smirks. "There are a lot of things you don't know about me, Riley. And yes, I can cook."

"Alex can't cook for shit," Aiden adds in his opinion. He closes the fridge and hands me a water bottle. "He lives in a fantasy world where he thinks he can be the perfect housewife."

I chuckle while Alex looks appalled. "I can cook!" Alex then looks at me. "Don't listen to him. I can make a mean macaroni and cheese."

Aiden and I laugh at Alex. I'm laughing next to him. I'm not much of a cook myself. Though my mom has shown me a few tricks in the kitchen, I don't think I could make a full-blown dinner.

"Which is exactly what I'm going to make. You don't mind macaroni, do you?" Alex asks.

I shake my head. "I don't mind at all."

"Great." He grins. "Why don't you and Aiden go watch TV while I start it then?"

"You sound like a parent." Aiden shakes his head like he can't believe his ears.

Alex shoos us out of the kitchen and into the living room. A particular memory involving Aiden and me, plus the couch, makes me blush. Aiden ends up plopping himself on the couch and makes himself comfortable. I sit on the smaller couch and *try* doing the same thing.

Aiden has the remote in his hands, flipping through the channels when he glances at me. "Why are you all the way over there?"

"Is it illegal to sit here?"

Aiden smiles and sits up. He stands up from the couch and makes his way over to the other side of the smaller couch. His legs find themselves on mine as he lays back. I stare at him for a moment.

"Riley," he says softly but never looking at me. "Are you checking me out?"

My cheeks warm and I look away. "No."

He chuckles and finally settles on a channel. I hardly pay attention to the TV though. Aiden moves himself so he's sitting directly next to me while he puts his arm around me. "I knew you couldn't control yourself around me," he whispers, his breath tickling my ear.

I inch away but hold my ground. "You obviously can't control yourself around me. Otherwise, you wouldn't have put your arm around me."

His eyes widen and I notice his grin is a bit wider this time. "I like this side of you. It's fun when you talk back." There's a ringing sound and Aiden reaches into his front pocket. With a quick glance at his screen, I see that Nicole is calling him. He stands up and sighs. "Let me take this real quick." He walks into a hallway and I hear his muffled voice answer the phone.

Disappointment builds up inside me, and I sink back into the couch. Aiden knows I'm not on solid ground with Nicole and vice versa. Does he have real feelings for her if he's willing to talk to her while I'm with him?

Of course, the voice in my head responded. *How could I have convinced myself that he had the slightest bit of feelings for me?*

I don't want to wait for Aiden to come back. Instead, I find myself walking towards the kitchen to talk to Alex to take my mind off it. When Alex comes into view, he's standing over the stove and turning one of the dials. "Hey." He smiles. "Where's Aiden?"

"On the phone." I sit in one of the bar stools. I rest my chin on my left hand and glance out the kitchen window. The sun is setting, leaving a beautiful orange glow outside.

"Aiden told me you've been hanging around his step-bro recently," Alex says suddenly.

My gaze is back on him, and I shrug. "We've gotten a bit close these past few weeks."

"Do you like him?" he asks, raising an eyebrow.

Aiden graces us with his presence again. His eyes land on me then flicker to Alex. "What are we talking about in here?" he asks as he makes his way next to me. "Gossiping?" He smirks.

"About Ryan." Alex pretends to gush while fanning himself. "His eyes! Oh, his eyes!" He bats his eyelashes.

Aiden scoffs and looks at me. "Why him?"

"Why not?" I challenge him.

"Don't worry, Riley. We can finish our discussion later." Alex winks at me.

***

"Aiden, think about your choices here." Alex pleads. "You've known me longer. That counts for something right?"

I roll my eyes at Alex. The drama queen is totally playing the part. "Alex, stop being such a drama queen. Aiden obviously wants to watch what I want to watch."

Aiden's cheeks turn a light shade of pink, which raises a whole lot of questions in my mind. But we have something at stake here. I want to watch a scary movie while Alex wants to watch an action film.

We leave it up to Aiden to choose the movie. He glances between each movie which we hold in our hands. "I don't know…why can't we just pick a movie we all agree on?"

"It's not that simple!" Alex exclaims. "Just pick one, Callaway!"

Aiden covers his eyes with one hand and with the other, he points to the movie in Alex's hand.

"*No!*"

"*Yes!*"

My arms fold across my chest as I sit back on the smaller couch. Alex smirks as he puts the disk in the DVD player.

Aiden, once again, sits next to me. I inch away, but he only scoots closer. I soon run out of room on my side. "Do you mind?" I ask, narrowing my eyes at him.

"Not really." He shakes his head.

Alex makes himself comfortable on the bigger couch. He glances at Riley and grins at her before looking back at the TV.

Aiden rests his chin on my shoulder. "Why do I get the feeling you're mad at me?"

"I'm not mad."

"Don't lie to me, Riley," he says in a more serious tone. "You're obviously ticked off about something. And I have the feeling it's not because I chose Alex's movie over yours."

Alex sighs. "Can you two, at least, whisper? Please?"

Aiden ignores Alex. "What's wrong?"

"Why don't you go ask Nicole what's wrong?"

Aiden runs a hand through his hair and lets out a long sigh. "That's what's bothering you?" I stay silent with my focus on the TV. "She won't leave me alone, Riley. I don't know how Ryan put up with her. She keeps calling me and texting me."

I glance at him. "That's your own fault."

Soon, he leaves my side and yanks me off the couch. "Come on," he mumbles. Alex is too entertained by the movie to notice we're exiting the living room and entering the hallway. Aiden stops when we're at the end of it, out of earshot from Alex. He pushes me against the wall and closes the distance between our bodies.

"What are you doing?" My voice is barely audible. I suddenly feel lightheaded.

He smirks. "This." His lips meet mine, surprising me. His hands plant themselves on my hips while my own rest on his chest. I can feel his heart beating rapidly in his chest, which makes mine beat faster. The kiss starts off soft, but Aiden pushes himself harder against me, and the kiss becomes rougher. He lets out a small groan.

My insides are on fire, and the pterodactyls in my stomach are flying around frantically. Aiden's fingers hooks around the belt loops on my pants and tugs on them. My hands travel up around his neck and into his hair, where I give a little yank. Aiden breaks the kiss and smiles at my small gesture. His lips kiss my jawline and down my neck while my eyes remain squeezed shut. He leaves a trail of kisses down my neck before I feel them on my ear.

"You're absolutely amazing." He's out of breath.

"I guess I could say the same about you."

His low chuckle makes me smile. His hands cup my cheeks and he places kisses all over my face. "Should we go back?" I nod mutely. He pulls away and grabs my hand. We walk back into the living room, where Alex gives us the side-eye.

"What were you two up to?" he asks, though I'm pretty sure he knows what we were doing.

Aiden smiles as we sit down on the small couch. "None of your business."

***

"C'mon, Riley. Don't you trust me?" Aiden asks me as he sits on his bed.

"I do," I say, trying to convince myself. "I-I've just never slept in the same bed with a guy before."

Aiden throws himself back and stares at me. "I'm not going to do anything. I have more respect than that, you know."

He wants me to sleep in here with him instead of the couch in the living room. "Why don't I just sleep on the floor?" I suggest. "I know how much you want me in here."

A grin sprouts on his face. "You know me so well." He sits up and makes his way towards the edge of the bed. He grabs my hands and looks at me seriously. "Just get under the covers," he says. "before I make you."

"And how are you going to make me?" I instantly regret asking.

Aiden pulls me forward and I land on the bed next to him. We struggle a bit and I end up on top of him.

"This works, don't you think?" He smirks.

I roll off him and sit on the bed. I play with the hem of my Red Hot Chili Peppers pajama shirt.

"What are you thinking?" Aiden asks as he puts his chin on my thigh.

I shrug. There are various thoughts running through my mind. "This is weird for me."

He sighs. "You don't trust me."

"I'm really sorry, Aiden." I hang my head. "I'm not used to making out with guys in hallways and sleeping in the same bed as them. I guess I'm not like everyone. I'm not normal."

At that, he picks himself up and sits directly in front of me. "There is no such thing as normal, Riley. Plus, I knew you weren't normal the second you opened your mouth that day I ran into you." He smiles teasingly. "And I'm glad you aren't used to this. I don't want to think about you spending the night with any other guy but me."

I stay silent but my heart beating in my chest is so loud I'm sure he can hear it.

"You're special, Riley. I'll go at the pace you want to go. I will never force you to do anything you're not comfortable with," he says.

"Thank you," I mumble as my cheeks grow warm.

He grins at me. "Riley, I want to ask you something..."

Aiden's next question has my mind racing and my heart beating at an unhealthy rate. I have never known this feeling before, but I know it's a good feeling and I like it a lot. I also know that I don't want this moment to end.

Chapter 32

Aiden

Sunlight seeps through the blinds in my room, indicating that it's already morning. I groan slightly and move around in my bed. I turn my body and I come face to face with a sleeping Riley. A smile instantly lands on my lips.

I study her features. Her bottom lip sticks out, making it look as if she's pouting. Her hair is sprawled out all over the pillow beneath her head. I honestly can't believe that I would end up falling for a girl like Riley.

She frowns in her sleep and moves around a bit. She yanks on the blankets, stealing the part covering me. I decide to mess with her and yank back. Her frown deepens as she yanks harder on the blankets. A laugh escapes my mouth as I watch her. Her eyes flutter open and they land on me. She yawns and then smiles.

"Good morning," I tell her.

"Morning," she says sleepily. She rubs her eyes and I scoot closer to her. "You were yanking the blankets from me," she says.

I chuckle. "You did it first."

"Well, you hogged all the blankets last night," she tells me.

"Sorry." I shrug. "I don't share blankets."

She grins. "I don't either."

"Well, that'll be a problem. As my girlfriend, you have to stay over more often," I tell her.

She closes her eyes and buries half her face into the pillow. "This girlfriend thing is hard."

I laugh. "How? You just continue being yourself, except you show your *undying affection* for me."

She's the one to laugh this time. "How do you know it's an undying affection?"

"Because I have an everlasting liking for you, so you must have an undying affection for me." I point out. "It's only logical."

She sighs. "If you say so."

I lean forward and kiss her forehead. "I'm lucky to have a girl like you in my life," I say truthfully.

"I guess I'm lucky to have a guy like you in my life then," she says, looking into my eyes.

"You guess?" I ask, amused. I can tell she's not a morning person.

She smiles and rolls her eyes. "You know what I mean."

I rub my chin. "Hmm, I'm afraid I don't know what you mean."

She groans, and I laugh. She sits up and leans against the headboard of the bed. It actually feels normal being like this with her. It feels like she always comes over to sleep in my bed and we're both used to it.

"You know, since you've slept in my bed, it's only fair that I sleep in yours," I comment as I sit up too.

Riley scoffs. "And if my mom sees you? I'll never hear the end of it."

"You're not acting like my girlfriend, Riley."

She holds her hands up in defense. "I told you, I'm new at this kind of stuff!"

I laugh at her and put my arm around her. "It's fine. Riley." I then release her from my grasp, and I stand up. "Want breakfast?"

"You can cook?" she questions.

I shrug. "I can't exactly cook, but I can make eggs and bacon."

She smiles. "Sounds good to me!" She hops out of the bed and we both walk to my bedroom door. I grab her hand before we exit.

Riley

Mondays are always awful. I wake up, and I don't want to go to school, but I kind of have to go.

Before I walk through the main entrance, I receive a text from Aiden.

I wish I could wake up with you beside me every morning :(

That manages to make my Monday a lot better. I feel the butterflies in my stomach, and I smile to myself as I make my way to my locker. Of course, me being clumsy, I succeed in bumping into someone.

"Sorry!" I say out of instinct.

My eyes immediately meet Nicole's gaze, and she sneers at me. "Well, look who it is. The nerdy whore."

I frown. I'm not going to deal with her today. "Speak for yourself," I retorted.

She raises her eyebrow. "Excuse me?"

Instead of responding, I walk around her. But she ends up grabbing onto my arm and yanking me back. "Don't walk away from me when I'm talking to you bitch." She seethes. "I heard you're dating Aiden now. Did he tell you he called me yesterday and asked me to go over to his house?" She smirks.

Don't listen to her Riley. She's just messing with you.

"I highly doubt that," I tell her, rolling my eyes.

"It's true," she says as she crosses her arms. "He said you were never going to be enough for him. You don't know anything about pleasuring a guy." She steps closer to me.

My hands clench into fists as I stare at her. "That's because I'm not a *slut* like you." I snap at her.

She doesn't even flinch. She actually looks amused. "You and Aiden won't last. Not as long as I'm around," she says. "You ruined my relationship with Ryan, and now I'm going to ruin yours with Aiden. Payback is a bitch, don't you think?"

"Just like you." I keep my hands at my sides.

She smirks. "You really suck at insulting someone you know. I don't know why I waste my time talking to you when I could be screwing Aiden right now."

That does it.

I lunge at her, and we both fall onto the ground. Nicole ends up on top and starts to yank at my hair and also throws in a few slaps and punches. But I'm not going to let her win this time. I'm sick and tired of her crap, and I release all my anger on her.

A crowd forms around us, but that doesn't distract me from trying to pull Nicole's perfect hair from her head. She digs her nails into my shoulders, and I reach out and slap her as hard as I can. She punches my left cheek. I ignore the pain and try to punch back.

I instantly feel someone pull me off her. I try to get out of their grasp, but I can't. Someone is also holding Nicole back.

"What is going on here?" A voice booms through the hallway.

I flinch and my arms fall to the side. The vice principal, Mr. Hawk, is standing there with his hands on his hips. He looks beyond angry.

"She attacked me!" Nicole automatically points at me.

"I did not!" I lie. "Okay, maybe I did, but she's been bullying me for weeks now!" I exclaim.

Whoever is holding me lets go and I catch a glimpse of who it is. It's Aiden. He looks at me with a small frown on his face. I turn away and see that Ryan had been the one to take Nicole away from me. She pushes him away once she sees it's him.

"Both of you, to my office. Now," Mr. Hawk says, sounding aggravated. "Mr. Dixon, Mr. Callaway, I suggest you move along to your first period classes."

Aiden looks at me before he leaves down the hallway with Ryan.

***

"And out of nowhere, she comes and attacks me like a mad person. I was just minding my own business when she did this." Nicole finishes her lie.

I roll my eyes. That was not what happened.

Mr. Hawk sits back in his chair and glances at me. "What's your side, Ms. Summers?"

"Nicole has been verbally attacking me for weeks now," I say, truthfully. "She's called me many names, and I got tired of hearing this crap from her. I'll admit I was the one who jumped at her, but it was because I'm sick of her bullying me like this."

Mr. Hawk then sits forward and clasps his hands together on his desk. "I'll tell you what, I'll have the security guards review the security cameras to see what really happened."

"Security cameras?" Nicole asks suddenly.

I want to smile. The cameras will show that Nicole lied about me randomly attacking her out of nowhere.

"But for now, I'm giving you after school detention today, which is from 3:35 to 4:45," he explains. I cross my arms but don't argue with the punishment.

"But, Mr. Hawk—" Nicole tries to pipe in.

He holds his hand up. "I don't want to hear it. You two failed to follow the rules, and now you are receiving the punishment."

"Are we going to detention just for today?" I ask curiously.

He nods. "We'll call you both into the office tomorrow after we've reviewed the tapes, then you will both receive the punishment you really deserve."

I internally groan. Can't they just send me home? I'm not one to really care about my looks, but my face is probably bruised and swollen, and I just want to sleep.

***

After the dreaded after school detention, I finally get home. I want to go straight to bed, but the school had called my mom and told her what happened. So now I'm getting a lecture from her.

"Riley, I just don't know what I'm going to do with you." My mom shakes her head. "Fighting? At school?" she asks, rubbing her temples.

"Mom, Nicole has basically been bullying me. Those times I came home claiming I wasn't feeling good were just lies. Nicole's words got to me, and I just wanted to leave school," I tell her. "I got tired of hearing crap from her."

She put her hands on her hips. "And going to a counselor or talking to me about it wouldn't have solved it?"

I shake my head. "Not really. That would've made it worse." I place my head in my hands. This conversation is going nowhere.

"Do you mind telling me what this girl has been saying to you?"

I really don't want to go too deep into this, but it looks like I don't have a choice. "She thinks it's my fault that Ryan broke up with her."

She raises her eyebrow. "Anna's Ryan?"

I nod. "He found out that she was harassing me and he broke it off with her. So ever since then, she's been calling me a whore and a slut and claiming that I stole him from her."

My mom sighs. "Riley, when someone starts talking that way about you, fighting them isn't the answer."

"It seemed like it at the moment," I mumble.

"I'm not going to punish you," she says to me. "But if you are ever in another situation like this, promise me you'll be the bigger person and just walk away."

I sigh. "I promise. Can I take a nap now?"

She shakes her head. "There's one more thing I would like to talk to you about."

I mentally groan. I just want to sleep. Today was a long day and I need rest. "Okay," I say.

She gave me a small smile. "I know you didn't spend the night with Kelly on Saturday."

Oh no! Busted!

"Um…" I don't know what to say.

"Riley, I know about you and Aiden," she says.

I rub my face. "I'm sorry, Mom. I promise I won't lie to you about it again. Aiden really wanted me to stay over and I kind of wanted to stay also. But I swear nothing bad happened. The only thing that happened was him asking me to be his girlfriend, and that's it," I ramble on.

My mom grins. She actually *grins*. "Riley, it's fine." She laughs slightly. "I know you're smart enough to make the right choices. I just want you to be careful. I also want you to know that you don't have to keep all these secrets from me. I'm your mom. I'm here for any advice you need."

I stand up from my spot at the table and go around to hug her. I squeeze her tightly and tell her I love her.

When we pull away from each other, she looks at me and smiles. "I want you to invite Aiden over for dinner sometime. I want to get to know the boy my daughter really likes."

I smile and nod. "Will do."

***

I sit in my bed and call Aiden. I try falling asleep, but my mind keeps buzzing from everything that happened today. I decide to call Aiden since I didn't really see him during the day.

"Hey, beautiful," he answers after two rings.

I look at my face that has a bruise on the left cheek. There are also scratch marks along the side of my face. "I look far from beautiful, especially after what happened today."

"You're always beautiful to me," he comments. "I will have you know that you did some pretty good damage to

Nicole's face too. Who knew you had it in you Led Zeppelin Girl?"

I smile. "I told you, don't mess with me."

He chuckles. "So, how much trouble did you get in with your mom?"

"Surprisingly, I didn't get punished. The only thing she told me was that she wants to have you over for dinner sometime."

"She knows about us?" he asks.

"I guess." I lay back on my bed. "She also knows that I was at your house Saturday night and she was fine with it."

He whistles. "Well damn. You do realize that you're going to be staying at my house more often then, right?"

I find myself grinning. "If you say so. As long as you come over to my house for dinner, so my mom won't bug me too much about it."

"I would love to go over for dinner. Tonight isn't a good night, but I'm free whenever," he says.

"I'll ask later. I'm getting sleepy," I say as I close my eyes.

"Get some rest, Riley. I'll pick you up in the morning," he tells me.

I sigh. "Okay."

That night, I dream of Aiden, Led Zeppelin concerts, and smashing Nicole's face into a brick wall.

Chapter 33

Ryan

I walk through the front doors of the school and make my way towards my locker. I had asked Riley if she needed a ride to school this morning, but she turned down my offer. So I'm at school a little earlier than usual.

I greet a few people who are in the halls. Once I'm at my locker, I open it and prepare for the day.

"Hey, Ryan." I feel someone put their hand on my arm.

I sigh when I hear the voice. "Nicole, what are you doing?" I stare at her hand on my arm still. I didn't sleep well last night and I'm tired and don't want to deal with people today. Especially people like Nicole.

"What? I can't say hi to an *old ex-boyfriend?*" She smiles. I can't see the bruises on her face from her fight with Riley, but that's probably because she's packed on the makeup to cover it up.

I pull my arm away from her. "Nicole, I told you, things aren't going back to the way they were." I really wish she will just get the hint.

"Why not? Things were fun." She tries slipping her arms around me. I slightly push her away and shut my locker. She instantly frowns. "It's because of that nerd girl, isn't it? You like her don't you?" she demands from me.

My eyebrows knit together. "We're friends, Nicole. And it's because of how you were treating her, along with everyone else," I tell her. "Don't you ever get tired of being a bitch to everyone?"

She scowls at me as soon as I say it. "You're an asshole, Ryan."

"Then why do you keep coming back?" I question.

She flicks her hair over her shoulder, turns around, and walks away. I sigh in relief.

Thank God that's over.

I walk in the opposite direction of Nicole and head for Riley's locker. As soon as her locker comes into view, I notice her standing in front of it, with Aiden next to her. He says something, making her smile and laugh a little. He then leans down and kisses her cheek, and I notice her cheeks turn a bright pink.

I walk up to them and grin. "Well, look at the happy couple," I comment.

Riley looks at me and smiles. "Hey, Ryan."

"Dixon." Aiden nods. I know Aiden still doesn't like me, but he'll just have to get over it since we are stepbrothers.

"So, your face looks healed up," I tell Riley. "How badly did you get punished for fighting Nicole?" I ask curiously.

"They reviewed the tapes and decided she would get a bigger punishment that I would. I just have after school detention for three days." She shrugs. "I don't know what her punishment was though."

I kind of feel proud of Riley for defending herself against Nicole. "Good for you then," I tell her. "And just so you know, most people are saying you won that fight."

She grins from ear to ear and looks up at Aiden. He smiles down at her, and I notice something different about him. It isn't appearance-wise, but something is definitely different.

He's completely in love with her. Sure, he's liked her for a while, but now you can see that this is something more.

Alex

"Come have some drinks with us tonight! It's guy's night!" Isaiah exclaims through the phone.

I chuckle at him. "Dude, I have work tomorrow—"

"Fuck work! Come hang out with us." I hear Jake yell in the background.

I look at the time and shake my head even though they can't see me. "You guys have fun. I'm staying in," I say, resuming flipping through the channels on TV.

My conversation ends with Isaiah right when I hear the front door open. Aiden comes into view and throws his backpack onto the floor. He jumps onto the couch and sighs in a good way.

"I guess you had a good day?" I raise my eyebrow. Riley has had a really positive effect on Aiden. I definitely approve of her for Aiden.

"You could say that." He smirks.

Who would have thought Aiden would like a girl like Riley. It surprised me when he brought her over the first time. But I'm glad he's found a girl like her. "You really like her, don't you?"

I notice him frown. "Obviously, I do. Otherwise, she wouldn't be my girlfriend."

I shake my head. "You don't understand what I'm saying. You *really* like her." It's so noticeable.

He raises his eyebrows. "Are you asking if I'm in love with her?"

I nod slowly.

He sits up on the couch and shrug. "I don't know."

He is. I know he's in love with her. But I don't think him nor Riley realizes it yet.

Aiden pulls out his phone suddenly and holds it up. "The girlfriend calls." He walks out of the living room and down the hall to his room.

I got him to confess his feelings for her. I'm pretty sure I can get him to admit he's in love with this girl.

Aiden

"I don't know, Riley..." I scratch the back of my head nervously. "What if she doesn't think I'm good enough for you?"

Riley is calling me to tell me that I still have to go over to her house for dinner some time to meet her mom. I tell her I will eventually, but I will admit that it is a little nerve-racking. I mean, I've met her mom before, but I didn't actually have a conversation with her. And not to mention that it was *my* fault that we got thrown in a holding cell after spray painting the wall.

"Oh please." I can imagine her rolling her eyes. "I'm sure she'll like you."

"What if I say something stupid and she doesn't want you with me anymore?" I question. We just got together; I don't want anything threatening our relationship. Especially since I really, *really* like Riley.

I hear her sigh. "She can't drive us apart you know."

I lay back on my bed and stare at the ceiling. "Okay. What day should I go over?" I find myself asking.

"Is Thursday okay?"

"Sounds good," I confirm. So it's done. I will be going over for dinner at the Summers' house Thursday night.

My phone beeps in my hand and I glance at the screen. "Seriously?"

"What?" Riley ask.

"My dad is calling me," I say shaking my head.

"Talk to him." She urges me. "I'm sure he'd be glad that you actually answered."

I sit up again. "I'm going to ignore the call."

"No, you're not." There's a click after she says that. I look at my phone and realize she hung up on me.

Of course, she will make me talk to him.

I groan and answer the call from my dad.

"Hello?" I ask slowly.

I hear him clear his throat. "Aiden."

"Dad."

"Uh, Anna and I were talking, and we want you to come over for dinner sometime this week."

My eyebrows shoot up upon hearing this. They actually want me to go over? "Um, what day were you guys planning this?" I ask curiously. I pace around my room as I speak with him.

"We were thinking Thursday or Friday."

"I can't do Thursday. I have plans," I say. I'm not going to blow off Riley and her mom.

"Then Friday?" he asks.

I purse my lips and sigh. "Can I bring a friend?" I'm not going without Riley.

"Sure."

After an awkward goodbye, I hang up with him. I think about the rest of the week, and I'm sure it will be interesting. Hopefully, things will turn out well when I meet Riley's mom. I wring my hands together nervously.

I've never met a girl's parents before. Will her mom like me? Will Riley tell her dad about us?

I rub my face and take a deep breath. I'm genuinely anxious about all of this. But I know it will be worth it.

Because I really, *really* like Riley.

Chapter 34

Riley

I'm actually excited for dinner tonight. I know my mom will like Aiden when she really gets to know him. I also know that Aiden is nervous about this evening. He doesn't say it out loud, but I can tell.

My mom is in the kitchen preparing a meal. She said dinner is a surprise, so I'm banned from the kitchen this evening. The aroma of food floats through the house and it smells delicious.

I'm sitting on the couch watching TV when the doorbell rings. I make my way to the front door and open it.

Standing there is Aiden, of course. He's wearing dark jeans with a black button down shirt. I smile when I see him.

"Hi." I grin.

He walks up to me and wraps his arms around my waist. "Led Zeppelin Girl." There's a small hint of cologne emitting from him. He smells heavenly.

"Is that Aiden?" I hear my mom ask from inside the house. I pull away from Aiden and pull him inside. My mom comes out from the kitchen and smiles when she sees Aiden and me. "Hello, Aiden," she greets. "I'm Carol, but we've met before, right?"

He nods slowly. "Yes, we have."

I'm not sure if she's referring to when he took me home that day after we spray painted our names on the library wall, or when we got put in a holding cell.

My mom smiles either way though. "Well, dinner is just about done. If you guys don't mind, can you set the table?"

"Sure." I nod. I grab Aiden's hand and pull him into the kitchen. We take out the napkins and the silverware then make our way back to the dining room. My mom stays in the kitchen to make sure everything is perfect.

"It's going pretty well so far, don't you think?" I ask as I lay out three napkins on the table.

He nods. "I think so. Do you think she'll grill me with questions though?" he asks as he puts the silverware on the table.

I don't think my mom will be too tough on him. "I think you'll survive."

Aiden walks around the table and stands in front of me. I look up at him. "I should've asked this yesterday," he says. "But I forgot, so I'm going to ask you now."

"What's wrong?" I ask, frowning a bit.

"Do you want to have dinner with me, my dad, and Anna tomorrow night?" he asks me.

I smile. "Sure." I feel happy for Aiden. I'm glad he decided to actually meet up with his dad. "Will Kelly and Ryan be there also?" I ask curiously.

He shrugs. "I don't know."

"Who's hungry?" my mom asks as she enters the dining room from the kitchen. She has a big plate in her hands. She sets it gently on the table and smiles to herself.

So the mystery dinner is chicken and rice. Simple but delicious.

"I am," Aiden answers her.

"Good." She grins. "I made plenty. Now, go wash up and I'll serve us."

We walk into the kitchen and wash our hands together. Aiden decides to be funny and put bubbles on my nose, so I put bubbles on his cheek too while we laugh at each other. We clean up and go back to the dining room.

Dinner turns out really well. My mom asks him a few questions about school and such. It turns slightly awkward when she asks about his family.

He visibly swallows and looks at her. "What would you like to know?" he asks politely.

"I know your father is married to Anna now, but what about your mom? If you don't mind me asking, of course," she adds in when I slightly glare at her.

"Mom, I don't—" I start to say but Aiden interrupts me.

"It's fine." He squeezes my hand then looks back at my mom. "She, um, she died of cancer when I was seven," he says.

I can see her shoulders slump slightly. "Oh, Aiden honey, I'm sorry. I wouldn't have asked if I had known…"

"It's fine." He shrugs.

"Well," my mom says, "I'm going to be honest with you, Aiden. I didn't like the idea of Riley hanging around you at first. But I understand why now. I didn't know your mom but I know every mom loves to see her child grow and find someone who makes them happy."

He grins. "Thank you. And I know for a fact that she would have loved Riley." He glances at me and winks. I smile and look away.

After saying goodbye to my mom, Aiden walks out to the car. I walk alongside him.

"I wish I still lived down the road." Aiden sighs. "Then you could walk me to my house instead of just walking me to the car."

I smile. "You make it sound as if this is the last time I'll see you."

"It will be the last time I see you today." He points out.

I chuckle. "I'll see you tomorrow, Aiden. Everything will be all right."

He slips his arms around my waist and pulls me closer to himself. "So you think your mom liked me?" he asks as he looks into my eyes.

Of course, she liked him. "I think she loved you." I grin. "Do you think your dad will like me?"

"Haven't you met him before?"

I shrug. "Kind of. But I've only had one conversation with him that time we took wedding pictures."

"Well, I don't care if he likes you or not," he says, squeezing me tighter against him. "I'm crazy about you and that's all that matters."

My heart flutters upon hearing those words leave his mouth. I wrap my own arms around him and hug him. "Can I tell you something?" I ask him.

"Go ahead."

"I think my mom is watching us through the kitchen window," I say as I pull away from him. He smiles and laughs slightly.

"Until tomorrow," he says as he opens the car door. After I wave to him, he drives off and disappears down the road.

When I enter the house again, I find my mom washing dishes in the kitchen.

"Need help?" I offer.

"Sure," my mom says.

I grab a towel and start to dry and put away the dishes she already washed and rinsed. We stay quiet until she breaks the silence.

"He's a nice boy," she comments. "I approve, Riley."

I smile as I dry a plate. "Thanks. But do you really have to be that nosy?" I ask, giving her an accusing look.

She holds her hands up. "I was not being nosy. I thought I saw a dog in the road."

She can't make it any more obvious.

***

"So I hear you're joining us for dinner tonight."

I turn and look at Ryan, who is standing next to me. I nod. "I am. Are you and Kelly going to be there?"

"Of course, we are. We live there too you know." He teases.

I roll my eyes. "I was just asking, jeez."

"You know," he says, "I'm surprised that Aiden agreed to go over tonight. I have the strong feeling that if you hadn't been able to come, he wouldn't be going over tonight."

I feel a pair of arms wrap themselves around me. "Talking about me?" Aiden's voice rings through my ears.

"Always," Ryan smirks. "I'll see you guys later." He then walks off in a different direction.

I spot Nicole walking down the hall with two of her friends. She glances at me for a split second then looks away and scowls. I take that as a sign that she's done bullying me around.

"Are you excited for tonight?" I turn and face Aiden.

"I'm excited that you're going with me." He steps closer to me and plants a kiss on my forehead. He then grabs my hand and holds it.

"I'm sure tonight will go fine," I assure him. I know he's a little uneasy about it.

He pulls me closer to himself, and his hands rest on my waist. He stares directly into my eyes and smiles slightly. "You know that I am crazy about you, right?"

I shrug. "I guess."

"Are you crazy about me also?"

I frown. "Of course, I am. Where is this coming from?" I question.

"I just want to make sure your feelings haven't changed." He looks to the side.

I go on my tiptoes and peck his lips. "I really, really like you Aiden," I tell him.

His eyes brighten up and he releases me. I shut my locker, and he wraps his arm around me as he walks me to class.

***

Aiden had picked me up at my house, and we're currently heading to Anna and Robert's house. Aiden grips the steering wheel a little tightly so I can tell he's anxious about tonight.

"You should calm down," I comment.

He visibly exhales. "Sorry."

"Don't apologize," I tell him. "You have every right to be nervous. I'm just saying, you shouldn't be as anxious as you are."

Aiden sighs. "I just want this night to go by as quickly as possible."

A few minutes later, he parks in the driveway, and we both get out at the same time. He holds my hand as we walk up to the front door.

Before Aiden can reach out to ring the doorbell, the door swings open, revealing a smiling Kelly.

"Look at the cute couple." She gushes. "I knew you two would end up together eventually. Team Raiden!" she exclaims.

I look at her like she's a lunatic. When I look at Aiden, he's giving her the same look I am. "Kelly," he says, "this isn't one of your cheesy teen novels. There are no teams. And what is Raiden?"

"Your couple name." She grins. "Come inside." She holds the door wider for us to enter the house.

When Kelly is out of hearing range, I lean over and whisper to Aiden, "We have a couple name?"

He looks at me and smirks. "I guess so."

We follow Kelly into the living room, where Ryan is sprawled out on the couch watching TV. He glances at us and smiles. "You guys made it," he says.

"Yes, we did." I nod. "No interferences."

"Unfortunately." Aiden coughs.

"Well, my mom and Robert are in the kitchen cooking still," Ryan says.

I pull Aiden in the direction of the kitchen. "Let's go say hi."

He groans slightly, but he complies. "I want to leave already."

"We're not going to leave just yet," I tell him. "Let's just see how things start off."

We continue towards the kitchen. And when we enter, someone runs right smack into us, sending whatever they're holding onto our shirts.

I gasp at the sudden sticky feeling. I look down and see that half my shirt is covered in spaghetti sauce. Aiden also has sauce on him; it looks like he got most of it.

"I am so sorry, you guys!" Kelly instantly apologizes. "I really didn't mean to!"

"I told you not to be carrying it around like that Kelly! Look what you did!" Anna exclaims.

Aiden looks ticked off by the way his jaw is set. He takes a deep breath to calm himself down.

I don't trust him to reply to Kelly. "It's fine." I assure her. I'm not wearing anything nice. And I'm not wearing one of my favorite band shirts, so it isn't that big of a deal for me.

Anna looks at Aiden and me, and she raises her eyebrows. "Well, this night is already interesting," she says.

"What happened in here?" I hear Robert ask. He enters the kitchen from another room and glances at Aiden and me.

"Kelly, why don't you lend Riley a shirt so she can get out of that one. And Aiden, you have a few shirts hanging in your closet still," Anna tells us, instead of answering Robert's question.

Aiden nods and looks at Kelly and me. Kelly makes her way to the stairs, and Aiden and I follow behind her.

"Oh yeah. This night won't end badly at all," Aiden says sarcastically next to me. "You shouldn't be as anxious as you are." He mocks me, repeating what I said earlier in the car. "Let's just see how things start off."

I frown at him and smack his arm. "I will walk out of this house if you keep mocking me like that," I threaten.

He slips an arm around my waist and pulls me close. "Don't leave." He snuggles his face into my neck.

"I couldn't, even if I tried," I tell him. "You have the keys and my house is too far to walk."

Kelly stops in front of a door down the hall. "I know you and I don't have the same style, Riley, so I'll let you rummage through my closet to find something comfortable for you."

"Thanks, Kelly." I smile at her. I pull myself away from Aiden and enter Kelly's room while he opens another door in the same hallway.

I follow Kelly to her closet, and she opens the door. "Go ahead." She gestures. I start going through the shirts and internally scowl at each of them. Kelly and I definitely don't have the same style.

I end up finding a Beatles shirt that I actually really like. I slip it on and hold my other shirt in my hands. I exit Kelly's room and go towards the room Aiden walked into. The door is slightly open, so I enter slowly.

***

Holy mother of Led Zeppelin.

I think it's pretty obvious that I am not like most girls. But I am still a girl, so the sight in front of me almost has me drooling.

A shirtless Aiden stands in front of me as I enter the bedroom.

He smirks when he sees me staring at his half-naked body. "Like what you see Led Zeppelin Girl?"

My cheeks instantly heat up and I look away. "Uh, no. Or, I mean, yes but—" I stammer.

Aiden walks up to me, the smirk still on his lips. "You're so adorable when you're nervous." He wraps his arms around me. "I'm just without a shirt." He chuckles into my hair.

I relax into his arms and wrap my arms around him also, making sure the sauce on my shirt doesn't get on him. "Don't laugh at me."

He continues to snicker. "Maybe I should go around shirtless more often."

Someone clears their throat behind us and we both turn. Anna stands in the doorway with a small smile. "Dinner is ready, if you two aren't busy." I know she wants to smirk.

I pull away from Aiden and blush even more.

"We'll be down in a minute," Aiden says to her.

Once she walks away, I put my face in my hands. This is going to be a long night.

Aiden and I walk into the dining room, where Ryan is setting out silverware. Anna walks in and sets a plate with garlic bread onto the table.

"If you want to, you can put those shirts in the laundry and I'll make sure to wash them for you two," she tells us.

"That'd be gr—"

"We're okay." Aiden interrupts me.

I glance up at him and give him a confused look. But he doesn't look down at me.

Something flashes in Anna's eyes and she purses her lips. "Okay." And with that, she escapes back into the kitchen.

I hit Aiden's arm again.

"Ow." He glimpses down at me. "What's with the abuse tonight?"

"Why are you being a jerk to Anna? She just offered to clean our shirts," I tell him.

He doesn't answer. Instead, he crosses his arms.

I grab his shirt and take it from him. Before he can react, I walk into the kitchen and find Anna by the stove. I approach her and smile slightly. "It would be great if you could wash these for us," I tell her.

She smiles at me. "Just set them on the washer and I'll get to them soon."

When I walk back into the dining room, Aiden glances at me and sighs. "Sorry."

"For?"

"Being a jerk," he mumbles. "I'll try to behave tonight."

I grin. "You better behave."

He rolls his eyes and grabs my hand. "And if I don't?"

"Please don't start being *that* kind of couple," Ryan says as he passes by us.

We both end up laughing slightly.

Chapter 35

"So, Riley, how've you been? I feel like I haven't seen you since the wedding!" Anna exclaims.

I look at her from my seat. The truth is I did see her after the wedding. I saw her when my mom picked me up from the police station. I remember snapping at her. "I've been alright." I nod. "Nothing has really changed."

"Do you have any classes with Aiden?" Robert asks me.

I shake my head. "I don't."

"Riley has advanced classes," Aiden tells him. "Which I'm obviously not taking."

I notice Robert's jaw tick, but he looks back at me. "I think it's great that you're taking advanced classes."

I nod. "It kind of preps us for college courses."

Kelly sighs. "I can't wait for college."

"You still have a couple more years." Ryan rolls his eyes. I chuckle at his response.

"Do you have any classes with Ryan?" Anna asks me.

Once again, I shake my head. "I don't."

"Aren't you in a couple advanced classes?" Robert asks Ryan.

Ryan nods. "Yeah, but Riley and I have the classes different periods."

"You're on your period Ryan?" Aiden asks. "I knew it."

My hand flies up to my mouth to muffle my laughs. Kelly, on the other hand, bursts out laughing and holds her stomach.

"Aiden." Robert warns.

Ryan smirks. "It's nice to know you haven't changed." I glance at Ryan when he says this. Ryan told me himself that Aiden has changed ever since Aiden and I have been hanging out.

"Boys, behave," Anna says.

As Anna tells Ryan something, I feel a hand on my knee. I glance at Aiden who's eating normally. But he has a slight smirk on his face. His grip on my knee tightens. I place my hand on his hand and slip it underneath it so we would be holding hands.

A smile breaks out onto his lips.

"Well, I'm full," Robert says, pushing his plate slightly away from him.

"Do you all want desert? I made brownies." Anna smiles.

"*One does not simply ask if we want brownies,*" Kelly says to Anna. "Of course, we want them."

Anna stands up and goes into the kitchen. Robert glances at Aiden then back at me. "So how long have you and Aiden known each other exactly?"

"Why does it matter?" Aiden asks him.

I look at Aiden and shake my head, trying to tell him to stop and just enjoy the night. I look over at Kelly and Ryan, and they're having their own conversation.

"I'm just curious," Robert replies.

"I'd say...a little over two and a half months," I answer him.

Robert looks at Aiden. "I'm going to take a wild guess and say that you didn't even know how long you've known Riley for."

Aiden sits forward in his seat and lets go of my hand. "Why can't you just accept the fact that things will never be normal around here? I don't even understand why we were invited if all you're going to do is interrogate us."

"Is it a crime wanting to know about your son's relationship?" Robert asks. "Quite frankly, it seems like you don't even know anything about this girl."

This dinner is taking a turn for the worst. And I'm caught off guard by Robert's statement. I don't really like being referred to as *this girl*.

Anna walks in and sets the brownies on the table. "The brownies came out delicious! Who wants one?"

"You don't know anything," Aiden says angrily to Robert, ignoring Anna. "You haven't known anything since Mom died."

Now *that* catches Robert off guard. Actually, I think it catches everyone off guard. I've never heard Aiden mention his mom around his dad.

"Aiden, I don't want to hear another word—"

"About what? About Mom? Why? Is your new family just so perfect that you don't even remember what you and Mom had?" Aiden explodes. He stands up as he yells at Robert.

Robert stands up too. "I do remember, Aiden! I remember every waking moment I spent with your mom! You don't know how hard it is to lose someone you'd thought you'd spend the rest of your life with." He starts to breathe heavily.

"You're right. I don't know," Aiden tells him. "But I have found that someone and I know that I would never do anything that would make me forget about her. I love Riley, and I *do* know everything about her. Maybe not the stupid little basic stuff, but the stuff that matters and makes her the way she is. Go ahead and think what you want about us, I don't care." Aiden reaches down and grabs my hand. "Let's go, Riley."

I don't even have time to respond. I get out of my seat and try to keep up with him as he storms off in the direction of the front door. He swings it open and pulls me along with him.

We make our way to the car and I yank my wrist away from him. He glances back at me. I see a single tear fall from the corner of his eye before he quickly wipes it away. "I want to get out of here, Riley."

"You're not driving like this," I tell him. "And we're not going anywhere until you explain to me why you just exploded back there."

"Is it not obvious?" he asks. "I hate the fact that he just acts normal around them like they were his first family. And where do I fit in all of this? Nowhere." He's breathing deeply.

I sigh and stand in front of him. "You need to calm down, Aiden." I try soothing him. He's acting hysterical. And we aren't going anywhere until he calms down.

He suddenly wraps his arms around me and hugs me tightly. I wrap my arms around him too and do the same. "I always feel like shit when I'm around them. I feel like I'm supposed to be exiled or something."

I pull back slightly and cup his face with my hands. "Hey, we're outcasts together, remember?" I offer him a small smile.

Aiden studies my face for a few seconds. "I love you, Riley Summers."

As soon as those words leave his mouth, my stomach fills with pterodactyls. I stand there in shock for a minute and I guess I made Aiden slightly nervous.

"Is that too soon?" Aiden asks me. "God, I'm an idiot. I should have just kept my mouth shut—"

I cover his mouth with my hand and smile at him. "Do you ever shut up?" I quote him from the first time we met. I feel him smile underneath my hand. "I love you too." I remove my hand.

"You do? Even after the whole dinner fiasco?" he asks me.

"I do." I nod.

He pulls me closer to him and smiles. "You are too perfect, Riley."

"And you're too kind." I laugh. "I'm sorry I pushed you to be on good terms with your dad."

Aiden sighs. "Things will never be the same with me and my dad. It's not your fault."

I let go of him and intertwine our fingers. "Let's go then."

"Where?" he asks.

I shrug. "Let's do something spontaneous."

He seems to think about this. "How about you let me sleep in your room this time?" I look at him skeptically. "We're dating, remember? But I promise I'll behave."

After debating over this in my head, I nod. "Okay."

We go straight to his house so he can get some clothes. We then go to my house and I explain to my mom that he will be sleeping over. Once I convince her that it would be fine, and agreeing to keep the blasted door open, she approves.

Tonight, Aiden and I talk about everything and anything. It's nice to just talk. No drama, no interruptions, and no bickering. I like being around Aiden like this.

I may not have liked him when we first met, but I am glad that we continued to talk. I'm glad that I agreed to be in the wedding because I probably wouldn't have known so much about Aiden. I don't regret one thing because everything that happened led up to this moment. And this moment can't be any more perfect.

Epilogue

The next few months go by in a blur. Kelly and I start hanging out more and she even gets me into watching *Glee* (shocking I know). Ryan recently started to hang out with a girl from his history class. He admitted to me that he really likes her and plans on really getting to know her. I found that really sweet. Lucas and I started to talk again and we've become pretty good friends. He has a girlfriend now and I think she is perfect for him.

Aiden and I are still together. I'm not going to lie though; I broke up with him last month. This whole thing started when I was partners with a guy from my chemistry class and Aiden complained that I was spending too much time with the guy. We got into a big argument and he went out and got drunk with Alex. He came to my house that night and admitted that he had kissed another girl out of anger. I got really hurt and I broke up with him. He begged me to take him back because he said he loved me and he's a total mess without me. I finally gave in after two days and ever since then, everything's been fine between us.

I took him to meet my dad about two weeks ago. Aiden was nervous the whole way up to my dad's house. Once they actually met, my dad really liked him. Alyssa adored him and Amanda basically clung onto him once she got comfortable around him.

Currently, Aiden and I are sitting in the grass in my backyard. He's lying next to me as I play with the grass in front of me.

"You're thinking hard about something," he says.

I shrug. "I'm just thinking."

"About?"

"Graduation. College. Everything." I sigh. "Just everything."

He sits up and wraps an arm around me. "You know graduation is in two months."

"I'm still nervous. Aren't you?" I ask him.

"I'm not going to think about it until I really have to," Aiden says. "For now, I just want to sit here and enjoy the afternoon with you."

I smile. "You're too great."

"I know." He grins. "And so are you. We are too great together."

I laugh at him. I lay back in the grass and stare at the sky above. He follows my actions and lays next to me.

"I love you," he says suddenly.

"I love you too."

He leans over and kisses my cheek, making me smile.

Aiden never got on good terms with his dad. He doesn't want to have any contact with them, other than Kelly and sometimes Ryan.

Aiden and I are so different, yet we're so alike. I never would have imagined us together at the beginning of the year, but now it feels so usual with him.

If there's such a thing as *normal*, I still wouldn't know what it feels like. I know what feels right and that's all that matters.

The End

Can't get enough of Riley and Aiden? Make sure you sign up for the author's blog to find out more about them!

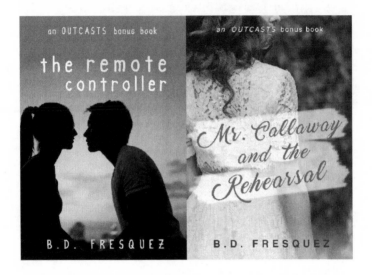

Get these two bonus chapters and more freebies when you sign up at bd-fresquez.awesomeauthors.org!

Here is a sample from another story you may enjoy:

AFTER

SCHOOL

❧ WITH ❧

MR.
OBNOXIOUS

♡
YOU'RE NOT EVEN
A GOOD KISSER!

FOR GOODNESS' SAKE
WOMAN, WILL YOU
SHUT UP ALREADY?

KIMTI ALEX

Prologue

"Hey, Aaron, you imbecile creature!"

Aaron Lanter stopped dead in his tracks as soon as he heard his name and the derogatory word that came after it. He did not like it. He's Aaron Lanter, the most popular guy in school; every girl's dream guy and every guy's object of jealousy. He was *the* Aaron of Lediville High. Who on earth would call his attention by calling him an imbecile?

The culprit was none other than Samantha Banks, who stood proudly by the countertop with her rather worried friends in the kitchen.

"What did you just call me?" Aaron asked. The party was beginning to bore him. He and his friend, Zack, decided to leave the party when they passed by the kitchen.

"Imbecile," Sam answered coolly. "Hey, spell imbecile, I-M-B-E-C-I-L-E."

"You're screwed, Sam, like down the sewer kind of screwed." A girl who looked like a gothic doll said.

Sam frowned at her. "That doesn't even make any sense, does it? Oh, I feel warm fuzzies."

Chloe was nodding her head between Sam and a gothic girl to the rap music blasting loudly. "This is an amazing party."

She has never been drunk in her entire existence. But in that gusty, Friday night, she let her best friend, Chloe, influence her decision on how she should spend her evening. If it were up to her, she would be curled up in bed and watched classic TV show reruns. In fact, it was what she had planned, but when Diana, one of Ledivilles cheerleaders, announced a house party before the first period even started Monday morning, everything changed.

For days, Chloe wouldn't let the topic rest; she begged Sam to go with her, promised her they would leave the party before midnight. And on Thursday, Sam finally gave in and agreed to go with her. Chloe victoriously manipulated Sam to join in on the fun with half of the population of Lediville High.

After a few arguments about the smell of alcohol in the entire house, Sam finally agreed to stay for four hours. It was the first party of the school year, and everyone was partying like it was their last. The place was already swamped, but surprisingly, the kitchen wasn't so they decided to hang out in there with two other girls from one of their morning classes.

It only took three bottles of beer to turn Sam as pink as salmon and a bit deaf, start to laugh and talk louder than normal. When boredom slowly crept in, the girl with the shiniest red hair they called Ginger suggested that they play *Truth or Dare.*

"Yes. Let's play that 'cause this party sucks." Another drunken girl agreed. She had her nose pierced and couldn't seem to stop playing with her pierced tongue. Her eyes were locked on a guy and a girl pinned on the walls, making out.

Chloe rolled her eyes. "Just because nobody wants to make out with you doesn't mean the party sucks, Martha."

The girl who got both her nose and tongue pierced frowned. "Who'd want to make out with jerks?" She started to stare at the two girls standing in front of them surrounded by four guys.

The redhead suddenly stood up and almost spilled her beer all over Sam. "Okay, let's entertain ourselves and play truth or dare," she suggested again.

"This is Diana's house. She's a popular cheerleader. Why don't we look around and maybe we'd find some weird stuff? Wouldn't it be fun to discover something about one of those perfect cheerleaders at our school?" The goth girl said.

Martha shook her head. "You have issues you need to fix, Luna." She said

Sam got up. "Chloe, I think we should go. I'm starting to feel weird. I can't feel my hands."

Chloe checked her watch. "Sam, it is a quarter to ten. We agreed to leave fifteen minutes before eleven." She offered Sam another bottle of beer while the other three had additional bottles too. After a couple more beers, Ginger proposed again that they play *Truth or Dare*.

And they all finally went for it. When it was Sam's turn, she didn't even hesitate to choose dare.

Dare. Samantha Banks chose dare, a choice she made which she would regret making for the rest of her senior year because as soon as Ginger saw Aaron and his other jock friend passed by, she was doomed.

Kiss Aaron Lanter, on the lips, with your tongue, for ten seconds — was the dare.

Chloe, Ginger, and gothic girl froze as Aaron walked to them.

"Oh, Sam, did you really have to call him imbecile?" Chloe muttered. She was growing nervous as few teens from the crowd started to gather around, waiting for what was about to happen.

"Who are you?" Aaron asked Sam. He looked really pissed.

Sam, on the other hand, was drunk and didn't really care what was going on. "My name is Samantha Banks, your majesty, a humble servant from nowhere land." She further ridiculed Aaron with a curtsy. "Actually, I know you know me because we had four classes together last school year. But you just pretend you don't have a clue since you're the so-called heartthrob, and you're brainlessly following this preposterous social structure, where a socially well-accepted person such as yourself would and should only acknowledge other popular people's existence. And since I am obviously neither cool nor popular, hence the '*Who are you?*'".

"Excuse me?" Aaron said.

"Is she drunk or high?" The Gothic girl whispered.

"Let's go, Sam. I think we drank more than enough booze for tonight." Chloe said. She had more than five bottles; however, Sam's alcohol tolerance was low compared to hers.

Sam had already turned red, not because of the tension everyone in the kitchen started to feel but rather due to the effect of the fourth bottle she had. She walked over to Aaron, smiling. "Listen, my friends and I are playing truth or dare. I chose dare. Now, I have to kiss you."

Some giggled, and some just stood there with *uh-oh* looks on their faces.

"Is she serious?"

"Where's Nicole? She's got to see this?"

"What did you just tell me?" Aaron couldn't believe what he was hearing.

"Whoa, dude. Nerdy got hots for you. *Respect!* " Zack mocked.

"Oh, please." Sam rolled her eyes. "Like you've never kissed before? It's simple. My tongue plays with your tongue and then we swap spit. Like this."

And before Aaron could even express his displeasure, Samantha Banks, Lediville High's nobody, grabbed his collar, and slammed her mouth against his before everyone's very eyes.

If you enjoyed this sample then look for **After School with Mr. Obnoxious.**

Introducing the Characters Magazine App

Download the app to get the free issues of interviews from famous fiction characters and find your next favorite book!

iTunes: bit.ly/CharactersApple
Google Play: bit.ly/CharactersAndroid

Acknowledgements

Thank you, Mom and Dad, for always supporting me and being there when I need you. Thank you, Serena, Tony, and Emery, for making my life just so much more entertaining, fun, and fulfilling. To the rest of my large and extended family, thank you for all the love and laughter you've brought me. I love all of you. Thank you to my best friends for all the inspiring adventures we've had and have yet to have. You guys are truly the best of the best. All of you have played an important role in my life, and I thank you from the bottom of my heart.

Author's Note

Hey there!

Thank you so much for reading *Outcasts*! I can't express how grateful I am for reading something that was once just a thought inside my head.

I'd love to hear from you! Please feel free to email me at bd_fresquez@awesomeauthors.org and sign up at bd-fresquez.awesomeauthors.org for freebies!

One last thing: I'd love to hear your thoughts on the book. Please leave a review on Amazon or Goodreads because I just love reading your comments and getting to know YOU!

Whether that review is good or bad, I'd still love to hear it!

Can't wait to hear from you!

B. D. Fresquez

About the Author

Just a 19-year-old girl who lives in Las Cruces, New Mexico, and loves chocolate and books with a passion.

58039048R00222

Made in the USA
Middletown, DE
18 December 2017